I0590685

CC'S ROAD HOME

LEAH B. ESKINE

Black Rose Writing | Texas

©2021 by Leah B. Eskine
All rights reserved. No part of this book may be reproduced, stored in a retrieval system or transmitted in any form or by any means without the prior written permission of the publishers, except by a reviewer who may quote brief passages in a review to be printed in a newspaper, magazine or journal.

The author grants the final approval for this literary material.

First printing

This is a work of fiction. Names, characters, businesses, places, events, and incidents are either the products of the author's imagination or used in a fictitious manner. Any resemblance to actual persons, living or dead, or actual events is purely coincidental.

ISBN: 978-1-68433-609-8
PUBLISHED BY BLACK ROSE WRITING
www.blackrosewriting.com

Printed in the United States of America
Suggested Retail Price (SRP) $19.95

CC's Road Home is printed in Cambria

*As a planet-friendly publisher, Black Rose Writing does its best to eliminate unnecessary waste to reduce paper usage and energy costs, while never compromising the reading experience. As a result, the final word count vs. page count may not meet common expectations.

Author photograph by Charles Marshall
Edited by Margo L. Dill, Editor 911

FOR PAUL

My best friend and my rock.

CC'S ROAD HOME

CHAPTER 1

CC followed her mother over to her new Chevy pleading, "Aren't you even going to stay and talk to Gran and Gramps?" Her mom continued to unlock the car without looking at her daughter. CC screamed, "What am I supposed to tell them?"

As usual her mother wasn't sympathetic. "Listen, CC. You made this mess. You talk to them. You're sixteen years old, old enough to start explaining yourself, all by yourself!" She plopped in the driver's seat and slammed the car door. Leaning out the open window, she hissed, "I talked to them on the phone before we came. They know why you're here, and they think they can help pick up the pieces from this mess you've made."

The contempt in Mama's eyes was withering and discouraged CC from any more screaming or arguing. She watched her mother drop the gearshift into drive and speed away from her grandparents' farm. The lonely sound of the tires on the gravel road could be heard after the billowing white powder shrouded Mama's view.

It was obvious Mama wanted to get away from her. The last week at home before they showed up at her grandparents, had evolved into dead silence between them and CC found that much worse than the screaming. She had hoped that at the last-minute Mama would hold her and tell her everything would be all right. But today when Mama gunned the engine on the new car and sped away, CC realized that would never happen.

They left New Orleans the day before in the afternoon after she told CC to throw her clothes in a bag and arrived at the farm after dark. Mama barely said hello to Gran and Gramps and went straight to bed. CC could tell she didn't want to stay at the farm and expected CC to manage for herself.

CC stumbled to the side of the road and fell on the grass. Pulling her knees to her chest, CC realized the tears could flow freely now, but she held back. *I'm not going to let anyone feel sorry for me. I hate being in Ruston, on a farm, in the middle of nowhere, and there's nothing Gran or Gramps can say to make it any better. This place is the pits. I can smell the cow manure. I miss New Orleans already.*

When she and Mama arrived on the farm, her grandparents' eyes widened in surprise. CC knew why because she was shocked at her own appearance. She had lost a lot of weight the last few months at home and her clothes were sagging on her tall, thin frame. Her normally pretty face was gaunt and expressionless and her chestnut brown hair was stringy and desperately needed trimming. She barely recognized herself in the hall mirror.

Footsteps in the grass behind her interrupted her train of thought. "Cicely, come on and help me pick some blackberries out here. You still like my pie?" Her grandmother was standing a few feet away with her hands in her apron pockets. CC started to correct her but thought better of it. *I'll let her know later about my name. She's uneasy like she doesn't know what to say to me. Well, it has been about three years.*

She noticed all the grey in Gran's hair and it seemed like there were more wrinkles on her face than CC remembered. She loved Gran but she didn't want to be stuck in the country.

"Course I still like your pie but can I help you later? I thought I'd walk around." CC searched for any disappointment in Gran's face. There was none.

Instead, Gran stared at her for a minute and then said, "Sure thing. You look around. You haven't been here in a long time." Gran leaned over and brushed a stray hair behind CC's ear. "Why don't you keep an eye out for your Uncle Bud? Bring him in for supper."

"Okay, Gran." CC felt an impulse to put her arms around her grandmother and hold on, but something held her back. Was she asking too much if she did? Did she deserve her love after what she had done? She didn't understand her feelings anymore. Was numbness a feeling, she wondered? She could name that. Forget it. How do you talk about numbness?

She watched her grandmother walking down the hill. CC could make out the white frame house below and recognized the aroma of peaches from the orchard. The blossoms were always out in June when she used to come to the farm before Mama's drinking got so bad. *God, I always loved that peach smell. Gramps used to take me out to the orchard to help pick them.* CC wandered over to a nearby tree. Leaning against the trunk, the memories of the farm drifted around in her head, but were overshadowed by her current life in the city and the terrible mistakes she had made.

She closed her eyes and held her long hair above her shoulders to get some relief from the heat. Aloud she moaned, "I wish I had a wet rag to wipe at this sweat."

Hot was not a strong enough description. Sitting alone you could actually hear the heat – the distant buzzing of bees and muted chirping of daytime crickets. And the gnats! They were always there, ready to get in your eyes until you waved them away. The heat just stuck to you while the sweat dripped down into your eyes.

Nearby voices interrupted the sounds of summer. She could make out men snickering and what sounded like teasing. Then she recognized the unmistakable mumbling of her Uncle Bud.

"Not stupid! I work over here just like you. Shut up. Leave me alone."

Oh God! Now what? That's Uncle Bud over there. And the other voices. Gran said to bring him in but I don't want to get in the middle of anything. I don't have the energy.

She squinted and could make out a few men near the fence. They were laughing and cutting up but she couldn't make out what they were saying.

CC wanted to sit by the tree and not get involved, but Uncle Bud appeared miserable. She knew how that felt, so she stood up and dusted her jeans off. "I can't believe I'm doing this. It's not my job. I don't have to do this. Gran would understand," she mumbled, making her way to the commotion.

The terrible heat made her feel confused and she could actually hear a buzzing in her head. *I came here because Mama made me. I came here to be left alone.*

But here she was within a few feet of Uncle Bud and three scraggly looking field hands by the fence. She stood in place and put on her meanest stare.

"What's going on, Uncle Bud? Everything all right?"

A voice from the group snickered and said, "We was just foolin' with him. He's used to it little lady."

"Yeah, we were just foolin' with him. Where you from? Saw you a while ago getting out of that new red '64 Chevy Impala." This boy got CC's attention. A six-foot tall, lean, jet black-haired boy leered at her from a pair of steely, sneering dark blue eyes.

Uncle Bud flailed his arms in the air and muttered. She could only make out a little of what he was saying, but she knew from watching him in the past he was worked up and there could be trouble if he jumped that fence. She remembered the times Gramps had to rescue him from fights.

"Calling me stupid! Crazy! Ain't done a thing. Make them stop, Sis!"

"Aww, you his sister?" They were practically doubled over with laughter. Only Tall Lean boy stood motionless, his sneering eyes never left her.

"You his little Sis? Ain't that sweet?" The question came from one of the scraggly guys.

"I'm not. He heard people calling me CC and he thought it was Sis," popped out of her mouth before she could stop it. *How the hell did I get into this? I don't want to have anything to do with these stupid hicks and I sure don't want them to know my name.*

"Aww, that is so sweet, ain't it fellas? The retard calls her Sis. Ain't that sweet?"

Tall Lean boy spoke up. "Come on. This here pretty gal don't need us making fun of her, too. Isn't that right pretty gal?"

"I am not your pretty gal and don't call him a retard. That's a terrible thing to call anyone. What's the matter with you idiots?"

"Idiots! We're idiots? You got that wrong miss. You're standing next to the idiot. It ain't us," one of the scraggly boys said as he doubled over with laughter.

CC felt her jaw drop. She couldn't believe she was in the middle of this. They must think she is a silly kid and that thought that made her mad. Furious! She felt her face getting red and her heart thumping so loud she thought she could hear it. She put her arms at her side so they wouldn't notice her fists were clamped shut. But no matter how hard she tried to hide her feelings Tall Lean boy was staring right through her. He had her number and his sneer proved it.

For the first time this summer, she was mad at somebody besides Mama.

CHAPTER 2

CC realized she was losing a battle she didn't want to be in anyway. "Come on, Uncle Bud. Let's go to the house."

"Hey, little Sis. Come on over anytime. We was just kiddin' around. Come on now."

She didn't turn around to see which of those fools was yelling at her but she figured it wasn't Tall Lean boy. He was too smooth.

Uncle Bud was stumbling along by her side and as hard as it was, she resisted the temptation to shoo him away. She felt responsible for him now that she saved him from the jerks. Her fists were still clenched. She rubbed her forehead hoping to push back another impending headache.

"Why's your face red, Sis?" Uncle Bud almost tripped trying to get in front of her.

"Just shut up, you hear me? I don't need any trouble from you. I just saved your butt. Why were you talking to those men?"

As soon as she said it, she knew it was a mistake. *What am I getting into? Uncle Bud sputtered like he could cry.*

She stared into her uncle's sad face. He had these eyes like a cocker spaniel and CC remembered how easily he could get upset. He could start bawling and then just take off, run away. One summer when she helped Gran look for him, they found him in the peach grove, all balled up under a tree and crying like a little kid. Gran told her a couple of years ago he was forty something but he sure didn't act like it.

"Uncle Bud, stand still, okay? I didn't mean to upset you. Don't tell Gramps. Look, let's hang out for a while. You want to sit in the clover? You still like that, don't you?"

CC plopped down near him. She used to watch him in the fields when she was a little kid. He still looked the same. Mama described his hair as sandy red. It had these yellow streaks in it, but it was his arms that caught your attention. There were red freckles all over his arms and you could see them because he always wore the same thing, every day. Short sleeved khaki shirts and pants, like a uniform. And he was so tall, his arms dangled like he was a giant. His face was all covered with those freckles too. CC used to wonder if he could wash them off and when she asked Gramps about it, he laughed so hard she figured no, they were there to stay.

One summer she snuck up where he was sitting in the grass and listened to him talking to something in the clover.

He made this sound like "Bzzz, bzzz," and then he giggled. He slid his finger down real slow and tried to get the honeybees to sit on his hand. Sometimes he succeeded. That same summer she watched him coax a little bird to sit on his finger. It stayed the longest until she sneezed and scared it away. She was sad about that at first, but then Uncle Bud grinned at her with that sweet simple smile of his.

A few years ago, she overheard her grandmother telling someone about him. He had been in an accident and hurt his head bad.

"That car rolled over and over. Miracle he lived. Then Dorothy, that was his wife, run off when she realized how bad he was. Took the three kids with her and married some Texas guy. His thinking never been right since. Guess it's better for her and the boys. We been taking care of him ever since.

CC couldn't remember Uncle Bud any other way. She stretched out on her back and rested her hands on her forehead to shield her eyes from the sun. She didn't want to be here babysitting her uncle. He had a rough life, but at least he had a home. For the second time that day, she wondered where her home would be.

Uncle Bud jumped up and started running toward the farmhouse. "Now what? What's he doing?

CC forced herself up and patted the back of her jeans. Then she shielded her eyes from the sun and realized where Uncle Bud was headed. "His garden. For cripes sake, why now?" She yelled, "Uncle Bud, let's just go to the kitchen. Gran wants you for supper, remember?'

She could make out his mumbling now as she got closer. "Gonna get beans. She'll like the beans."

CC ambled to the garden with her hands in her pockets, talking to herself. "I guess this is what I'm doomed for now. Following my crazy uncle around and getting sneered at by a bunch of country fools. This is my life!"

She leaned over the wire fence to gaze out over his little garden. Jeez, she thought, this is how a person spends his time. This is something. The rows are as straight as a ruler, and it's filled with these vegetables, like who would eat all this stuff? Tomatoes and green beans. Yuk! I wonder what those big purple things are.

Her thoughts were interrupted by his mumbling. "Got to get her some" was all CC could make out but she guessed he meant Gran. She watched him fill his little pail with green beans. He turned towards CC and a big smile replaced the sad face of earlier.

"Okay, Uncle Bud, you ready to go in?"

"Yep, yep, yep." He liked to repeat himself. CC tried not to, but she felt herself grinning at his response.

They walked across the yard. At the back door, he put the pail on a step, leaned over and started taking his boots off. Placing them neatly by the door, he picked up the beans and they walked into the kitchen.

The room was big and sunny and clean with a round oak table in the center of the space. CC had loved sitting on the floor when she was little and playing with her paper dolls. Gran used to stir up chocolate milk for her and a bowl of fresh peaches ready to peel sat in the middle of the table.

"I saw you out there picking those beans, Bud. You get enough for supper?" Gran was standing in her usual spot at the kitchen sink washing dishes.

Uncle Bud started to put the pail down on the oak table when Gran called out. "Now where does that pail go, Bud? How many times have I reminded you? Don't set anything dirty on my table. That's where we eat."

He grabbed the pail and brought it over to the kitchen counter and stood waiting, shifting from one foot to the other.

Her grandfather's gravelly voice came from behind the newspaper. "He forgets 'cause he's been talking' to them bees. What'd they have to say today, son?"

Gramps let his paper slide down a few inches as he stole a glance at Gran. It was obvious he enjoyed teasing his son. Uncle Bud stood by the counter with his head down but his giggle made CC think he liked the banter.

Gran dried her hands with one of her bright kitchen towels and looked at CC. "Bud, supper's another thirty minutes or so. Why don't you go out and sit in the shade and wait for me to call you in. Chicken's almost ready."

Bud started for the door and CC could see him putting his boots back on, lickety split. She didn't feel like going outside again, but her sensory cells were on full charge. She sensed a conversation with Gran. Before they could say anything to her, CC announced, "Think I'll go back out too. It's cooler now."

Outside, she strolled past the well and, stopping to stretch, CC looked up and couldn't help but notice a beautiful sky filled with streaks of purple and blue. Funny, she thought, you just didn't notice the sky at home. In the country, the sky looked like it sat right on top of you, like it had been painted there. She wondered if people who lived here looked up much or if they took it for granted.

CC continued her walk to the barn and thought about trying to saddle Lady up for a quick ride, but decided against it. "Couldn't do it by myself after being away so long. Too late anyway. It'll be dark soon."

Instead, she strode over to the side of the barn and jumped up to straddle the nearby fence. "It's quiet out here." As soon as she spoke out loud, she heard Lady whinnying from her stall in the barn. "I wonder if she knows it's me."

"Sure, she does, Sis. Anyone would be crazy not to sense your good lookin' presence."

CC recognized his voice. Tall Lean boy was already paying her a visit.

CHAPTER 3

Startled by his voice over her shoulder, CC tried to swivel her body and almost fell, but the boy from earlier in the afternoon grabbed her to break her fall. He was fast, placing one arm around her middle while the other covered her arm.

Forced to face him, she brushed against his cheek and felt his warm breath. Those steely, blue eyes bore into hers but didn't feel as threatening. Before she could regain her composure, he flashed another smile, asking, "You okay?"

She pulled back but felt his hands on her arms with just the slightest pressure. It was enough to signal that he was in command and preferred that she stay where she was. She thought he would let her go if she pulled back. Instead she heard herself say, "I need to jump down."

Almost laughing, he challenged her. "Really? Is there a rule that New *Orleens* gals can't sit on the fence?"

"How'd you know I'm from New Orleans?"

"I checked." And there was that sneer again. "I checked with my dad, Clay, your grandfather's farm hand. I think that's what they call him."

"You checked on me?" CC thought if she came up with anymore lame questions like this one, she may as well give up. She felt ridiculous. Trying to sound more in control, "It's very nice of you to keep me from falling, but I can take care of myself now."

Still holding her arms with the same slight pressure, "Well, yes'm. I wanted to know you. I decided that this afternoon." Leaning over the fence, he almost touched her face. She sensed a slight whiff of something, not cologne, more like an outdoorsy smell. Like fresh hay. He was too close. CC wasn't totally naïve and something told her to back off so things didn't get out of hand. She was breathing faster now, and she figured Tall Lean boy knew it.

She pulled away from his clutch abruptly so he would know she wasn't that easy. "What is your name anyway? You seem to know a lot about me, I don't even know your name."

Before he could answer, she heard Uncle Bud yelling, "No! Trouble! He's not nice! Trouble! He's trouble! Dad said so, Sis!" Grabbing CC's arm, Uncle Bud pulled her so hard, she lost her balance, teetered, and fell.

"Ouch! What the hell? Uncle Bud, what's wrong with you? You hurt me! You grabbed my arm too tight."

Tall Lean boy jumped the fence and started shoving Uncle Bud back by ramming him in the chest. "You idiot. What's the matter with you?" Almost knocking Uncle Bud down, he threatened. "You better not have hurt her!" Looking at CC, he yelled, "You alright? We told you he's a retard. You see that. You can't trust him," and shoved her uncle again.

"Stop! Stop. Back off! He didn't mean it. He can get rough, but he thought he was protecting me." CC stepped towards the pair and patted her uncle on the shoulder, hoping to calm him down.

Not so sure about Tall Lean boy, she asked him again, "I need to know your name. What is it?"

He looked at her and the grin was gone. The intensity from his dark blue eyes deflated any self -control she had mustered. "Name's Eric, Miss CC, Eric Ralston." His expression and his hold on her uncle did not falter. The three of them stayed in that stance until Uncle Bud broke loose and started running to the house.

"Well, I guess I'm in for it. Your retard uncle is going to the house to tell your folks I hurt you." His grin returned and betrayed any real feeling of concern.

"I told you, Eric, stop calling him or anyone 'retard.' That's awful, and why did you call me Miss CC?"

Eric shifted his weight to stand in front of her again which seemed to be his favorite position. Arms loosely at his side, legs spread a slight distance apart, black curly hair tousled – CC was almost jealous of his self-confidence and his control of the situation. His ability to make her feel inadequate seemed epic.

She swallowed and hoped the next few words didn't make her seem nervous. "Look, I need to go back to my grandparents and make sure this isn't blown out of proportion. It got out of hand, but I guess you were just trying to help. I'll explain."

Eric stared at her with the same cocky expression. "I called you 'Miss' out of respect. Trying to get on your good side."

CC didn't know what to say to that, so she turned and started back to the house. She felt unsure of herself and needed to get back some self-control before she talked to her grandparents.

Why did he find her anyway? She just got here and she knew he was older than she was. He must be at least eighteen. He was good looking, but not her type. What was she saying? She didn't have a type, did she? What about Marcus? Was he her type?

She hadn't thought about Marcus in a while, but Eric had made her think of him. Mama made her call him up to tell him she was leaving New Orleans. She felt crappy when she did call him because he sounded so sad. Marcus was only seventeen and didn't know what to say to her. She understood. She didn't know what else to say to him.

She stopped and shook her head to clear it of those thoughts. *Stay focused. Don't give in to any need to explain myself. I didn't do anything wrong with Eric and Uncle Bud.*

As she walked around the house, she could hear the television through the window. It was the news from New Orleans. She smiled as she looked up at the TV antennae her Gramps put up in the backyard. He was so proud of it when it worked right away. It picked up all three channels.

She could hear a man talking about the King guy being in a jail in St. Augustine, Florida. What she heard next surprised her.

Several Negroes were arrested today in St. Augustine for organizing sit-ins at the McCrory's Five and Dime and the Woolworth's lunch counters. After staging the sit-ins, the managers of the establishments refused service and police were called. The arrest followed without incident. This remains a continuation of the Greensboro, North Carolina sit-ins last year where several students were arrested following a peaceful protest at city lunch counters.

CC knew kids at school talked about the Negroes trying to eat in white restaurants. It seemed ridiculous that people had to get arrested for trying to eat, but she remembered seeing Negroes going to neighborhood places to eat in New Orleans. She thought people made a big deal out of this stuff. CC liked Negroes. She didn't care where they ate.

She took a deep breath and started for the back door.

"He's bad! You know he is. Bad. You told me to stay away."

There Uncle Bud goes, CC thought, talking about that boy. Damn! It's my first day here and already I feel like I'm in for it. CC walked through the door deciding to go on the offense.

"Hi. I guess Uncle Bud is telling you about the little incident by the barn." Her grandparents stared at her and caused CC to keep talking. "Gramps, I don't know anything about this boy. I was just sitting around looking at the sky, and wham! There he was. Out of nowhere. Who is he anyway?"

Her grandparents looked at each other and Gramps smiled, but Gran looked kind of serious. She did this thing with her eyebrows that made you think she was on the verge of saying something stern. CC's throat went dry but she couldn't understand why she felt nervous. She didn't do anything, right?

"Gran, I just sat there on the fence. I think he tried to get Uncle Bud to back off, but he was so upset and thrashing around, Eric, I mean this boy, shoved him a little." CC cleared her throat and decided to stop talking. It felt like she was digging herself in.

They looked at each other again but Gran's face looked different. "Cicely, your Gramps and I know you didn't cause anything. Eric is Clay's son. Hadn't been around here until recently. We don't know much about him, but Ethan, your Gramps, may want to ..." she paused and looked at Gramps who jumped in.

"Cicely, it's fine, but we can't have any pushing and shoving. I'll talk to Eric and Clay tomorrow. Bud is upset because he thinks he might have hurt you. What's that about?"

"He grabbed me. Pulled me off the fence. I mean I was sitting on the fence. I think he thought I might fall off or something like that. He didn't hurt me." CC finished with a weak smile.

Gran took over. "Well, it's your first day here. Eric is older, seventeen or eighteen I think Clay said, and he dropped out of school. Maybe you ought to steer clear of him."

CC surveyed the room and decided to stop explaining. Uncle Bud yanked her off the fence and Eric shoved Uncle Bud and she was fed up with the whole thing. Actually, she was very tired and needed something to eat. Thankfully, Uncle Bud seemed calm now and was sitting next to Gramps.

"Is that chicken? It smells delicious." She smiled at her grandmother. She hoped she could end this discussion by complimenting Gran on her cooking. She walked over to the sink and washed her hands and hoped she smoothed the incident over by smiling sweetly and asking, "You want me to set the table, Gran?"

"Ethan, why don't you keep an eye on that pot? Cicely and I are going to have a talk on the back porch."

CHAPTER 4

CC took a deep breath as she followed Gran and reminded herself to breathe.

Thank God Gramps was nearby if this talk got too intense.

The back porch was actually a sleeping porch. CC used to love sleeping out here on a pullout couch, listening to the crickets at night and occasional howling from somewhere in the nearby woods. It could be hot even with the breezes through the windows and she remembered thinking it was her very own space, better than a bedroom because it felt like camping, without the bugs.

She watched as Gran picked a dead leaf from a hanging basket and put it in her apron pocket. That made CC smile. It reminded her of Gran's favorite saying, "everything in its place."

Gran turned to face CC and brush stray hair from her granddaughter's face. In spite of CC's impending fear of what might happen next, she instinctively closed her eyes and enjoyed the momentary soft touch. She felt tears welling up and willed herself to take a deep breath. She gave herself a silent warning - *Don't do it. Don't cry. Don't.*

"Let's sit down over here on the couch, Okay Cicely?"

"Gran, it's fine, but could you call me CC. Everyone does."

"And who's everyone, Sweetheart?"

CC frowned at Gran. This wasn't off to a great start.

"Uh oh, I made a mistake. Too nosy. You mean your friends and teachers, right?" Without waiting for an answer, she sat on the worn sofa and patted the seat next to her.

CC sat at a safe distance so that they weren't touching but faced each other.

Breathe. Breathe. She reminded herself.

Gran leaned over and folded her hands on her knees. Looking straight in CC's eyes for the second time that day, she started over. "Cicely, I mean CC. I'll get it, Sweetheart. What I want to say is that your Gramps and I are glad you're here. You know we've always loved having you around. You're our favorite granddaughter."

CC felt the tension ease with the little joke they always shared. "I'm your only granddaughter, Gran, but you're my favorite Gran, too." They both smiled.

"Yep, I'm your only grandmother. That makes us both special, right? I know you never knew your father or his parents, so we love each other special, real special."

Here it comes. Here's the talk. CC put on a blank face and told herself to get through this without getting too upset.

"First, we aren't angry with you about talking to Clay's son. You're going to meet people now that you're back on the farm. We just wanted you to know he dropped out of school and we don't know very much about him."

"It's all right, Gran. We just talked. I won't see him much."

Gran smiled. "We'll see about that. I hope you're right." Gran cleared her throat before the next question. "Sweetheart, have you thought about staying here with us and going to school next year?"

CC was not expecting that question. "Gran, I'm here for the summer. I'm going back home to finish school in New Orleans." She took a deep breath and reminded herself to stay calm. "No, I haven't given that idea any thought. Why would I?"

"Your Gramps and I were talking, and we thought you might want to stay here. You could have your own room, and we would pay for everything, and..."

CC wondered if this was her mother's idea. Did Mama want her to stay here?

"Your mother just mentioned you could stay longer. We didn't discuss it any further. I wanted to talk with you first."

Almost inaudibly as though she was thinking out loud, CC asked, "What's going on? What's happening?" CC's voice was still level. But then she sat up straighter, and her eyes widened. She was beginning to understand. "Wait, is this my mother's idea? Is she trying to get rid of me?"

CC couldn't sit any longer. She had to stand up and move around the room. She walked to the window and leaned over the sill trying to get some air. The room felt stuffy and warm. She felt closed in and needed air. "What's going on? What's happening? Did you talk to Mama before she left this morning? Is she tired of dealing with me?"

"Sweetheart, just a minute. I'm just trying to talk to you about your future. We haven't had any serious talk with your mother since she picked you up in Shreveport the end of March."

"It's been awful with her in New Orleans since then. She barely speaks to me. Randy still lives with her and he's a creep. They went out every night and left me alone."

CC's face flushed at the mention of Randy. She swung around to ask, "Is that what this is about? Am I being dumped here so Mama can have the house to herself with him?" CC felt a burning in her chest replacing the tears that threatened earlier. Her mind raced to sort out what was going on, as she struggled to gather her thoughts.

She tried to calm down and turned to face Gran again. "What did Mama tell you about what happened at home before I went away? Did she tell you about Randy?" CC spit out his name unable to hide her contempt.

Gran swallowed. "I know a lot has happened, but..."

"What else did Mama tell you?" CC's eyes widened with shocked recognition. Unable to hold back the thought that tumbled out next, she hissed, "Is she punishing me? I can't go home, is that it? Of course, that's it." CC stood and paced around the room.

"Cicely, calm down. You're not listening to me." Gran reached for her, but she pulled away.

"Mama. Mama." It was as though the sound of that word made her want to scream. "Mama is jealous of me, Gran. She doesn't want me around because of him. Randy! I can't believe this!" She spit his name out so viciously, she wiped her mouth with the back of her hand. "What does she think? If I stay in her house, I will steal that shit face from her?"

Gran couldn't hide the shock she felt and uttered, a soft, "Please Cicely, wait. I need to say..."

"Say what? You still think I'm some little kid who doesn't say stuff like that? I've been through a lot, Gran, and I'm telling you he is a shit-face, and more!" CC was breathing hard. Her heart was beating so fast she could hear it thumping. "I'm a little bitch who flirts with her live-in boyfriend? Is that what Mama told you?" CC could feel the tightness of tears in the back of her throat as more anger bubbled to the surface.

"Sweetheart, no one here is saying any of those things about you. We love you. We want you here."

"And what are you going to tell your friends, Gran? Are you going to say, 'Well, she's here because she flunked out of school? She's here because her mama doesn't want her. She's here because she's a bad girl. She's here because her mama's jealous of her?'"

And then the final question came from a place deep inside her and through the back of her throat like a roar. "She's here because she had a baby. She's here because she got knocked up." CC felt her knees buckle. She held onto the back of the sofa.

CC heard footsteps and could tell someone was entering the room. Glancing to her left, she saw Gramps standing in the doorway. He spoke so clearly and softly, she had to strain to hear him. "Cicely, we are going to tell our friends our beautiful granddaughter is here because we love her. She is here because we need her. She is here because she needs us." CC saw tears forming round her Gramp's eyes and a sweet smile on his face that reminded her of Uncle Bud.

Nothing could stop CC's wall of sadness and tears as she looked into Gramps' eyes. She thought her restraint from crying had been a badge of strength, but she collapsed on the sofa and let the sobs come. She wouldn't be able to tell anyone how much she hurt these last months, but in that moment with her grandparents, she felt safe enough to weep and hope she wouldn't die from all the pain in her heart.

CHAPTER 5

Gran put her arm over CC's shoulder as the gulping sobs subsided. She held her for a while rocking ever so gently and whispering, "You are here, for however long you want to be. This is family, Sweetheart. This is your family, and we are always here for you. Family is everything, and it means putting our arms around each other and loving each other no matter what. That's what you get from us, CC, always. No matter what."

CC couldn't be sure how long they sat there, but it was well past the time they usually ate supper. The crickets started chirping and she could feel the darkness settling in around her. As her sobbing became sniffles, she could feel the exhaustion from all the emotion of the last few minutes. She wanted to ask Gran if she could just go upstairs to her room, but before she could say anything, Gran took over.

"CC, why don't you wash up? Take your time. We'll wait for you, but I would feel better if you ate a little something and I think you would too. Want to give it a try?"

CC was all out of words for now. She looked up and blinked at Gran managing a weak smile. She nuzzled one more time in Gran's shoulder and managed to say, "I think I will. I haven't eaten all day." The thought of food actually made her stomach turn but she knew her grandmother wouldn't let it go.

They stood up and Gran stole one last hug before starting for the kitchen. "See you in a bit?"

"Yes ma'am. I'll be in soon. Gran, I'm going to sit on the steps for just a minute.

"Sure, but don't take too long, please. Your Gramps must be starving."

CC opened the back-screen door, hearing its familiar screech. She needed to be outside on the concrete steps alone. The stars were out and there was a breeze even though it was June. It felt good. She sat down and put her head in her hands and her elbows on her knees and swayed back and forth.

What's happened? After everything, I am dumped here in the middle of nowhere and Randy and Mama are at some favorite hangout getting drunk. Why me? I got in this situation because of him. The bastard.

She thought about the first time Randy scared her.

That night Mama had been working the late shift at the Spotlight making drinks for some other creeps. Randy was supposed to be home but had gone out. CC remembered falling asleep on the couch and waking up late knowing immediately there was something wrong. She rolled over on her side and there he was. Randy was sitting on the coffee table right next to her. She realized immediately that she was hemmed in by him. He was staring at her with a look easy to recognize. It was threatening. It was a look of a man who wanted something. His eyes watered from the booze and the smell of beer filled the room.

Spit dribbled from his mouth as he sneered at her and drawled, "Hey, CC. Went to bed early, huh? Well, I'm here now," The whisper and the booze and the funny look in his eyes gave CC all the warning she needed. He tried blocking her escape by leaning in even closer to her, but she was agile and faster than him. She pulled her upper body up and swung her leg over the coffee table which allowed her to get to the floor. Before he could move, she sprung up, teetered slightly and then ran for her room.

Locking the door, she started screaming, "Go away! I'm going to tell Mama. She'll have you outta here so fast!"

She could hear his drunken laugh and imagined him leaning against her door. "Say, whatcha getting all riled up for, Gal? I'm just trying to be a good step-daddy to you."

CC tried not to heave. The thought of him being in the house permanently was an awful idea. "Mama would never marry you. You will never be related to me. Get away from my door. I'm going to tell Mama what you did."

"Whatta you gonna tell her. That I woke you up? You're a firecracker and she knows it." Randy had said. "She ain't never gonna believe anything you say."

And Mama hadn't believed her. Thought she was exaggerating.

"What are you telling me, Cicely? That he tried to do something to you? Listen, he was drinking. Just fooling around. Grow up. He didn't mean anything. He takes good care of me, girl. I don't need you to mess things up around here."

Thinking about Mama's answer to the whole thing was just as bad as what Randy had done.

CC put her hands over her eyes as though she could rub out the memory of that night. She wanted to forget all the stuff that happened since Randy moved in, but it was like a nightmare that she kept dreaming over and over again.

"Cicely, you want to come in now and get a little something to eat?" Gramps was holding the screen door open and speaking low. "Your Gran said your name is now CC. You're gonna have to explain that new twist to me, but how about doing it over some homemade mashed potatoes? You think you can do that?"

CC remembered Gramps words from earlier and thought she might cry again, but she fought the tears by rubbing her eyes and standing. "Oh, Gramps, I'm sure glad you're here. You make me feel so, like, safe. I don't know. I guess I needed my Gramps." She stood facing him with her arms folded across her chest and her head down.

"Remember what I said. We need you too." As she looked up, she saw tears forming in his eyes again. CC was struck by the memory of Randy and the contrast now with Gramps standing right in front of her with that sweet expression of his.

Without a word, CC put her arms around Gramps and squeezed. It felt right and she held on for a few seconds. When she pulled away, she looked into his eyes and thought how different it felt to be held by someone like Gramps. She realized she hadn't been held like that in a long time. The moment passed and she followed him into the kitchen.

The kitchen was so bright; it took a minute for her eyes to adjust. When it did, she saw Gran back at the sink, her favorite spot, and Uncle Bud sitting in his chair by the window. He looked up when CC walked in, and he peeked at her with that wonderful shy smile of his. She had a brief thought about the encounter earlier and felt guilty about letting him get slapped. She could have kicked that boy or something, but she could barely fight her own battles.

Gramps pulled out a chair and motioned for her to sit down. "Don't think I'm going to be so, what's the word, polite or something, every time we eat."

"Gallant is the word, Ethan. Or at least I think it is. That right, CC?"

Before she could answer, she felt a couple of big paws on her legs, and the big golden retriever licked her right in the face. CC held on to the large dog and wanted to get down on the floor with him, but he had her trapped in her chair. "Oh wow! Champ! Champ! You big old thing. I forgot about you today. Where you been? I missed you. I'm sorry. I didn't go looking for you."

Gran was at the table wiping her hands. "He was with Clay in the back field to help with some baling. Came in here a little while ago and sensed you on the back steps. Started carrying on, but Bud kept him in here by the hardest."

"Yep. Had to keep him. He wants you, Sis." CC glanced over at her uncle and could see he was proud of taking care of Champ.

I'm glad to see you, Champ. You doing good? You sure look like it."

"All right, Champ, down." Gran was taking over in her domain. "You can lie down by Bud while Cicely eats. Come on now. Over to Bud."

Champ trotted over and settled in around Uncle Bud's feet. CC was excited to see him but she knew she better eat something for Gran's sake or she would just get more pressure.

CC started with a bite of mashed potatoes. Minutes ago, she thought she might throw up if she had to eat, but now she relished the taste of the warm soft homemade dish. She eyed the big stick of butter in the middle of the table and cut off a swath and plopped it on top. She mixed it around a little bit and then dove in.

"You think you could try a little chicken, Sweetheart?" Gran didn't wait for an answer. "Here, just take a little bite and eat it with your potatoes. And when you finish that, I have some of that pie we talked about earlier."

Now Gran had a big grin. She accomplished what she wanted. Her granddaughter was sitting at her table eating and enjoying her meal.

"This is good, Gran, but I'm not sure about the pie."

"Oh, you want the pie. If you don't, it'll be all gone before daybreak. I'm taking a big slice to work." Gramps was grinning too.

"What work, Gramps? Where are you going?"

"We didn't get a chance to tell you. I'm working in town at Uncle Red's gas station. Helping fill gas tanks and tires and such. Bringing in some extra money."

They heard a car door slam and Champ sprung up and growled.

Gran was the first to ask, "Who could that be this time of night?"

"Let's find out." Gramps was almost to the door when they heard a knock.

Opening the door, Gramps stood back and squinted. Then his whole face lit up. "I can't believe it! Bess, come see who showed up on our doorstep."

A tall, brown haired, lanky boy stood by the door. He had a huge grin and twirled a cream-colored cowboy hat with his big hands. CC thought he looked familiar but wasn't sure.

Gran edged over from the table and looked over Gramps' shoulder. She let out a yell and pushed Gramps over so she could get a good look. "Oh, I can't believe you got here so soon. We just got your letter. Son, how did you… where are your… Oh, I don't care, come here and let me look at you."

CC saw her Gran grab him for a big hug. She didn't know if Gran was crying or just overjoyed, but whatever it was, they were happy to see him. Gran turned around and pulled him in the kitchen. She thought she heard Uncle Bud make a sound because he was standing nearer her now. Champ stood next to her uncle and was wagging his tail cautiously.

Gramps couldn't hold back anymore. He grabbed the young man and hugged him too. He muttered, "You came all this way to see us, son. This is too good to be true."

The three of them turned around and realized CC was sitting at the table staring at the little group. "This is Johnny, Cicely. You remember him, don't you? This is your cousin all the way from Texas."

CC heard Uncle Bud murmur, "John. Johnny. From Texas."

She remembered him as a little kid, but he was definitely older than her. He was much taller and looked like he was eighteen or nineteen.

Johnny didn't acknowledge any of the comments. His face broke into a crooked smile and his eyes twinkled. He walked straight up to Uncle Bud and said, "Hi, Dad."

CHAPTER 6

CC watched the hullabaloo from her perch on the kitchen chair. Uncle Bud grinned from ear to ear and kept repeating "Johnny, Johnny." Gran still had her arm over Johnny's shoulder and CC wondered how long it would take Gran to make him sit down and eat supper.

CC recognized Johnny from past summers on the farm. He was the nicest of all her cousins. She was the youngest and the only girl and he always stood up for her when they teased her.

She squirmed when Johnny recognized her by loudly calling out her name, "Cicely. You sure have grown up."

"Aw, come on, CC, stand up and say hello. He won't bite."

Aggravated looks were CC's specialty. She rolled her eyes and scowled. She managed a very brief, 'hi' with a slight wave of her hand and then plopped back down in her chair.

It didn't bother Johnny. He was still looking at her with a big grin and wasn't ready to back down. "You sure look different than the little kid who kicked Tommy and shut him up. Let's see. I'm eighteen so you must be at least sixteen, huh?"

"Yep." So far Johnny was just like she remembered. Always finding something friendly to say. He was very tall, a couple of inches taller than Uncle Bud. CC thought he was six something, but he didn't look like his father at all because he didn't have red hair or freckles. His brownish hair curled up on the ends, and he had laugh lines around his brown eyes when he smiled.

Gran started talking to Johnny taking the attention off her. She felt uncomfortable and irritated by the chit chat that was going on and wanted an escape. Lifting herself off the chair, she started tiptoeing out of the kitchen, hoping they wouldn't notice.

No such luck. Gramps spotted her and wasn't going to let her give up so easily. "Hey, CC. You going up to your room? Why don't you stick around and have a piece of that pie before it disappears?"

When she looked across the room, she was surprised to see Johnny eyeing her with an understanding stare. She didn't know why, but she could tell he understood she needed to leave. All he said was "See you in the morning, Cicely." She felt relieved that someone could tell she had to get out of there.

CC bounded up the stairs to the bedroom. When she got to the top of the stairs, she leaned her head against the closed door and fought to catch her breath. *Oh God. What's wrong with me? I had to get out of there. They're so happy and I'm an idiot. I can't even act like a normal kid anymore. I need some time by myself.*

She straightened and took a deep breath. CC knew what was waiting on the other side of the door. It was hard to relax in this bedroom. It had been Mama's room and she always felt like she stepped into the 1950's.

"Good grief!" she said as she took in the room. Gran had turned the light in the center of the ceiling on and it made the room so bright, she had to blink to adjust her eyes. "What the hell?" She found the lamp on the bedside table and flipped the overhead off.

"This room is like it's from *The Donna Reed Show.* Sweet and frilly. Not like Mama at all." CC laughed out loud. "This is too much. Mama couldn't have gone for this stuff. She's no Donna Reed. That's for sure. She's all rough and loud. More like *Whatever Happened to Baby Jane?* She would fit in Baby Jane's room. "

CC stood at the end of a very white bed and let her eyes roam from the pillows to a dresser to windows covered in white frilly curtains. It seemed like everything in the room had ruffles. Lots and lots of them. On the curtains, on the bedspread, on the cloth that covered the front of the table. She sat down on a chair near the table and immediately hopped up again. It was very soft and the seat was covered in pink fabric with little dogs and cats in different colors.

At home Mama didn't always make it to her own bedroom. She thought of the time she was about eleven and found her mother passed out in the morning asleep on the sofa. It was the first time she admitted to herself her mother drank too much. Way too much. She got up to go to school and knew she was late. Mama didn't wake her up. No surprise there. When she went into the living room, there was Mama sound asleep on the couch. She had rolled over on her side and her leg hung over the side. What stood out in CC's mind was the loud snoring with her mouth wide open and the half empty liquor bottle on the floor next to her. CC started to wake her up, but changed her mind, instead dressing quietly and slipping out the door. She always walked to school, but that morning she felt so alone.

CC spotted her bag, the one Gran had brought up for her. She unzipped it and rooted around for something of her own to toss on the bed.

"Ahhh! I forgot about this." CC pulled out a small blanket she had thrown in at the last minute. "I'm glad I brought this." She used to roll it up and use it for her pillow when she was in Shreveport.

She reached in the bag again and pulled out her transistor radio. "Let the batteries work, please." Turning it on only produced a lot of static so she moved closer to the window and positioned it on the top of the bed frame. The only station she could find was someone talking but at least she had some kind of noise.

CC lay back on her blanket. She was exhausted and closed her eyes. The announcer droned on and on about music and she drifted off into a light sleep. She wasn't sure how much later it was when she woke to the Platters' "Only You."

The house was night quiet; you know it's late without looking at a clock. She rolled over and faced the white pillow with the ruffles.

Then she sat up, stretched, and thought about having to sleep in this room. "Not sure I can sleep in here," she whispered. She got up, grabbed her radio and blanket and headed for the hallway. She tiptoed down the stairs lit by a hallway lamp. At the foot of the stairs, she checked again, but there was no sound. She felt her way through the kitchen to the back door and safely out to the sleeping porch.

CC looked around trying to adjust her vision and trying to find a lamp or a light switch. She felt around on the wall with no luck.

"Hey, Cicely. Is that you?"

CC jumped and let out a little yelp. "What? Johnny, is that you? You scared me half to death." She dropped her radio, but held on to the blanket.

"You woke me up. I'm the one who's surprised," Johnny countered while he switched on the lamp next to the sofa. "What are you doing down here? Can't you sleep?'

"No, I can't." CC started to say something about the room, but decided not to get into that. "You're as bad as I am though. You're sleeping in your clothes, too."

Johnny sat up and swung his legs over. He still had that smile on his face.

CC couldn't resist. "Do you smile all the time? How 'bout in your sleep?"

"I wouldn't know. No one ever told me if I do, but I know people tell me I smile a lot."

CC felt bad about teasing him. She could tell he was trying to be nice to her. "I can go back upstairs if you want. I used to sleep down here."

"I remember. You always got dibs on this room. It's okay. Don't go. I wasn't sound asleep yet anyway. Here, sit down." He pulled his blanket over to make room for her next to him. CC sat at the very end so she wouldn't be too close.

"Are you hungry? By the way, why is everyone calling you CC?"

"Yep, that's my name now. Do you know if there's any pie left?"

There was that grin again. "Sure is. Come on."

CC followed her cousin into the kitchen and he turned on the stove light. The room was bathed in a soft glow, and CC thought how nice it looked. Kind of homey. The covered pie was in the middle of the table. Johnny poked around for a knife while CC got the plates. They faced each other at the table and dug into the delicious slices.

"This is cool," CC managed with a full mouth. She was surprised at how hungry she was.

Johnny motioned with his hand and got up to retrieve two glasses and milk from the icebox. "Can't have pie without milk."

"I guess we have to leave the rest for Gramps' lunch," CC moaned.

"I know for a fact Gran already packed a slice for him."

It only took a second for them to look at each other and dive in for more.

CC took the final gulps of milk and leaned back in her chair. She played with the glass by turning it around with her fingers and avoided looking at

Johnny. "Why did you come here? I mean is there anything in particular. I know how much you love it around here, but is there anything going on?"

Johnny took his time to answer. "I guess there's a lot. I graduated early and…"

"You are already out of school? Wow, that's cool."

"I guess it is. My mother, Dorothy, wanted me to stay in Waco and apply for a scholarship to Baylor, but I wanted to come here. I applied to Tech and got a scholarship if I major in a science program.'

"You did all that? Did anyone help you?" CC wondered how people made things happen.

"I had a lot of help from my counselor and my calculus teacher." He noticed CC's astonishment. "Yeah, calculus. That was my favorite last year. Good thing, too. He knows the dean here at Tech."

CC felt like she was talking to a total stranger. This didn't seem like the kid who ran around the farm and told her cousins to shut up.

Johnny explained, "But I want to be here to help Gramps with the farm so Dad can stay here."

"Why? Is he going somewhere?"

Johnny's expression changed. He looked very serious. "My mom told me Gramps and Gran started talking about finding an institution for him. They're getting older and they're not able to keep working the farm. They want him to be cared for."

CC was shocked at how determined Johnny sounded. "I'm going to take care of my dad. I'm going to school so I can keep this farm and keep him here too. I don't want Dad going to one of those places. I'm going to take care of all three of them."

CHAPTER 7

CC laid on the couch listening to the farm wake up. The crickets gradually faded out to the sounds of frogs near the pond as the rooster crowed. She even heard Lady's whinnying from the barn and Gramps' truck on the gravel road as he left for work.

CC and Johnny had stayed up late talking after they finished the pie. He told her about his last year in Waco studying hard so he could graduate. She asked him why he called his mother by her first name instead of Mom or Mama and he had this faraway look before he said he just did, wasn't sure why.

She thought they got a little loopy staying up so late talking about the kind of music they loved. Johnny told her about Patsy Cline who died last March in an accident. He said she was a famous country singer, but CC never heard of her so Johnny broke into a song called "Crazy." He said it was famous, and he was so funny singing a few lines about somebody being crazy for feeling blue.

She remembered hearing it once on the radio, but told him she wasn't a country music gal. When he asked her about her favorite singer, she had to admit she loved Elvis.

"Ah! But he sings country, too."

"No, no he sings rock and roll," CC protested.

"What about *Loving You?*

CC hummed the melody and Johnny asked, "Can't you hear the country in that song, CC?"

"This is too stupid. You're from Texas. You think it's all country. What is it, like three in the morning or something?"

CC couldn't stifle a big yawn, so they agreed to call it a night. She started for the stairs and Johnny called out to her. "Where are you going? Thought you were sleeping on the porch."

"I wanted to, but where will you sleep?"

"No problem," Johnny answered. "My dad's room has twin beds. I'm go bunk with him. Rather do that anyway. See you in the morning."

It didn't take long for CC to collapse and fall sound asleep after Johnny said good night. Listening to the morning sounds now, she thought about Johnny coming all the way here to help Uncle Bud and their grandparents. She remembered how Mama dumped her here and wondered if Mama even knew about the problems on the farm.

She decided to creep up the stairs to get some clean clothes and use the upstairs bathroom. Even though she dreaded going back in Mama's old bedroom, she dreaded even more spending another day in the same clothes. She grabbed fresh jeans and a shirt and washed up in record time.

The fragrant smell of coffee drifted from the kitchen. CC wasn't a big coffee drinker, but this morning it beckoned her. Entering the kitchen, she saw Johnny standing by Gran giving her a smack on the cheek.

Johnny shouted, "Hey, Cuz, I mean CC, you up already? Gran, this gal can put away some pie. And she can carry a tune too."

"You did all the singing, remember?" Gran was beaming at the both of them. CC didn't know what she had done to make Gran so happy, but she had done something right.

Johnny was out the door taking a cup of steaming brew with him. "See you later, Gran, I'm going to catch up with Dad. CC, come on down to the orchard if you want to catch up with us."

"Good morning, CC. You sleep OK?" Gran asked. "I see you came down to the sleeping porch, your favorite spot."

"Yeah, I did, Gran. We can talk about redecorating the bedroom later."

"You know, CC, I was thinking. It needs a little facelift. Looks old, don't you think?"

CC avoided Gran's eyes. "Gran, you don't have to do anything special for me. Especially since I'm just here for a little while." She kept her back turned as she poured a cup for herself.

"Gran, I was wondering. Did you say anything to Johnny about me and... you know, me and the... what we talked about last night? I just want to know because I forgot to say let's keep it to ourselves."

Gran wiped her hands on a towel and walked over to CC. She put each hand against CC's cheeks and kissed her on the forehead. "You don't have to say anything you don't want to. And no, your Gramps and I haven't talked about it." She searched CC's eyes. "How about some breakfast? Think you can eat fresh eggs and toast. You used to love bread toasted in the oven?"

CC turned away as she fought to hide her embarrassment. She heard herself ask in a soft voice, "Will I ever be normal again, Gran?"

"What do you mean normal, child? Depends on what you mean by normal."

She immediately felt sorry she asked that question and turned back to Gran. "I don't know what I meant. It was a stupid question, I guess." Before her gran could say anything, CC added, "I think I'll hold off on any breakfast. I'm not used to it. Usually wait to eat lunch at school. I'm going to go saddle Lady and catch up with Johnny. OK?"

The look of concern on Gran's face disappeared. "Sure thing. Let me know if you want something later."

CC hurried to the barn and heard Clay whistling near the loft. "Hey, Clay, how you doing?"

"I'm doing fine, Cicely. Hear you met my boy, Eric. How'd that go?"

"Went fine, Clay. We didn't talk much." CC wanted to avoid any more discussion about him. "I'm going to saddle Lady, but I'm glad you're here to check the harness for me."

"Sure thing. You was good at it last time you were here."

"Thanks, Clay."

It was a source of pride for CC to get on Lady by herself. Lady was the old family mare that all the kids rode, but CC always loved to gallop on her. It didn't take long to get her ready. After Clay checked the girth and the bit, she was riding out of the barn, past Uncle Bud's garden, waving at Gran though the kitchen window and trotting toward the peach trees.

She had to admit it felt good to be outside. As hot as it was it wasn't as noticeable on top of Lady. She pulled back on the harness and sat for a minute to take in the smell of the peach trees and give her a chance to listen for Johnny. She heard him talking to Uncle Bud.

"Dad, what do you mean? What about birds?" Johnny was asking Uncle Bud.

"Birds dead. Near trees. All over," mumbled her uncle.

"We'll have to look around, but I'd be surprised if we found very many." CC heard Johnny pulling on branches as he talked.

She clicked for Lady to move in to the clearing. Johnny turned and flashed a big smile and Uncle Bud jumped slightly in surprise. "Glad you made it," Johnny said. "Dad and I are talking about some damage around here. He's come across a dead bird and I'm looking at these trees. They don't look as healthy as they usually do."

Uncle Bud was kneeling on the ground. "Not just this one. I found more," Uncle Bud chimed in. He took a handkerchief out of his pocket and wrapped it around the bird.

"What're you gonna do with it now, Uncle Bud? You're not going to put it in your pocket, are you?"

He peered at her with his usual gentle smile. Before he could answer, Johnny told him to put it in a small pile of brush next to one of the trees. "We'll take care of it later, Dad."

Johnny motioned for CC to follow him. She looped Lady's bridle casually around a branch to keep her in place and followed Johnny. The orchard was always one of CC's favorite spots when she was a little kid. It was fun to hide among the trees because the aroma from the peaches was so great. Gramps would walk down when they ripened, and they would always pick a bushel together. He used to let her ride in the truck to take the fruit to the market in town.

"Are you on another planet, Cuz?" Johnny hollered from the edge of the tree line.

"No, I am not, and please don't call me Cuz. That sounds so icky and countrified," CC countered.

"I am countrified, CeeeCeee," exaggerating her name. "Hey, do you smell smoke?"

CC walked over to Johnny. "Yeah," but she couldn't see anything. They were near the barbed wire fence between Gramps' property and his neighbors.

"It's coming from that field across that fence, isn't it, Johnny?"

Johnny was busy surveying the field and his smile had vanished. "Yes, it is. I don't see any crop over there. It's an open field so they must range cows here. It smells like a brush fire and you're not supposed to light those in the summer. Fall and spring only. Wonder why they're taking that risk."

CC heard Uncle Bud mumble, "Hate fires. Dangerous. Stay away."

She watched Johnny walk along the fence and stop a ways from her. He leaned over and then crouched. "Hey, what do you see?" she asked.

He shouted, "There's a big hole here in the bottom of the wire. Been cut with shears. Clean cut, not torn though by an animal which would be darn near impossible anyway."

"So what? You can tell Gramps when he gets home." CC felt like she was being pulled into something again. Just like yesterday.

Johnny stared at CC. "I'm here to help on the farm, remember? I just want to find out what's going on with this hole and with the brush fires in the middle of summer."

Uncle Bud and CC stood around while Johnny remained crouched looking at the fence and then staring at the smoke. She saw Uncle Bud look over her shoulder. Suddenly his face turned to a frown. CC heard galloping behind her. She turned and spotted Eric sitting atop a beautiful ebony horse riding along the fence on the neighbor's side.

CC groaned. "Now what? I can't believe it. I just saw him yesterday at the fence. Is he following me?"

CHAPTER 8

"Hey, CC. Thought I saw you over here. Up early, huh?" Eric pulled the reins in a few feet away from her. "Talked to Clay a little while ago, and he said you were already riding Lady."

CC's back was to Johnny but she heard him approaching her. She tensed up. She knew she couldn't help getting in the middle of the skirmish between Uncle Bud and Eric yesterday. What would happen now when Johnny found out about it? He sure wouldn't like hearing about Eric pushing his father around.

"Hey, Eric. I saddled Lady to meet up with my cousin. I thought Clay was your dad."

Eric swung his leg over the saddle and jumped down with a thud. "Yep, Clay's my dad."

CC wasn't surprised that he didn't explain why he called his dad by his first name any more than Johnny not explaining why he called his mother Dorothy. She was beginning to think it was a custom. She wondered how her mother would feel if she called her Loreen. *Probably wouldn't care.*

"So, who's your cousin?" Eric stood next to his steed holding his bridle casually. She hadn't noticed before, but he had a straw in his mouth and he wore a cowboy hat. At least that's what CC called it. She thought the fact that it was cocked to one side was not an accident. Eric knew it looked sexy that way. He knew he was good looking. There was something about some boys where you could just tell that they knew they were good looking. They walked like they owned the world, and they talked like everyone was hanging on to every word.

And CC was.

Eric looked even better in the morning sunlight. He dismounted and stood near the fence. He took the straw out of his mouth and twirled it in his hand, and the sneer that matched those steely blue eyes was plastered on his mouth.

"Who's your friend?" Johnny was standing next to her now. She had almost forgotten him as she stared at Eric.

CC still felt funny about Eric showing up. *This is crazy. I haven't done anything and I don't owe any explanations.*

"Oh, Johnny, this is Clay's son, Eric."

Johnny moved closer and held out his hand. Eric hesitated for a second and then shook hands. He looked self-confident, too, CC thought, but in a different way, like he was sure of himself, but not in a cocky way like Eric.

"I don't remember you around here. My brothers and I used to come every summer." Johnny seemed curious, but he was still smiling.

CC noticed a dark expression spread over Eric's face as he stood there silently. She wondered why he didn't respond, but his face cleared and he turned to CC. "How 'bout that ride? I could show you the Gibbs' property on this side. He has a pond across this field."

Johnny ignored the fact that he was talking to CC. "You work for Mr. Gibbs?"

This time Eric glared at Johnny. "You sure are asking a lot of questions this morning. Why do you want to know that? You need a job?"

CC could sense Johnny getting his back up a little, but he sounded normal. "Just wanting to know who's talking to us."

Eric was quick on his reply, "I think I was talking to the gal from the big city. Not you."

CC was almost knocked over as Uncle Bud ran up between her and Johnny and started screaming. "Can't fight again. Leave us alone. Go! Leave!"

"Hey, not again. I'm not going to put up with you today. I told you yesterday to keep back and leave your hands to yourself," Eric shouted.

Uncle Bud flailed his arms above Johnny's head and yelled what sounded like gibberish. With Uncle Bud's back to CC, she had trouble understanding him, but Johnny was holding his father's shoulders trying to calm him. "Dad. Dad. It's all right. Nothing will happen to you while I'm here."

Turning to Eric, Johnny's brows furrowed, now dead serious, and he spoke like he was measuring every word. "You don't know this, but he is my dad. What's going on? Why is he so upset?"

Eric stretched to his full height and attempted to stare Johnny down before he said, "Just a little tiff yesterday. Nothing to worry about, isn't that right, CC?" He never looked at her as he spoke. The two men glared at each other.

This must be what they call a standoff, CC thought, and they look like idiots. She was grateful Eric didn't call her uncle a retard in front of Johnny. It would've been a real disaster if he had.

She admitted, "It got out of hand, Johnny. Your dad misunderstood what was going on. I don't think he was hurt." She avoided looking at her uncle. She could tell he was looking at her with those sad puppy eyes. That made her annoyed with having to explain herself.

"Look, Johnny, I was just trying to take care of your dad, and now I'm in the middle of this mess."

Turning from the three of them, she made her way back to Lady and announced as she mounted her, "I'm going back to the house."

She knew Johnny was riled up, but he kept his cool as she heard him ask Eric, "You know anything about this hole in the fence over here? Somebody's cut it."

"I don't know nothin' about it. Now getting back to you, Miss Cicely."

Sitting atop Lady, she was quick to tell him, "Actually, my name is CC, remember? And I don't have time for a ride. Like I said, I have to get back." She glanced at Uncle Bud again and was relieved to see he looked calm. He stood by the tree, stooped, with his head down while he picked bark with his fingers.

Eric shouted after her, "Plenty of time for riding, CC. Dad says you might be staying on round here."

CC bristled at that comment. *Why does Clay think I'm staying here? Who said that? Am I the topic of conversation around here or what? Eric may be good looking, but he's way too much trouble for me. He's nosy, and I sure don't want to get involved with anyone who thinks they know too much about me.*

She aimed Lady for the house and called to Johnny, "Y'all coming on now or you staying? I need to get back."

"Yeah, we'll be on our way, but I'm going to the barn." Johnny looked at Eric as he said going to the barn. CC thought for sure Johnny was gonna talk to Clay.

CC trotted along being careful not to look in Eric's direction. She didn't hear another horse behind her, so she guessed he galloped off by himself. As she left the orchard, she felt the nice breeze coming towards her in the open field. She laughed to herself thinking that she had seen Eric three times, and all three times, it was at a fence. But her laugh dwindled as she thought about the tension between Johnny and Eric.

"That sure looks like it's gonna be bad between them," CC mumbled to herself. "Those two are like oil and water. If Eric keeps taunting Uncle Bud, there'll be trouble for sure."

CHAPTER 9

CC led Lady to the water bucket and let her take her fill. Clay walked over to them saying, "Hey CC, did you have a nice ride?"

She nodded and tried to hide her annoyance after Eric's comments about her sticking around. He took Lady back to the barn for her, and CC headed back to the house relieved to get out of the heat.

CC's thoughts about Clay and Eric were interrupted when she stumbled over a basket of Uncle Bud's vegetables by the back steps. Gran heard her and yelled out the kitchen window, "Glad you're back from the ride. Want to come in for a little breakfast now?"

Stretching her back and arms she answered, "I think I'm just going to have coffee or juice and toast."

While she washed and dried her hands at the sink, Gran puttered. "Sounds all right. It's too hot to have the oven on, but you can fix a piece in this toaster. Fresh juice in the icebox and coffee's still warm."

She grabbed a cup, and popped a slice of bread in the toaster. "Say, Gran, now that you have this modern toaster, does that mean you buy jelly? Or do you still make those fresh peach preserves?"

Gran smiled. "There's a fresh jar I made in the icebox. Help yourself."

CC grabbed the bread when it popped up and started heaping butter on the slice. She spread the golden preserves over it, and bit right in before sitting down. With her mouth full, she muttered, "Damn, this is good."

"Excuse me?" Gran exclaimed with tilted brows. "What was that?"

"I mean this is wicked, Gran," and was amazed at how hungry she was. She couldn't remember the last time she was this hungry.

Gran interrupted her thoughts. "CC, I would rather you sleep in your mother's old room upstairs. I told Johnny to take the porch last night, Okay?"

CC put her cup down and looked at Gran. "Johnny and I decided he would bunk with his dad. He said there are twin beds in his room."

Gran's look let CC know the plans had changed. "There are twin beds, but it's very crowded in there. I told Johnny to sleep on the porch. You need to have your own room with some privacy and a proper bathroom. The bathroom down here is for Bud, and now Johnny, of course."

Suddenly the toast didn't taste as yummy. CC felt her stomach flip a little and her mouth went dry. She wasn't used to being told what to do. Mama was always at work or passed out or with Randy. As she twirled the coffee cup around, she murmured a reluctant, "All right. I guess so. Gran, what about...?"

Before she could finish her question, Gran sat down in the chair opposite her. "There's something else I want to talk to you about, CC."

Now what? I can't handle too much talking with her about the room or anything. What does she want from me now?

CC sat at attention while Gran began explaining, "I know you don't want to stay here and go to school, at least that's what you think now..." She held up her hand to stop CC from protesting. CC felt that churning in her stomach again.

"Like I said you want to go back to New Orleans, but I think you need to do something about your schooling. I know you missed some time this spring. My friend, Jessica Boudreaux, works at the high school here. I've been talking to her about you and trying to make some plans for you this summer."

Her mouth fell open as she gaped at Gran. "What do you mean discussing me with your friend? What does that mean? Does she know all about me now?"

Gran leaned in and slid her hands over the table. CC hadn't noticed before but her grandmother's hands, wrinkled with veins popping out, looked even older than her face. Gran's face wasn't terribly wrinkled, but she always pulled her hair back in a bun. Even though it was grey, she had these little tendrils that gathered around the side of her face making her seem a little younger.

Why is she taking over my life? She's old, I guess, but that doesn't make her know everything, does it?

Gran started in again. "You always did good in school. You made your grades and liked your teachers, didn't you?"

CC managed to swallow and nod "Yeah, I guess so. But what does that have to do with my visit here this summer?"

"It has everything to do with it. It's almost the end of June. Don't you want to keep up in school? "

CC thought of telling her Gran the truth. She didn't want to be here at all. But where would she go if she couldn't stay here? Could she go home? What home? The hall radio played some old fifties song, and she thought, this is what I'm going to be hearing if I stay here. Who is that? That guy Perry Como? God.

"What are you saying, Gran? What can I do about school here? I didn't finish all my credits so I guess I'm going to stay in tenth grade." She felt her eyes watering.

"That's what I mean. We can do something about your credits. Miss Jessica said so. She wants to help."

"Help how, Gran? How? I'm in the middle of nowhere and I don't have any way to change what happened last year. I'm stuck. And I know. It's all my fault. Okay? Why won't everyone stop reminding me I messed up! God!"

CC sprung from her chair. She couldn't hold back her frustration any longer. How did her Gran think talking about failing school and some teacher she didn't even know could help her? Nothing could help her

She paced across the kitchen a couple of times, before turning back to Gran.

"So now what, Gran, what do you want me to do? Do I have any say so in this or is this some kind of punishment?"

Gran settled in her chair and brushed the crumbs from the table. CC could tell she wasn't about to back down. Her face took on that stern look where she arched one eyebrow and made her eyes look like they were missiles coming right at you. "When you calm down, I'll tell you what you can do and what I can do to help you. You interested or you just want to keep pacing around the room?"

CC sat in her chair, crossed her arms and stared at the unfinished coffee in front of her.

"Well, I'm telling you, the granddaughter I've always known is smart as a whip. You still are, aren't you?" She didn't wait for CC to answer. "I know you are, and Miss Jessica wants to give you some work to turn in to your school next year, wherever that is, so you can move on to eleventh grade next year. What's so bad about that?"

CC uncrossed her arms and rubbed her hands back and forth on her jeans. Before she could answer Gran, the back screen swung open and Johnny walked in.

He walked over to the sink and filled a glass with water. Turning and leaning against the cabinet, he swallowed the whole glass's contents. He acknowledged them sitting at the table, "Thirsty, you know?" He put the glass down and spread his arms over the counter. He stared at the floor and CC could tell he was bothered about something.

Gran broke the awkward silence. "Something' on your mind, Johnny? You seem deep in thought."

Johnny stared at CC for a minute and she wondered if he and Eric had gotten into a fight after she left the orchard. It was already uneasy in the kitchen what with Gran throwing the stuff about school at her. She hoped she wouldn't have to defend herself about Uncle Bud getting slapped around.

"I was just wondering how much you know about that boy Eric, Gran? Has he been around a while or what?"

When Gran pushed her chair away from the table, it screeched and CC jumped. She looked at CC and teased, "You jumpy about something? Johnny, I told CC last night, he's Clay's son and we don't know much about him except that he dropped out of school. He's seventeen. Clay told us he came here to live to get to know Clay. He hasn't had any time with him. Lives with his mother up north somewhere."

Johnny's eyes narrowed. He focused on CC. "You haven't seen much of him, huh Cuz?"

CC hid the fact that she was irked about being questioned and about being called Cuz again. She was glad to get the attention off her talk with

Gran. "I just met him a couple of days ago. Don't know him. Don't plan on knowing him."

Gran seized the moment to bring Johnny into the previous conversation. "Speaking of school, I was just telling CC that she can make up her credits while she's here this summer."

CC protested, "Gran, I was asking you if I had a say in this. I'm not sure how long I'm going to be here. What if I get started with this stuff and can't finish?"

"Then you can take it with you wherever you go. Look, CC, this is a good plan to keep you from getting behind in your studies."

CC looked from Gran to Johnny to Gran and back to Johnny again. He broke into a grin and that made CC annoyed with him again. Gran was taking over her life and Johnny stood there grinning like he had the upper hand. Not only was she backed into a corner, but Johnny was enjoying it.

Gran stood and announced, "CC, I'm going to call Miss Jessica and set up a time for you and me to go see her. Then we can make a decision. Just meet her." Her back was to CC as she said "You're going to love her. This is a great idea, you'll see."

"Do I have any choice? At all?" There was no answer as Gran was already down the hall to make a phone call. "Johnny, couldn't you say anything? You used to take up for me with our cousins. Can't you see? Gran is pushing me into this. I don't want to study with some stranger in this hick place. Are you laughing Johnny? Look, I'm not doing this. She can't make me."

Johnny stopped laughing and folded his hands over his chest. He kicked back against the counter. "Are we talking about our Gran? I think she already decided this for you. You ought to just roll with it. Sounds like a good idea actually. Making up some school work in your free time. Getting ahead for school next year? Anyway, after what happened with Clay's son and Dad yesterday, do you want to just hang out around the farm this summer by yourself? I'm going to be busy. Have to help Gramps and get ready for college next fall."

Gran returned and was standing at the doorway. "Good news, CC, she can see us tomorrow afternoon after lunch." And with that Gran turned and made her way down the hall again. CC was sure she was humming. To make it even worse, she heard Johnny laughing again.

CC felt her face flush. She wasn't sure where this was going, but it felt like her life was now in Gran's hands. And she didn't like it. *This is going to be a real drag.*

CHAPTER 10

Trapped. Cornered. Those were the words running though CC's head as she bathed. Not only did Gran make an appointment for her, but she suggested she take a bath before they left because CC had been outside all morning in the sun. She mumbled all the way up the stairs about being treated like a child. "Telling me to take a bath. Change clothes. Go see some lady I don't know. Damn."

When CC finished bathing, she put on her other pair of jeans and a blouse from the bottom of her suitcase. "Gran will have something to say about this outfit. The top is wrinkled." Looking in the mirror she noticed the buttons on the top were tighter than before. "Have I put on weight? I guess so, but I wore this all the time last fall. Say it. Say it out loud. "Okay, I had a baby" There. I said it. "I had a baby and my boobs are bigger. I'm bigger."

Holding on to that thought, she trudged down the stairs. She saw Gran whispering to Johnny. She intentionally coughed loud enough for them to hear her. Gran turned and without skipping a beat asked, "Would you want to put your hair up in a ponytail?"

CC noticed Johnny actually roll his eyes and to CC's relief came to her rescue. "You look fine, CC." Turning to Gran, "She's only going to the school."

CC kept quiet. She just wanted to get this over with.

Gran brought the car around. CC climbed into the passenger seat and rolled her window down. Gran still had her steel gray fifties Ford. They said they bought it used. It was nothing like the new Impala she arrived in with Mama. This was totally stripped down with no air, no radio, no power steering, no power transmission, actually no power anything. It was just a hot box, but Gran handled it expertly. CC watched how she shifted effortlessly to keep the old Ford moving.

They started down the same gravel driveway where CC arrived a few days before. The corn field was on her right and cows grazed in a nearby pasture. It looked the same as it had in all the summers before. The cows looked like a painting. They stood perfectly still only moving to lower their heads to graze. CC could actually see the blistering heat rising from the corn stalks. Gramps used to joke about the corn popping by itself with these summer temperatures.

When they got on the two-lane road going into town, the breeze coming through CC's window felt good on her face. She ignored the land on the drive coming here, but now she scanned the rolling country hills. It was so different here than in New Orleans. In northern Louisiana, there was a lot of open land with hills and trees. Everything was green and you could go for miles without seeing anything but another farm.

She laid her head back and wished the car had a radio. "Gran, don't you miss having a radio. You could listen to some music."

Gran smiled at her. "I don't miss it. You know, we have television at home and it's nice to get away from the noise. I like to drive and clear my head."

"What do you clear out of your head?"

Gran snickered at that question. "Whatever may be bothering me, I guess.

As the car glided down another hill, what looked like a school came into view. "Is that where we're going to see this lady?"

Gran took a sidelong glance at CC. "Yep, it is. That's Ruston High School."

CC thought it looked bigger than she expected. There were a lot of windows on the three large grey buildings, and no trees anywhere around. The big red school letters showed up on the building's sides. Made her think it was a new school. There were boys in uniforms on a large field who liked like they were practicing for football season.

Gran came to a stop at the entrance to a one-story building and looked around to find a parking space. She spotted one with a sign that said, 'Visitor' and she eased the Ford in the slot. Gran told CC to leave the windows down and she climbed out.

"CC, you coming?"

CC sat with her hands folded in her lap with her head bowed. When she looked up, she knew she seemed pitiful as she turned to Gran. "I don't know what to say to her. Gran, what did you tell her about my being out of school?"

"I just told her you had to drop out the last few weeks cause of a personal emergency. I don't expect her to ask you why, but if she does, you can repeat that. It's true, isn't it? Now, are you coming or not?"

It was very hot in the car already and CC could feel the sweat dripping down her back. She thought it might be because she was nervous, but she decided either way, she better get out of the car. She slid out and slammed the door. As she felt the sweat on her neck, she said, "I should have put my hair up," and was grateful Gran didn't say 'told you so.'

They walked through the big doors in the front of the building and immediately saw a sign that said OFFICE on the right. CC peeked through the big glass window. "Where is she?"

"You mean Miss Jessica Boudreaux? She said to come over to her office and knock." Gran walked a few feet down the hall, and there was another office on the left, with a sign that said, J. Boudreaux, Assistant Principal. The door was open but Gran stopped and made a motion with her arm to show Miss Jessica was on the phone. "Let's sit in these chairs and wait."

CC knew about these chairs. You sat there if you were in trouble and had to see the principal or somebody like him. Kids passed by on purpose to tease you and make faces at you. She wanted to move around. "Gran, how about I walk around a little? I haven't been in school for a while. Just want to go down the hall."

"All right, but stay within shouting range. We don't want to make her wait."

CC started down the hall. It seemed eerie without any kids roaming around. She heard music from down the hallway but couldn't make it out. She tiptoed so as not to make a sound. CC thought it was kind of like being in a church, all quiet and clean. The doors to the classrooms were all closed, but she noticed a door at the end of the hall was propped open with a box and it seemed the music was coming from that room.

As she approached there was no mistaking that sound. Laughing to herself, CC said out loud, "Can't believe it. The Beach Boys." The familiar voices of the California sound echoed through the doorway.

When she peered into the room, a girl bounced to the music and held a book in her hands. CC thought she might be the same age as her, but a totally different look. She had these blond curls that looked like they sprang out of her head in all different directions. That was the first thing you noticed about California girl.

When CC got past the hair, she realized the girl was shorter than she appeared at first. She had on jeans and a red shirt that set off her hair. As she glanced down, she saw the girl was wearing boots that CC would trade her prize possessions for in a heartbeat. They were real worn leather that looked like natural calfskin. She had seen a pair at Godchaux's Department Store in New Orleans. Definitely out of her price range.

Just as she was admiring the boots, California girl saw her standing there and yelled out, "Hey! Come on in!" You here to help me?" Then she bolted for the portable phonograph and turned the music down.

CC couldn't resist. "You can turn it off. I'm definitely not a Beach Boys fan."

"Oh wow! Why not? They're the hottest thing around except for that new group in England." And then she smiled the widest smile CC could imagine. It was the kind of look that made you smile back even if you didn't feel like it.

"Oh, I know. I like the Beatles. I still like Elvis too. I know, he's a fifties guy, but I love him." As soon as CC said it, that stupid feeling came back. She didn't even know this person, and she was disclosing personal music tastes. *I must seem like a real idiot.*

It didn't matter. California girl had already turned the phonograph off. "Hey, that's fab, too. My big brother has the biggest Elvis record collection and he's away at college. I could bring some of those here. He'd kill me if he knew. I don't know why he didn't take them with him, but..." and then she stopped talking, and that big grin that filled up her whole face was back.

"I see you two have already met. I was going to bring you down here to meet Addy." CC guessed the woman who walked in was Miss Jessica

Boudreaux. "Hello, you must be Cicely, or is it CC? Sorry, I was on the phone when you and your grandmother got here."

CC shook the woman's hand She was very tall and thin and looked more like a model than an assistant principal.

California girl walked over to CC and Miss Boudreaux. She was so close CC almost bumped into her when she turned around. "No, we were just talking, Miss Jessica. Hey, I'm Addy. Addy Forrester. I go to school here and I'm working on a volunteer program this summer." She was still grinning.

CC looked from Miss Boudreaux to Addy. She felt out of place and squeezed in between the two of them. She wondered where Gran was. Before she could ask, Miss Boudreaux said, "Your grandmother went over to the office to talk to her friend Stella, the school secretary."

"Oh, okay." She looked at Addy. That big smile of hers was reassuring.

Miss Boudreaux touched CC's arm lightly. "Why don't we go back to my office to talk, CC? Addy, we'll catch up with you later if CC has time."

"Yes, ma'am. See you later, CC. Miss Jessica, these are the books I'm taking to the church tomorrow. You need to check them out?"

"We'll talk about that later, Addy." Then she turned to CC, "Come on, CC. I'm glad you're here."

CC followed Miss Boudreaux out of the room and down the hall to her office. The hallway was nice and clean and it reminded her of the Shreveport hospital. The thought made her feel alone just like the time Mama dropped her off in Shreveport at the maternity home. She remembered thinking she would be alone for a long time. She had to depend on people she didn't know, and now Gran wanted her to rely on Miss Boudreaux, someone she didn't know at all.

What's the matter with me? I feel like I don't fit in anywhere.

CHAPTER 11

CC walked with Miss Boudreaux back to her office. She wished Gran had stayed with her because she could use a friendly, familiar face right now. Her palms were sweating and she wished she could have some water. Her throat was like sandpaper.

The phone rang in the office and Miss Boudreaux ran to pick it up. After speaking for a minute in almost a whisper, she turned to CC and said, "I apologize CC, but I must take this call. Can you please wait in the hall and I will be with you as soon as possible?"

Miss Boudreaux shut the door and CC couldn't help but wonder if the phone call concerned her in some way. She looked at her hands that shook a little from her nervousness as she remembered the last time she sat in a counselor's office. It was in her school in New Orleans.

Even with small meals she had gained weight last winter. That was the signal that alerted her school counselor, Mrs. Kepler, to send for her during homeroom in November.

What a talk that turned out to be. As soon as CC sat down, Mrs. Kepler began with, "Cicely, what have you and your parents decided to do about your condition?"

CC could be a smart ass and couldn't resist asking Mrs. Kepler, "What parents and what condition?" She had put her head between her hands and rubbed her forehead. That was the first time CC had to talk about her pregnancy out loud. She kept it to herself for the first months.

When CC realized she was pregnant, she thought it would be hard to hide, but the kids at school didn't pay attention to anything other than who was going out with who and the new Motown music, of course. She was able to keep it from Mama easily because she wasn't at home in the evening. She was either too tired or too drunk to notice her condition.

CC felt trapped, but she mumbled, "I haven't told anyone, not a living soul."

Mrs. Kepler had been shocked. "Wait. You mean your mother doesn't even know you're pregnant?"

CC didn't want to look up. Her secret was out in the open but she didn't want to explain her home situation to a stranger.

The conversation evolved into a barrage of questions. "You haven't had any prenatal care? Have you ever seen a doctor? When were you planning on telling your mother?"

Mrs. Kepler informed CC she had to call her parents. It was a counselor's responsibility to advise them since she was a minor. CC decided to confide in her. She told the woman there was no father and she better call her mother early in the morning to catch her sober. CC turned away from the look of pity on Mrs. Kepler's face.

CC held her breath when her counselor called Mama that next morning and asked her to come in to school for a conference. She was eating her usual breakfast of crackers and heard Mama answer the phone with a slur. "Conference? Conference for what? What'd she do? Look Lady, I'm not coming 'less you tell me whas's up."

There was a long quiet pause, and then Mama yelled into the phone, "She's what? What'd you say? Are you crazy?"

Mama slammed the phone down and stormed into the kitchen. The tirade had begun.

"CC, did you hear me? I said you could come in now."

CC looked up at Miss Boudreaux and followed her into the office. She could not seem to focus on anything Miss Jessica was asking her. She stared at a large, glass jar filled with candy and the different posters with animals and quotes all over the walls.

"CC, dear, I was asking if you knew anything about your credits." Miss Boudreaux was in her chair and looking at a folder.

CC shook herself back into the present and tried to focus. Before CC could ask her about the posters, Miss Boudreaux told her the plan.

"First of all, everyone just calls me Miss Jessica. You can, too, if you like. Your gran told me you might be interested in making up some credits this summer and I've checked. We can do that through the summer program and I can certify that you'll complete your tenth grade English and social studies from here. Would you be interested in doing that? If you do, you can definitely go on to eleventh grade. You completed your math and electives before you left New Orleans."

Once again, CC felt propelled along by other forces. She wasn't sure whether this would work out, but she decided she wanted to do something other than work around the farm in the blistering sun. She hated working in the gardens. The orchard wasn't so bad as long as she did it with Gramps. Doing school work wouldn't be so bad.

Also, Miss Jessica looked interesting. She had jet black hair that was cut short around her face and large dark eyes lit up her creamy complexion. It was her voice too. Like she was from someplace other than Ruston. It made CC think she could look right through a person.

She heard herself say, "Sure, Miss Boudreaux, I mean Jessica. Miss Jessica, that is. Sounds good. What do we do?"

Miss Jessica told her about a new book that had just come out. She had a copy on her desk. It was by a woman named Harper Lee. CC told her she liked the title and wanted to know why anyone would kill a mockingbird.

Miss Jessica seemed to like that question. "Yes, *To Kill A Mockingbird* is an interesting title. Why don't you read the first fifty pages and we'll talk about it? You may not find the answer there, but it will come."

They agreed on what seemed like some easy stuff to begin the work. CC was to start reading the novel and to watch the news or read the newspaper every day to summarize major news stories. Miss Jessica gave her two notebooks for each assignment and told her it was important to write about the book and the news.

CC couldn't get Addy out of her mind, so she asked Miss Jessica, "What's the girl down the hall doing here? Does she work with some kids?"

"You mean Addy? She does, but as a volunteer. Addy found out that some Negro children at the Vacation Bible School can't read. She's taking books out there this summer a couple of mornings every week to help teach them to read. I've found books she can take with her."

CC tried to picture the girl she just met sitting around teaching reading. She wondered if Addy could sit still very long, but her only response to Miss Jessica was, "That's nice."

Miss Jessica smiled and stood up. "You want to find your grandmother?"

Gran was sitting in the other offices with an older lady. When Miss Jessica said good- bye, she also mentioned Addy. "I'll tell her you'll see her some other time, CC."

"Sure." CC just wanted to leave the school and get back in the car. That girl looked like she might be fun, But CC wasn't ready to make friends around here.

Gran backed the car out slowly and started home. CC waited for her to start asking some questions, but they were quiet for a while. CC broke the silence, "You didn't ask me anything about Miss Jessica."

"I thought you would fill me in when you're ready."

CC kept her thoughts to herself until she couldn't stand it anymore and blurted out, "Why do people find things to do? You know, things they don't get paid for or anything?"

Gran was quick to respond. "Are you thinking about anyone in particular? Anyone I know?"

CC didn't answer her grandmother at first. She was trying to figure out why learning about Addy bothered her. She didn't even know her, but it nagged at her. She didn't understand why a young girl would spend her summer working for nothing.

"Seems like kids here want to be different. Johnny came to help on the farm and take care of Uncle Bud. Addy teaches Negro kids at a church."

Gran didn't say a word, and CC began to get frustrated. "I mean, they have some kind of special something they want to do, right?" She paused for a minute and then added, "Is there something wrong with me? I'm just trying to get back to where I was. Am I supposed to do something else?"

Gran glanced at her, but remained quiet.

CC turned her head to the window wondering what bothered her so much. The breeze was refreshing. She put her head back and closed her eyes.

Gran asked again, "Is there anything in…?"

CC's eyes popped open and suddenly she had to ask Gran a question. Before she lost her nerve, she blurted out, "Why doesn't anyone ask me how I feel about giving that baby up? I mean giving her up for adoption?"

Gran slowed the car and slid into a gravel clearing on the side of the road. "This is a little roadside park. Let's get out and sit there. There's a little bench between those trees. I stop here sometimes."

They climbed out of the car and walked over to the bench. Gran sat down and CC sat at the end putting her head down between her hands. Keeping her back to Gran, she asked again, "Why hasn't anyone talked to me? It's weird. What am I supposed to do? Just go on like nothing happened? Read some book and ride Lady and pick peaches? What should I do, Gran?"

"Did Miss Jessica ask you some questions that got you upset?"

"No, she didn't ask me anything. She's nice, but she was all business. But I met this girl, Addy, a little older than me, a senior next year. All bubbly and stuff. I felt out of place around her."

She faced Gran. CC pleaded, "I'm not a kid anymore, am I? I had a baby. I gave up a baby I thought I didn't even want to keep. And now I'm talking to some girl who's dancing around to a Beach Boys song and I can't even understand why I don't feel like a kid anymore. I feel like I'm all by myself and if I talk too much, I will just blurt it all out."

CC stood up and walked to a tall pine tree nearby and started picking at its bark. The strong fragrance of the pine reminded her of Christmas. Her feelings were all mixed up. Minutes before she was talking about rock music and school work. Now she felt even more alone and out of place. After the baby was born, all she could think about was getting home and going to school and hanging out. Here she was and she still didn't know how to act or where she fit in.

She sensed Gran getting up from the bench. CC pushed against the tree and held her emotions in check so she wouldn't start crying again.

Gran stood behind CC and wrapped her arms around her shoulders. The hug felt warm and comforting. After a few minutes, CC turned and looked into her grandmother's eyes and asked the question that she knew was inside her but she had been afraid to ask, "Am I terrible for giving up the baby? Am I terrible for trying to forget her? Gran, what am I supposed to do? Is it even possible to forget the whole baby thing? Can I ever be a kid again? Will I ever feel like that girl Addy?"

CHAPTER 12

CC sniffled quietly as she stood against the towering tree. She wiped her eyes with the back of her hand so Gran offered her a Kleenex as she said, "Here, your nose is running."

She shuddered as she took a sidelong glance at Gran. "Thanks. I didn't know I was going to get into that. I haven't talked about the adoption to anyone."

"You haven't had much time to think. You had your baby and left the maternity home and went back to New Orleans. It must have been hard. Kids didn't ask where you were?"

CC didn't know how to answer that. Mama didn't make her go back to school right away, and when she did no one asked her anything. Only Marcus. He looked at her with those sad eyes. She could hardly stand it.

Gran put her arm around CC's shoulders to guide her to the car. As she slid into the passenger seat, Gran leaned in to look into her granddaughter's eyes. "This is hard to talk about, but I think you did the right thing. You made sure the baby has a good home. We can talk some more about this when you're ready."

"Good. I don't want to talk about this anymore. Let's just drop it for now. Okay?"

"Okay," as she patted her back. "Let's go home. I need to make some supper."

Gran slammed the heavy car door and walked around to the driver's side. Easing into her seat, she started up the old Ford. CC noticed the car's musty smell and how different it was from the freshness of the woods they just left. The car smelled like motor oil and, for a second, reminded her of

Mama's boyfriend, Randy. He seldom changed out of his coveralls from his mechanic's job until he went to bed.

When Gran shifted into first gear, she turned to CC again and announced, "I didn't let go of the clutch yet. You know what the clutch is?"

"It's that pedal on the floor. Right under your foot?"

"Yep, next to the brake. Brakes on the right, clutch on the left."

A puzzled look crossed CC's face. "Why are you telling me about that, Gran?"

"Maybe you'd like to learn how to drive while you're here. I could teach you."

CC shot up in her seat. "Learn to drive? Are you serious, Gran?" CC's dark mood suddenly evaporated. If anything could get her mind off the adoption, it was this proposal. "I used to think about driving a car like some of the kids at school. They already have licenses and act like they own the road. But wait. You mean on this car, with this stick?"

Gran laughed out loud. "Is that what it's called? A stick? I had no idea. But yes, on this car. We have open roads and it's better if you learn on a regular shift before you start using that new 1964 Impala your mother's driving."

CC sat back again. That would be like so cool. "That is wicked, Gran! When can we start?"

"Let's get you started on this school work and I'll take you out on the road tomorrow afternoon? Did you say wicked?"

"Yeah, like out of sight, Gran! Learn to drive! Cool!"

CC let it sink in. This was the first time in a while she had that rush of excitement. *Who would have thought? I was all mixed up and sad, and wham! Learning to drive. Gran hit it. Like she's hip. Who knew?*

This was the closest CC had come to wanting to grab Gran and give her a big hug. Since they were heading down the road, she gave her a big smile instead. "Gran, thanks. I mean, - thanks." CC leaned back in her seat. Her window was still down and the wind on her face made her hair fly in all directions. She thought about how it would feel to drive a car. She could be free as a bird. Driving. Wow.

As excited as she felt, she knew she needed to say something to Gran about their talk. "Gran, I hope it's okay. I mean, that I don't want to talk about the baby or the adoption anymore. At least, not now. I mean, it's not that I don't care what you think. I just can't talk about it. For now, anyway."

"Understood. But CC, at some point you and I are going to have to talk about your mother. She may not be perfect, but it bothers me that you two are fighting so much. I'd like to see you try to talk to her. You think you could try?"

CC threw her head back against the hard seat as she closed her eyes against the thought of her mother. "Okay, Gran. But can we discuss that later?"

They drove the rest of the way in silence. CC wanted to enjoy thinking about learning to drive. She looked out over the rolling green hills thinking how cool it would be to drive. What would be even cooler is if Gramps would let her drive his old green pickup truck. She always wanted to drive a truck.

The odor of manure hung in the air, but it wasn't as pungent as it was when she arrived. It was mixed with the faint scent of the peach trees she loved as a child. They grew all over the area and the fragrance floated through the air and made her feel even happier.

Opening up to Gran and her offering to teach CC to drive made the trip back to the farm seem shorter. As they neared the gate, CC realized it looked worn. The iron entrance was painted white, but it was chipped and one side of the gate leaned heavily into the ground. From a distance the wooden farm house looked old and sagged, but the flowers in the front yard gave it some life.

She saw her uncle leaning over the flowers. Uncle Bud took pride in tending the gardens by weeding and watering them. Looking over at the barn she spotted her lanky cousin walking out of the horse ring. He wasn't on Lady so CC assumed he was taking a shortcut from the barn. Gran slowed when she hit the gravel driveway.

CC spoke up. "Gran, I think I'm gonna talk to Johnny. Is it okay to tell him about the driving?"

"That's fine. You want me to take your school stuff in the house?"

"Yes ma'am. That'd be good."

She bolted from the old car and felt a soft breeze drift towards her. CC hurried towards Johnny. "Hey, are you heading to the house?" Johnny squinted from the afternoon sun as he stared at her.

"Oh, you're back from the high school. How'd it go?" As he walked closer, CC saw the work gloves in his hands. As he faced her, CC had to look up to him even though she was almost as tall.

"It's okay, I guess. Not much to it. I met this lady and we talked for a little while. She gave me this book to read. Something about killing a mockingbird. Strange, huh?"

Johnny smiled and said, "Harper Lee. I know about that book. It was just published a couple of years ago."

"Yep, she said it's a 1960's book, but I just heard about it today." She looked down to kick some dirt from her tennis shoe. Looking back at him, she bit her lip as she said, "You know an awful lot, don't you? Did you read a lot in school?"

Johnny snorted, "Nope, not books like that. Just read science books for my science project."

CC decided to let that go. She didn't want to get into talking about school projects again, so she announced, "I think I'll take that ride. I'm going to saddle Lady up."

Johnny didn't answer and just stood with his arms folded over his chest, staring off toward the fields. CC decided to turn and start for the barn.

"Wait. Hold up. I want to talk to you about something." As Johnny spoke, he looked off toward the north field and bit his lower lip. CC could tell he had something on his mind.

He was still looking off toward the field as he told her, "I went all the way back to the fence on the north end of the orchard."

"OK, what about it?" CC didn't know where he was headed.

"I could see through the fence and there were two dead robins just lying there"

"You mean like Uncle Bud talked about? He said he saw a couple of dead birds, but he meant up here by the house, right?"

Johnny pushed his hat back and wiped some sweat from his forehead with a crumpled handkerchief. Jerking his hat down, he announced, "There's something going on around here. I can feel it. Those birds don't just up and die. Not in that number. And why is that back property so wilted? It's not green like it should be."

She didn't understand why he was so worried about the birds. Don't birds die? All CC could think about now was the driving lesson Gran promised.

Who wants to look at dead birds when I could learn to drive? That's what I want to do.

CHAPTER 13

CC came to the farm to get away from trouble and didn't want to get caught up in some mystery about dead birds. The serious look on Johnny's face felt like trouble. Aggravated, she started kicking loose dirt on the ground. She decided to cut him off and muttered, "You better talk to Gramps about this. He might have an explanation."

Johnny shifted his feet and shoved his hands in his front pockets. "Okay, I guess you're right. I'll wait and talk to him." An awkward pause stretched out between them. "You going to take that ride?"

CC glanced at the barn. "No, not now. I think I'll take a walk instead. It's getting close to supper. Maybe ride tomorrow."

Johnny walked over to his dad who squatted in the clover and patted him on the back. "Come on, Dad. Let's take a walk."

Slapping Uncle Bud on the back again, Johnny and his dad sauntered off towards the garden as CC strolled towards the clump of Japanese plum trees in the back of the barn. She remembered hiding in the middle of the thicket when she played hide and seek with her cousins.

She wondered if Eric looked for her today. He was sure good looking. And then she silently reprimanded herself for even thinking about him. *I've been in enough trouble and he sure is trouble with a capital T.*

No sooner did that thought cross her mind when she heard a shrill whistle, the kind her friends called a wolf whistle. She saw Eric coming from the back of the barn. As she looked towards Johnny, she was happy to see they had walked in the other direction. She didn't want another confrontation between the two of them.

"Hey there, Miss *New Orleens.* How's it going today?"

Turning to face him, she again felt the need to correct his pronunciation. "It's not Orleens, Eric. It's more like 'Or lee ans.' That's how the locals say it."

There was that grin again. And as soon as she finished her sentence, she stumbled and almost fell all over herself. He grabbed her arm, breaking her fall and pulling her up straight.

He was quick. She had to give him that.

"You know, I ought to get rewarded for rescuing you from falling. Ain't this a second time? Yep. I think it is." He flashed a big smile, lighting up his dark eyes and showing off bright white teeth.

"Rewarded? Rewarded, how?" The minute she said it she was sorry. *I keep saying these stupid things around this boy.* "What do you mean anyway? Just for keeping me from falling all over myself?"

This time he let out a hearty laugh and she chuckled a little in return. "There you go. That wasn't so hard, was it? Laughing with me a little bit?"

CC stood up straight and took a quick glance at the house to make sure no one was spying on them. "No, I guess not."

"Say, Miss CC," and with that he took his wide brimmed cowboy hat off and held it in his hands, kind of twirling it at the same time. "You think you might want to go out with me sometime this week. Take a ride in my truck and go over to the Dairy Queen for a hot dog and a sundae?"

CC's mouth practically fell to the ground. She felt her face turning red and there was a tingling on her scalp that wasn't there earlier. She had never been officially asked on a date. All she ever did with Marcus was work on school stuff. They never dated. She didn't say anything to Eric for fear of stumbling all over her words. When she did talk, all she could muster was, "Uh, I don't know. My gran might not let me. I guess I could ask her. Not sure though."

"Well, we could take off in the afternoon when nobody's watching. What do think?'

She noticed a different kind of smile on his face. There was a glint in his eyes now that prompted her to say, "I don't know about sneaking off. That doesn't feel right."

He snickered, and she sensed contempt in the sound. Before she could react, he grabbed her around the waist, pulling her towards him. As he tightened his grip over her shoulder with his other hand, CC felt his warm breath on her cheek and the faint odor of sweat filled her nostrils.

"What do you say? Does this feel right?" His breathing was faster as he mumbled in her ear. CC felt his hardness pressed on her belly.

"What are you doing? I don't even know you! God!" She managed to shove him enough to regain some control. Her heart was beating so fast she could hardly catch her breath. Shock was replaced by anger swelling up inside her.

Eric backed up a few steps and sneered at her. That hard glint in his black eyes she had seen earlier was back as he spit out, "Why don't you just stay here then and pick beans with that Bud fella?" He turned and strode off towards the barn. His cocky gait showed off his arrogance.

CC glared at his back until he was out of sight. She rubbed the arm he held still able to feel his tight grip. Standing alone her confusion clouded her thinking, wondering if she caused him to try to force himself on her. She shook her head to clear the feeling of guilt.

No, I didn't do anything. I didn't egg him on. Did he think that's what I was doing?

She shook her head again. *No. That's crazy. I didn't give him any reason to think I wanted him – not that way.*

CC started towards the house in a daze walking as though she was a robot. She wasn't sure she wanted to tell anyone. *I shouldn't make a big deal out of it. Guys try stuff all the time, don't they?* She answered her own question. *How should I know? I've only been with Marcus. He was more innocent than me. We had never even kissed before that night.*

As she stumbled to the house, Johnny was coming out of the double doors on the front of the barn. "Hey, back already?"

She kept walking with her head down, still in a daze left from the encounter with Eric. "Hey, CC. Did you hear me? What's up?"

With that she turned slightly to face her cousin. "I guess I did. I was thinking about something."

"CC, you look upset. What's wrong?"

She tried to regain some composure hoping for now she could keep Johnny out of it. She needed time to figure it out. "I'm fine, Johnny. Guess I got too hot out here. What's up with you?"

"Thinking I would go in and wash up." He still looked suspicious not taking his eyes off her.

CC was still distracted. She wanted to avoid any more questions and as she glanced over towards the house, she saw Uncle Bud sitting near his garden. "Hey, there's your dad. He's sitting on the ground and he's doing that swaying thing he does when he's upset or sad. Don't you want to check on him? He's talking to those bees. His favorite thing."

Johnny ignored her comment, and had already started for the yard. CC followed him and as they got closer, she saw Uncle Bud had his head down low and rocked back and forth. He wasn't smiling or giggling like when he talked to the bees. Johnny put his hand on Uncle Bud's shoulder. "Hey, Dad, what's going on?"

As he raised his head, CC saw the saddest expression on her uncle's face. Tears streamed down his cheeks as he raised his hands and opened them. A lifeless bird sat in his palms. Uncle Bud moaned, "Gone, gone. My little friend is gone."

Johnny sat on the ground next to his father still patting him on the back. "I'm sorry, Dad." He looked up at CC and mouthed the word "Dead."

"Dad, we have to do something with him. Let me look at him." Johnny grabbed his father's arm and as he did, Uncle Bud dropped the dead bird. Johnny tried to pick him up, but his father shoved him hard knocking him to the ground.

"Leave us alone. Mine." Uncle Bud picked the bird up and snuggled it to his chest. His face turned crimson and his freckles were so red, they looked like they were drawn on his cheeks as he shouted, "Leave us alone! Alone!"

Johnny tried to reason with him. "Let's sit for a few minutes and we'll decide what to do."

CC felt lost standing above the two of them. Still shell-shocked from her encounter with Eric, she grappled with wanting to make Uncle Bud feel better. A light bulb went off in her head and she found herself saying, "I'll be back in a minute. I remember seeing a little box in the barn on the shelf next to the feed. I'll go get it."

Uncle Bud clearly heard her cause he looked up and had that familiar sweet smile through his tears. He nodded and she could barely hear him say "OK, Sis, OK." He continued stroking the dead bird.

CC headed for the barn and the shelf she remembered. Clay entered through the side door and asked in a gravelly voice, "Hey, CC, you going to do some late evening riding?" CC didn't turn and answer him, afraid she might give away any feelings about his son or rat on him. She wasn't ready to talk to anyone about that encounter.

Keeping her back to Clay, she told him about Bud and the dead bird. "Yeah, he wasn't going to give him up, but Johnny's calming him down. I'm going to find that little box to bury him."

"Is this it, this little red one over here? It was on that shelf but I moved some stuff this morning."

"Thanks, Clay. That's the one."

"Tell Johnny I'll talk to him about the dead bird. I found one too. We have that old tom cat that stays in the barn, but he don't hunt much anymore. It was just lying there on the ground, but ol' Tom's too lazy to do anything else with him."

She looked at Clay and managed, "OK, I'll mention it to Johnny. I have to do this and then get inside and help Gran with supper."

CC walked back to the garden and was relieved to see Uncle Bud smiling up at her. "Here's the little box I was talking about. Think it's big enough."

Johnny stood up, brushing his seat off and lumbered over to the garden where a shovel was propped against the white fence. "Dad, would you like to put him in the box and we'll bury him all nice and proper like I told you."

Bud looked up at them and CC could tell he was thinking it through. He took the box from her and slowly and carefully laid the little bird in the box. Johnny looked at him and CC heard him say, "Come on, Dad, we'll bury him over here by the side of your garden."

CC had seen enough. She raised a halfhearted wave to Johnny and trudged to the house. Between helping Uncle Bud with the dead bird and being ambushed by Eric, she felt drained. She knew she had to put on her game face cause if she didn't, Gran would know something was wrong.

I guess I can distract her over the story of Uncle Bud and the dead bird. I sure don't want her to find out about Eric and what he just tried on me.

CHAPTER 14

CC rolled over in bed and pushed the hair from her face. It had been a restless night and it took her forever to fall asleep. She kept reliving the awful scene with Eric and couldn't believe he tried to take advantage of her after he had just met her.

Yesterday she had walked in the kitchen after the episode with Eric at the barn hoping to help Gran with supper and avoid any discussion of her afternoon. She thought she was in luck because Gran was on the phone.

"Loreen, that's not what I meant and you know it. Don't start up with…" Gran stopped in mid-sentence when she saw CC in the doorway.

Gran held the black phone receiver out to CC and mouthed 'It's your Mama. Talk to her." CC's emotional beeper went off. She knew she didn't have it in her after everything that just happened to have a conversation with her mother.

Shaking her head violently, she mouthed back, "No. No. Please, no. Gran, not now, please."

Gran looked puzzled and arched her eyebrows into a question that easily read, "Why not?" Dropping the phone to her midriff while covering the receiver, she pleaded, "CC, how about a simple hello? Here," as she held out the receiver.

Dragging her feet and keeping her head down, CC grabbed the black receiver and mumbled, "Hello, Mama." She hoped her mother sounded sober. She did.

"Hello, Cicely. You know I told you to call me anytime you wanted to." Pause. "I guess you didn't need to."

CC could detect some hurt in Mama's voice. "Mama, I guess Gran and Gramps are keeping me busy around here." Pause. "I don't have much to say."

Big pause. "Cicely, Mother said she took you to someone to talk about making up some credits for high school. That's good. I hope you take advantage of their help."

The old guilt routine. I'm supposed to roll over and play reformed country girl. "Mama, I'm trying." She realized she raised her voice so she intentionally lowered it, "Listen, I have to help with supper. I need to go." She shoved the receiver to Gran and started to storm out of the kitchen.

"What is the matter with you?" Gran asked in a loud whisper at CC's back. CC turned slowly to face her grandmother. There was a long silence and finally Gran said into the phone, "Loreen, I'll talk to you later. Have to go now. Yes, we'll talk again soon," and hung up.

There was a long silence as Gran leaned against the counter and folded her arms over her middle. "CC, can't you show some respect for your mother. It's hard I know, but she seems worried about you."

The silence continued until CC mumbled something incoherent about how hard it was to talk on the phone. By some miracle Gran decided to let it go and the two of them worked in more silence setting the table and cooking supper.

As soon as she helped with the dishes, she went upstairs, but the second she lay down, she imagined Eric's face. She couldn't get his dark eyes and cocky smile out of her mind. When she tried to go to sleep, she could still feel him against her middle. His warm breath lingered on her face.

Eric was so different than her one and only time with Marcus. That had been a quick encounter where they fumbled with each other and struggled to get their clothes off, totally inexperienced with how to connect as young lovers. Marcus had been her friend for a while and shared her distrust for other kids at school. They were both loners, but the other students thought Marcus was a drag because he was a brain. Most of the colored kids didn't do well in school, but Marcus was an exception. She was more of an outcast because she was so withdrawn and she was one of the few whites who hung out with kids like Marcus.

Everything changed for the pair when CC ran to her friend's house the night Randy tried to break into her room. Marcus tried to comfort her as she cried and their intimacy became passionate. They woke up before daybreak and she clumsily dressed and crawled out his window. The next day in school they avoided each other. She knew he cared about her but this didn't feel like young love to her, and she wanted to forget their having sex as much as she wanted to forget Randy's attempt at molesting her.

It seemed impossible to CC that she could be pregnant after one night, but as her stomach grew and she missed her second period, she was terrified. Not about telling Marcus, but about facing her mother. Mama hated her even hanging out with Marcus.

Not only was she pregnant, but CC's baby was going to be half Negro.

CHAPTER 15

She resorted to secrecy and didn't talk to anyone, but when her counselor comforted her about being pregnant, she had to tell Mama. What an explosion that had been. Pregnant and carrying a colored baby. Mama stormed to Marcus's house and lowered the boom on his mother.

CC was relieved her mother knew she was pregnant because now she could figure out what to do. Abortions were illegal and dangerous and she did not want to marry Marcus. It was illegal anyway for Negroes and whites to marry in most states, including Louisiana.

Both mothers agreed there should be no more contact between Marcus and CC. They were worried about repercussions since they were a mixed couple. What would happen when other kids found out about them?

CC didn't talk much about her pregnancy, but when Mama came up with the home for unwed mothers, it seemed like a solution.

"You'll just be in the home for a couple of months. It's already December and you're due in March. I can drive you there around New Year's while it's still a holiday from school. Less questions I guess." Mama had said to her.

"Yeah, no one will miss me at school. Those kids won't notice I'm gone." When she saw Mama's sad expression, she added. "It's all right, Mama. You're right. It's not forever."

CC knew it would be hard. She didn't have any close girlfriends. It was too embarrassing to have girls around her house. She would miss being in New Orleans, but at least she would get away from Randy.

CC sat up in bed and let her long hair fall over her face trying to push back the memories. She stretched her full frame and let out a loud grunt.

Jumping into a clean pair of jeans, she pulled a white shirt from the pile of clothes on the chair next to her bed.

She thought about going out and sitting on the porch to avoid Gran dredging up the phone conversation, but as she glanced out her window, she saw Johnny lumbering toward the porch. That could be a godsend if Johnny is downstairs. Gran will talk to him instead of bringing up the phone call. She hoped she could just make some coffee-milk and get out the door without any more hassles. Peeking around the doorframe, she heard them talking.

"Dad's already out in his garden, Gran. Went out early this morning."

"Johnny, where did you find the bird exactly?" Gran asked him.

"I didn't find it, Gran. Dad was holding it when I walked up. Already dead."

Gran looked at Johnny with a suspicious look. "Was it already dead when Bud found it? Do you know that for a fact, Johnny?"

Johnny pulled away from the counter he was leaning on and stood erect as he answered Gran. "Why're you asking me these questions? What are you thinking?"

She picked the kitchen towel up from the counter and started wiping the table. "I'm just remembering not so long-ago Bud held one of those birds in his hands. I saw him near his garden and realized what he was doing. Told him to let it go, but it was already dead. He usually is gentle with animals. Sometimes Bud doesn't realize how strong he can be and he crushed that little bird."

Johnny stood even straighter and raised his voice. "What exactly are you saying? You think he killed that bird himself? He wouldn't do that. He loves those birds."

Gran was still talking. "I'm not saying it's on purpose. I just want you to know. He can get rough without realizing his own strength. Sometimes, though..."

CC's throat went dry. Looking at Johnny, she could tell he was getting too upset. Jumping from behind the door frame, she almost shouted, "When I got that box last night, Clay mentioned something about finding a dead bird around here. Said that old cat may be killing them."

It got quiet in the kitchen. Johnny glanced at CC as she said, "Or you think it could be that smoke coming from those brush fires from the Gibbs' property? That could kill them too, couldn't it?"

"Why don't you ask your Gramps about all of it when he gets home?" Gran suggested. "He called a while ago and said he would be home early from work."

Johnny started for the back door and called over his shoulder to CC. "You want to ride out to the orchard with Dad and me? We're going to look around."

Before she could answer, he was out the door.

Gran swiveled around to the sink and started rinsing the few dishes from the morning. "CC, you want breakfast before you go?"

"I think I'll just make some coffee-milk and take it outside, Gran."

She heard Gran mumble something under her breath but she couldn't make it out. She thought she better let that go. Instead, she clattered around the cupboard to find an old mug. As she poured the coffee, she noticed Gran was already heating the milk on the stove. She waited a minute and held the mug out to Gran. Their eyes met for the first time and CC read a look of sadness in her eyes, not anger.

"Gran, I'm sorry about that phone call. I just need some more time."

Gran poured the steaming white liquid into her cup, and stared at CC. "You can only work things out by talking to each other, not running away or ignoring a person."

CC noticed the grey tendrils of hair around Gran's face were already damp from the morning heat. A bead of sweat formed on her upper lip. Once again, she fought the urge to put the coffee down and give Gran a big hug. Instead she mumbled "sorry" again and headed for the back door. CC knew she needed to fight back whatever feelings might come up when she talked about Mama, especially with Gran, because she didn't want to make her feel bad.

Holding the coffee in both hands, CC stood on the porch stoop and heard the chickens clucking from the coop near the barn. The morning smells of chicken poop and horse manure blended in with the freshly cut grass and her coffee. The summer heat already formed for the day.

She thought about Eric again and the incident at the barn yesterday and her thoughts about Marcus and their baby. It was disgusting that Eric thought he could do that to her. Eric might be attracted to her, but how would he feel if he knew she had a baby last March? And what would he say if he found out the baby was half colored?

She knew the answer to that question. She had to keep it to herself!

CHAPTER 16

Minutes later CC led Lady from the barn, saddled up and ready to go. She cupped the reins in one hand and prepared to swing over and mount her when she heard a loud sound coming from somewhere on the driveway along the cow pasture.

"That is like blaring. Sounds like music coming from a car." CC raised her free hand to shield the sun from her eyes to try and figure out whose car it was. It didn't take long. Whoever was driving was getting closer and from the looks of the dust clouding up in the distance.

CC heard the gravel spitting from a vehicle. As it came down the driveway, she recognized the unmistakable sound of Elvis. It was a faster song of his, but even with the racket, she recognized the lines about not kissing him once but kissing him twice to be the hit from a few years before, *Treat Me Nice.*

"Well, I know who's singing one of my favorites on the radio. But that is some loud, and who's driving?"

She could make out a red truck. The music blared and the truck slid to a stop spewing gravel from its back tires. As soon as it stopped, out jumped Addy, the girl she met yesterday afternoon.

"What's she doing here?" Addy put her hands on her back and stretched a little. When she saw CC, she broke out into a full grin CC remembered. She waved and yelled something CC couldn't make out because the radio still blared. She made a motion to Addy who turned back, opened the truck door and turned it off. All of a sudden it seemed deafening quiet.

CC walked closer. "Hey, Addy. What brings you here?"

"Miss Jessica said you were staying here so I drove out to say hi. We didn't get a chance to talk yesterday."

"I thought you were tutoring those little kids. By the way, do you always listen to Elvis so loud?" CC asked.

Addy took over the conversation. "Yep, I do, but I don't go back to the church until tomorrow. And yep, I listen to the King every chance I get. That's WRUS, the local radio station. They play all Elvis for two hours every morning."

Addy took a breath and started again. "What are you up to now? You want to take a drive? I can show you around." She didn't wait for an answer. She looked over at Lady and grinned some more. "I have horses over at our place. We could go riding together. Or take a drive."

CC thought Addy was very enthusiastic to say the least. She felt Lady nuzzling her back. "I think Lady is getting impatient. I was going to take a walk with my cousin and his dad."

"Who's your cousin?"

"He's Johnny from Texas," CC explained. "Just got here a few days ago."

"Oh. Who's his dad?"

CC didn't hesitate. "You sure ask a lot of questions." Addy grinned even wider, but waited this time for an answer.

"It's my Uncle Bud. That's his dad."

"Oh, wow. Bud with the red hair and lots of freckles? I know him. Your grandpa brings him over to our farm sometimes to help out in our garden. He's a cool guy. I sure like him." As she spoke, Addy glanced over CC's shoulder and her large blue eyes got even wider. The grin turned into a half smile. "Who is that?"

"Who is who?" CC asked. As she turned, she saw Johnny walking back from the pasture with Uncle Bud. His tall lanky frame was in contrast to his father's fuller body and ruddy complexion.

"Who is that tall, gorgeous boy?" CC heard her ask again.

Before she could answer, Addy exclaimed, "He is some cute. Is that Johnny from Texas?"

CC knew her mouth fell open. As she looked at Johnny, she tried to see him as Addy did, but what she saw was a boy who used to tease her and chase her through the chicken coop trying to get old Ben the rooster stirred up. She popped out laughing. "You think he's cute?" CC's head tilted, and she just shook it back and forth as she laughed to herself.

"Yes, indeed. He is some good looking. At least I think so. Especially for around here. All we have here are some hickey-looking farm guys."

CC felt her opening. "You mean like that dark-haired guy, Eric?" She looked over at the fence so as not to look too interested.

Addy for once didn't answer right away. By the way her big eyes slanted suspiciously, CC wished she could take the question back. "When did you meet him? Was he over here?"

She waited for CC's response, then Addy added, "That boy came over to make a delivery for Mr. Gibbs at our place. He got out of line. I didn't say anything to Dad, but I shooed him off."

Addy seemed to be watching her, so CC tried to brush it off. "Yeah, he talked to me over the fence a couple of times. He just didn't look like your ordinary farm boy. Like you said before, you know, about the boys here. What did he do?"

"Oh, he tried to ask me out with that sneery look on his face. I said no, of course. I meant 'hell, no.'"

"Oh, that's pretty sly." CC decided to drop it.

Addy was already taking long strides over to Johnny and Uncle Bud. "Hi there, Mr. Bud."

Johnny looked at Addy and then at his father and smiled ear to ear. "That's the first time I heard anyone call him Mister. Usually they just say Bud."

CC caught up with them. She noticed Uncle Bud was grinning at Addy and seemed perfectly comfortable standing there with her. He mumbled something about liking bees and flowers.

Johnny chuckled as he looked at CC and back at Addy. He held out his hand and offered, "Hi, I'm Johnny Scott." Addy looked down at his open palm and took it pumping a little too hard.

"I'm CC's friend, Addy."

Johnny, of course, couldn't resist. "Oh, OK. When did y'all meet? Like this morning?" He looked at Addy with that teasing look in his eyes. "What does Addy stand for?"

For the first time since she arrived, Addy looked uncomfortable. She stared at the ground and shifted one of her boots into the grass, and whispered, "Adelaide." Looking up she saw Johnny's eyes meet hers and she drew up to her full height. "Adelaide, but everyone, and I mean everyone, calls me Addy."

Now Johnny had a half teasing look while Uncle Bud, mumbled that little half laugh of his, seeming to enjoy the moment. "Well, that's settled. Addy, it is." Turning to CC with a more serious expression, "OK, Cousin, we're going to go ahead and get out to the front field like I talked about. I guess we'll see you later."

CC tried not to let her surprise show. "Addy just stopped by. I'm still going with y'all. I saddled Lady and I'm ready to ride. Grinning herself, she turned to Addy to say, "You have to go, right?"

Not missing a beat, Addy's look circled the little group as she announced, "I can walk with y'all. I have plenty of time. And I know the land around here. Can I help?"

Before CC could protest, Johnny impatiently said, "Let's just go, all right? I want to check this out."

He turned and led Uncle Bud by the arm who turned back to Addy and asked, "Coming?"

It was Addy who started giving orders. "Ready? I'm all in. Come on, CC."

CC found herself taking orders from Addy. She mounted Lady and purposely trotted at a slow pace in the back of the others. *This is something. Here I am on a farm I don't want to be on, following my cousin and his dad and a girl I I don't know. She is super friendly, but loud and bossy. Not sure about her."*

To make things worse, now they were laughing and Addy was slapping Uncle Bud on the back. Johnny seemed to be enjoying the banter. *I guess she's entertaining. Hell, she is cute. Those boots and that tan. Does have a nice figure. Shorter than me of course. And that hair. All blonde and curly. Wish I had some curls.* Thinking of her hair, CC blew her bangs away from her eyes and wished she had her stringy hair in a ponytail.

They walked through the peach trees and CC soaked in that wonderful scent again. CC swung her leg over Lady's rump and landed on the ground near Johnny. She wrapped the horse's reins lightly around a tree limb.

Addy moved closer and picked up a branch and twirled it in her hands "What's going on? It looks different around here," she exclaimed.

"You come back here much, Addy?" CC asked.

The girl stared at CC and then at Johnny. Before she could answer, Johnny told them, "I'm going to go over in the back of the tree line and check it out." He stood near his dad and touched him affectionately on the shoulder before walking to the edge of the peach orchard.

Addy followed him. "That's Mr. Gibbs' barbed wire fence. Very sturdy and strong, built so it's not easy to cut though. Hard to climb over too. And he doesn't have this sign posted near the field by our property."

Addy, CC, and Johnny stood in front of the sign.

NO TRESSPASSING

Johnny didn't answer. He turned and looked back at the trees. "Those trees near our side of his fence don't have any fruit. Did you notice that, CC? And the leaves are looking wilted." He studied the foliage some more and picked a leaf from the nearest tree. Holding it up, Johnny looked toward the tall fence and crushed the small leaf in his hands, tossing it to the ground.

"The trees look kind of sickly too, but no peach trees."

Johnny knelt down where the hole had been cut. "This was done with metal shears. There's a big enough space to get a man through or even some small equipment."

There was till the faint odor of burnt brush in the air. "Where is that smell coming from, Johnny?" Addy asked.

Johnny looked at her. "Mr. Gibbs farm hands are setting brush fires over there on his land. Don't understand why in the summer."

Addy looked puzzled. "Yeah. It's dangerous. Easy to start fires and kills insects like ladybugs and mosquito hawks. Bad for the whole system."

Johnny looked at her with what seemed to CC to be admiration. Uncle Bud just kept grinning at her.

"Yep. We studied that in science last..." Johnny didn't get to finish his sentence.

"Hey, what are you kids up to? I saw you trying to cross that state fence. Can't you read?" Mr. Gibbs appeared suddenly all red faced and out of breath. "I'm going to tell your grandparents you're trying to sneak around on government property and on my farm. I seen you over here today, young man. You trespassed on my side." He spotted Addy. "And you little lady, what're you doing out here with this bunch? You sneaking around, too? I'll sure tell your dad."

Addy drew her back up and took a few steps towards Mr. Gibbs. "We're investigating something. Something important."

"What in the hell are you kids investigating? What do you know about anything? Bud, you better high tail it outta here or I'll get you in trouble with your dad. You been in enough messes already! Scott won't like these shenanigans."

"Don't threaten my dad. He has a right to be here on this side." Johnny stood in front of Uncle Bud.

Addy jumped in too. "We're just hanging out here. My dad wouldn't mind my being here. He likes Mr. Scott and he likes Bud." She smiled at Johnny.

"Anyways, Mr. Gibbs, why are you lighting those brush fires? What are you burning?" Johnny held on to the fence as he questioned Mr. Gibbs.

Mr. Gibbs sputtered and pulled his hat over his eyes. "None of your damn business. Who'd you say you are? You better get on outta here. You got no business here. This land is posted."

Johnny retorted. "Not my grandpa's."

CC spoke up this time. "Let's get out of here." She held onto Lady's reins and did her best to look at the old man straight in the eye as she commanded, "We have better things to do than stand around here. Come on, Addy. Let's head back and hop in your truck and go cruising."

"That sounds like a good idea, ladies," said a familiar voice behind them, "You need to say something to me, Harold?"

They all swung around to face Gramps standing a few feet away.

CHAPTER 17

"These kids are up to something, Scott." Gibb's face turned beet red as he shook his fist at Gramps.

"What exactly did they do?" Gramps spoke to Gibbs while looking at Johnny and CC. She shifted from one foot to another and squinted. When she glanced sideways at Johnny, he grimaced and shoved his hands in his jean's pocket.

Johnny started to speak but Gramps held up his hand to silence him. CC heard Addy grunt like she wanted to butt in, so CC stared her down to shush her.

Gibbs sputtered, "I saw your boy on my property today poking around. What were you looking for anyway?" Johnny started to answer, but Mr. Gibbs continued to rant. "They started climbing over the state posted fence. What are y'all nosing round for?"

Gramps held up his hand again. "I'll talk to my grandkids and Bud when I'm ready, but what are you all up and bothered about? Just cause Johnny looked around? I remember when your farm hands snuck over here a lot of times to pick peaches. I never said nothing. Just tried to be neighborly. Now you're carrying on about Johnny looking around."

Gibbs wouldn't let it go. "I don't remember that. But you better warn your kids to stay away from that state land that's posted. He was gonna jump over." Gibbs pointed a finger at Johnny.

"No, I wasn't. I was just looking. Never jumped over." Johnny faced Gramps as he spoke.

"I'll talk to my grandkids, Gibbs. We don't need to be yelling' and arguing."

"Keep them away, Scott. That's final." He turned after letting out a loud 'humph.' CC watched the big man strut back to his tractor.

Gramps spoke to the group. "Come on. Let's head home and we'll talk then." He looked at Addy like he just saw her, "Adelaide, when did you get here?"

"Oh God, Mr. Scott. How could you? Really? It's Addy now." She put her hand to her forehead and rolled her eyes to the sky to exaggerate being insulted. CC admitted it was kind of funny, and it broke the ice.

Everyone was silent on the walk back. CC decided to lead Lady back rather than riding her. Gramps looked back at the group and caught her eye. She detected that little twinkle in his eyes and smiled back at him.

When they got to the house, Gramps went straight to the barn. They stood around looking at each other, except for Uncle Bud. He ambled over to his garden and started picking at the beans in the front row.

After a few minutes, Gramps and Clay walked from the barn. Gramps was the first to speak. "Clay and me been talking about the birds and he backs up what y'all are saying. We don't know what's causing' it."

Johnny broke in with, "I have an idea, Gramps, but..."

Gramps held his hand again and Johnny stopped talking. "Son, we're gonna look into this, but right now, leave it to me. Understand? Gibbs told y'all to stay out of his land and posted area."

"Yes, Sir." Johnny's response was halfhearted. CC could tell he wanted to get into the action.

CC decided to jump in this time. "Gramps, can I ask you something' about the fires?"

Gramps sounded surprised when he asked, "What fires?"

"Mr. Gibbs had one going yesterday when I was walking with Uncle Bud."

Gramps smoothed his salt and pepper hair back, a gesture he used when he started explaining something. "We usually don't have fires going in the summer. Brush fires on the farm are started in the spring when the ground is damp and there's less wind. In the summer they're dangerous cause it's so hot. Other fires can be sparked."

"So, why's he doing' them, Gramps? It's hot as blazes already." Johnny mopped the sweat from his forehead with his red bandana.

"Well, it's his land and he has a right. It's a problem though cause the fires scorch the ground and burn up lady bugs, butterflies, earthworms and such. They're all insects that help the land."

Addy couldn't resist. "Even the butterflies, Mr. Scott? That's awful. What about the dead birds? Is that from the fires?" CC watched Addy glance Johnny's way and she rolled her eyes.

"Birds usually fly away from the smoke. Clay and I need to talk some more about it, find out how long this has been going on. First time I've heard there are so many. Gran was telling' me bout the ones Bud found." Gramps looked at Clay as he talked and ran his fingers through his hair again. Then he turned back to Johnny and CC. "Y'all gonna have to stay on our side of the fence. Let me handle any problems with Mr. Gibbs. There's plenty to keep you busy over here."

CC wondered what he meant by being busy, but decided not to ask. He let her know by giving directions to Johnny first. "Son, I need you to pitch in with Clay. Those peaches are coming in and the fields need work every day. Can you do that, Johnny?"

"Course, Gramps, you know I will. And the pasture, too."

CC waited her turn and couldn't help noticing Addy snicker. "CC, you getting' on them books yet?"

"Gramps, I just got them," CC moaned. But when she saw the serious expression on Gramps' face, she added, "But I will. Right away. I'll start reading tonight."

"That's real good, CC. And you can help with the peach crop. Bushel some with Clay and Johnny."

CC's mouth fell open. She hoped to get out of more work since she had school work too, but she shook her head up and down to let him know she would help out.

Addy jumped in again. "Mr. Scott, could CC go with me to the colored church? I do some tutoring there. Help the kids with reading during Vacation Bible School."

Gramps grinned at CC again. "What do you think, CC? Wanna give it a try? I'll leave that up to you."

This time CC glared at Addy. She wondered why the girl would take it on herself to plan her summer for her, but she decided to play along.

"Adelaide and I can talk about it. I might go with her sometime, but not a lot since I have so much school work."

The smile CC flashed at Addy said it all. It dripped with sarcasm and she couldn't wait to get the little curly-headed know-it-all alone. Addy seemed to get the message and was quiet for a change, at least for the time being.

Gramps appeared satisfied that everyone would be busy. "I'm on my way back to work at the gas station."

Johnny said, "Yes, Sir," and headed towards the barn with Clay. After a few steps, he turned to tell Addy good-bye. CC watched her absolutely melt when she answered with a yucky, sweet-sounding, "Bye, Johnny."

CC wanted to yell at Addy right there on the spot. She was tired of people telling her what to do, and to have this girl jump in without checking with her first was too much. "Listen, Adelaide, I don't know what's wrong with you, but you keep your ideas to yourself. Now, how do you think I'm gonna get out of this running around with you to some church? You have a lot of nerve." The more CC railed at her, the madder she felt.

Addy stood there and took it. She meekly said, "I checked with Miss Jessica first. If you want to go with me, she'll give you some extra credit."

CC reeled around and got right up in Addy's face. "Listen, that's what I mean. Where do you get off fixing things for me? Who told you I want to go with you, anywhere?"

Addy didn't back down. She answered calmly, "I was trying to help. You're new here and I thought you might want to ride around, get off the farm, you know. Just trying to get to know you."

CC 's fuming subsided as she thought about riding around in Addy's new red truck and having time away from the farm. While she was thinking it might not be too bad and this girl might be fun, Addy broke into that big grin again. Her blue eyes got wider and even though she was a head shorter, CC looked into her eyes and worked to suppress her own smile.

She sighed. "Okay, Addy, maybe I got a little overheated after the comments from Gramps. Can you pick me in a couple of days? And will you stop making plans for me?"

"I will. And yes, I can pick you up Thursday around nine. The kids will be through with breakfast by the time we get there."

Without another word Addy turned and sauntered back to her truck. When she turned on the ignition, CC could hear the blaring music. Instead of Elvis, it was some country singer. She wondered if Addy was thinking about Johnny. As the trail of dust grew dimmer, CC wandered into the kitchen. The room was empty so she decided it was a good time to get upstairs and start reading her book.

CC opened the bedroom door and could tell it had changed. It looked brighter and certainly cleaner. It had a fresh smell about it, so she knew Gran must have been cleaning it. She felt a little pang of guilt after the way she complained about Mama's room earlier, but she had to admit it looked more comfortable than sleeping on the cot downstairs.

A different spread covered the double bed. It didn't look as girly and Gran had taken down the plastic flowers on the chest of drawers. She walked over to the dressing table and caught her reflection in the mirror. Surprised and pleased to notice that after a few days, she was already tanning. She could also tell there were a few gold streaks in her brownish hair.

Next to the table, there was an old bulletin board like the ones in her classrooms, but this one held Mama's high school pictures. She noticed the pictures and clippings earlier, but hadn't paid much attention. Now she saw a black and white picture of a few girls in costumes. CC peered closer. She blurted out, "Are you kidding me? That's Mama in a Ruston High School outfit. She's a cheerleader. I can't believe it. Damn!"

CC sat on the bed and tried to digest what she looked at. "Mama as a cheerleader. Fancy that. Ha!" Mama sure didn't act like some all-American girl. She had to ask Gran about that.

Her book and papers were neatly sitting on the table next to her bed. "That has to be Gran's doing. Right there, where I won't forget."

She picked up her novel and flipped through the pages. She felt grateful that it wasn't too awfully long and thought *what the heck? I may as well read a few pages.* CC rolled over, stretched her long frame out and pulled a strand of her brunette hair over her face. Turning to the first page, she read the first line. "When he turned nearly thirteen, my brother Jem got his arm badly broken at the elbow." She tossed the book to the side.

She looked at the ceiling and asked herself what in the world was she doing here? Ruston of all places. And a farm? Would she ever get to go home? Does she want to go home?

What home? Did she want to go back to Mama and Randy?

She picked up the book again. She knew the answer to that last question. No way.

CHAPTER 18

CC headed downstairs to find Gran already hanging over the stove. The aroma of fresh vegetables hung in the air and she figured there was a pot of beans already cooking. Gran liked to cook in the morning before the heat confiscated the room especially since there was no air conditioning. Back home, Mama put in a couple of window units which helped to cool things off.

As she neared the stove, the heat from the gas flames brushed over her. "Whew. I don't know how you can stand over this stove. It is absolutely sweltering."

Gran glanced at her and tapped the big spoon on the edge of the pot. She turned around to face CC and exaggerated a 'good morning' since CC hadn't bothered with a greeting.

"Sorry, Gran. Good morning," CC said as she swept a bow in return. Then without giving it a thought, she wrapped her arms around Gran and gave her a short hug. Pulling back, she smiled and asked, "That better?"

The good mood had come out of nowhere. CC woke up thinking about sleeping in Mama's room and wondering what it must have been like long ago. She wondered what year Mama graduated from high school and then she thought about what her mother's dreams might have been or if she even had any. Did she just run away to New Orleans? She thought about asking Gran, but it felt strange to think about her mother that way. And then she realized she had never talked to her mother about her life. What would she say to her?

Anyway, coming downstairs this morning, it was like she wanted to give her grandmother a break. She knew she had been kind of standoffish.

When she finished pouring her coffee, she saw Gran staring at her. She brushed her hair back before saying, "I figured maybe you wanted to keep me from asking questions about what you were doing down by Gibbs land the other day. We never talked about it, but that hug felt really nice, so I'm not gonna poke around. Your gramps said you might go off with Adelaide this morning."

CC half swung around. A look of surprise registered on her face but she countered her feeling with a smile. "Yep. She's supposed to pick me up in a while. Going to that Negro church. Addy helps with the kids' reading."

"How do you feel about that? You want to go?"

This time CC didn't mask the surprise. "Why would I say I'd go if I didn't want to?"

Gran shifted her weight to lean on the counter. "I don't know. I guess I got the idea you wanted some time alone."

Bringing the coffee mug to her mouth, CC blew on the steaming liquid before she answered. She wasn't quite sure what to say.

Before she could say anything, a horn blared in the backyard. CC grinned at Gran and said, "I'm surprised she doesn't have an Elvis Presley-sounding horn."

Gran snickered at that remark. "She sure likes that man. You want something to take with you to eat on the way?"

"Nah, I'm good." She put her cup in the sink and grabbed her purse. She started out and then thought Gran deserved some respect. "Should I be back at a certain time?"

Gran's face softened as she looked at CC. "You just go on and enjoy yourself. See you later today."

CC couldn't help thinking it was a good move to ask Gran that last question. Her attention turned to Addy's red truck. She could see Addy tuning the radio and wondered how long it would take her to find Elvis. No sooner did CC have that thought when the familiar chords of "Loving You" floated through the truck passenger window.

CC put both hands on the door frame, leaned in, and teased, "Something nice and mellow. What happened to early morning "Hound Dog"?"

Addy started for the radio knob and CC wailed jokingly, "Oh no! Just kidding! I can live with Elvis in love. Leave it on."

CC climbed up in the seat and caught a whiff of new car smell. "Nice. New, huh? When'd you get it?"

"On my seventeenth." CC looked at Addy and was again struck by her mop of blonde curls and her eyelashes so spidery long, they batted at you when you got close enough. That's what made Addy's blue eyes stand out and when she blinked them at you, it was like she beamed just for you.

Clearing her throat, CC glanced at her side mirror and checked her own hair. *Well, it might be straight but I've already picked up some, like gold streaks from the sun.* She looked back at Addy, gave her a smile, and announced, "Let's go."

As they drove down the familiar gravel driveway, the girls peeked at each other when

"Lonely Teardrops" geared up on the radio. Addy asked CC, "Okay, I gotta turn this up. You like Jackie Wilson?"

CC hooted. "You're kidding right? That's some good music. Turn her up."

She couldn't help thinking about Marcus as they listened to Jackie Wilson. He was a favorite of Marcus and they used to sing along and argue about who were the best male singers. He loved Marvin Gaye and that whole Motown sound. No sooner did she think of Gaye when they played "Hitchhike," and CC smiled as she remembered their trying the Hitchhike dance they saw on American Bandstand.

The two girls spent time riding through the countryside singing away to Martha and the Vandellas, Roy Orbison, and some more Elvis. CC hooted some more when Elvis "Return to Sender" played. They even got into a little argument about who recorded it first. CC thought another singer introduced it, but they couldn't resist singing along to Elvis' lyrics.

"Admit it, CC. It's fun singing with Elvis."

CC just grinned at Addy, but she had to admit it was fun. She hadn't noticed they pulled up in front of a church. A pristine, white, wooden building sat in a grove of tall oaks. Sitting atop the building, a black steeple housed a large silver bell. It reminded CC of pictures in her readers when she was a little kid. When she hopped out of the truck, a cool breeze from the trees embraced her. She leaned against the door, and, with the radio off, was struck by the silence. She heard the soft rush of leaves and had a fleeting thought that she could stay in this spot for a while.

She heard a slight 'uh hum' and realized Addy stood nearby observing her. When she turned sideways, Addy broke out in that remarkable smile and CC mumbled, "Just looking at the church."

"Wanna go in?" Addy acted like it was perfectly normal thing to stand there.

CC followed Addy as she walked around to the back of the church. A path bordered by summer flowers led to an entrance with a small cross mounted in the middle of the door. Addy led her through the entrance and CC immediately got an unmistakable whiff of paste. CC recognized construction paper mobiles of birds and flowers floating aimlessly above the children's heads. Everyone was colored except for CC and Addy.

The children, bent over their tasks, glued colorful cut-outs on their pictures by dipping wooden sticks into the white sticky paste. Others drew their own pictures with oversized crayons while some children sat in a small group on the floor listening to an older kid read from a big picture book.

A voice from the front of the room called out to Addy. "Hey, girl, glad you're here. Who's your friend?"

CC looked over to see an older woman sitting at a wooden desk holding a large book. One small child sat on her lap and another stood behind her peering over her shoulder. CC was struck by the bright colors in the room and the woman at the desk was no exception. She had on a vibrant yellow blouse and a red and yellow scarf hanging from her neck. She slicked her hair back into a pony-tail and her full lips were accentuated by a bright red lipstick. CC could feel herself smiling. She was reminded of the Norman Rockwell pictures her English teacher always brought to class.

"Hi, Miss Eugenia. This is my new friend CC from New Orleans."

"Hello, CC. Welcome. You want to help us out here?" The teacher's eyes widened into the question and made her whole face light up.

Addy looked at CC who shrugged nonchalantly and motioned to CC to follow her. She plopped on the wooden floor in the midst of kids' reading and patted the wooden floor next to her. CC sat down and crossed her legs Indian style, burying her hands in her lap to hide her nervousness.

"Hey, you little summer soldiers. This is my friend CC. She's going to help us with the reading group today." Addy glanced sideways at CC and flashed a warm smile.

CC looked out at the kids and as usual wished she could be as lighthearted as someone like Addy. The kids back home accused her of being too serious and keeping things in. She felt it now sitting next to Addy, who was obviously having a good time. A little girl with pigtails jumped in Addy's lap and looked up at her with an adoring grin. Addy returned the favor by kissing her on the forehead. She was a pretty, light-skinned Negro with a gingham dress that looked like it had been starched and ironed.

The child who had been reading the book stood up and handed it to Addy. "All right, you little munchkins, I'm gonna read the next couple of pages and then we'll take turns, right? We wanna show CC here how well we all read."

A sudden cacophony of voices cried out.

"Me, me! I want to read."

"No, me! It's my turn, 'member Addy?"

The children cried out begging for turns and Addy laughed and shushed them. "We'll all have a turn today. Just wait."

CC marveled at Addy's enthusiasm for everything. She encouraged each child especially the one boy who struggled with the words. "You're getting better, Eddie."

As they read, CC noticed not all the children had starched pretty clothes. The boy who had trouble reading had a faded shirt and a pair of pants which billowed over his small frame. When his turn came, he read clearly without mispronouncing a word and beamed when the group clapped for him.

When Addy caught CC staring at a girl sitting by herself in the corner, she whispered, "That's Star. She likes someone to read to her. Wanna give it a try?" Without waiting for an answer, she handed CC a copy of *Charlotte's Web.*

CC grunted slightly as she stood and mouthed "I know this book well," to Addy. Actually, she loved this story having read it several times in fourth grade, but couldn't help wondering if this child could relate to the spider and to Fern. Her concern was short lived. The tiny girl jumped up obviously delighted over the choice and grabbed the book out of CC's hands.

She opened the book and flipped through the pages as CC watched. After a few moments, she sat down next to her and said, "Hi. I'm CC, Addy's friend. What's your name?"

CC looked down on a charming mocha -skinned face with undoubtedly the biggest eyes you could imagine. The child closed the book and held it to her chest. "My name is Star." It was almost a whisper and when she said it, CC saw her beautiful brown eyes widen as she blinked very slowly almost as though she ordered the lids to drop at a slow pace.

As CC leaned in closer, she noticed a faint aroma of soap and starch and realized the little girl's pink dress, while faded, was perfectly ironed. CC had never spent time with little kids before and she fought an impulse to pick Star up and hold her closely. She felt drawn to this child.

"What a perfect name. The name Star fits you perfectly." CC was rewarded with a shy smile and Star slowly handed the book back to her. "You want me to read it to you?"

Star shook her head slowly and CC settled in to read. "*Charlotte's Web* by Mr. E. B. White. Chapter 1. Before Breakfast. Where's Papa going with that ax?" Star sat with her legs crossed and eyes focused intently on CC.

When CC finished the first chapter, she looked around and noticed the room became very quiet and everyone stared at the two of them. She looked back at Star, who smiled up at her and said, "Keep reading." A voice from the front of the room said, "Please." Miss Eugenia smiled and repeated, "Please. Star, say please."

CC hurriedly looked down at the book, but Star touched her on the leg and whispered, "Please."

They read a while longer until her legs got stiff. She stretched out and started to hand the book to Star. "Here. You want to read for a while?"

Star shoved the book aside and scooted back into the corner. Her eyes widened with fear as she crunched into a small figure and shook her head back and forth. "No. No." Then she turned her back to the room and CC could see her tiny frame shaking from soft sobbing.

CC's helpless expression conveyed her despair to Addy and Miss Eugenia. The teacher glided across the room and knelt behind Star.

"It's all right, Star. You were listening to CC and we know you love that book. You will learn. We will help you."

Star swung around and threw her little arms around Miss Eugenia, burying her face in the teacher's brightly colored blouse.

CC heard Addy's voice behind her saying, "She doesn't read yet, CC. That's why we read to her."

"Why didn't you tell me that? How could you let me hurt this child?" She jumped up and stormed out the door not bothering to close it. Her eyes misted with tears of rage as she stumbled down the flower-covered pathway and found her way to one of the huge oak trees in the front of the church.

Dropping on the ground, CC's anger was again replaced by despair at Addy and herself for being stupid enough to think she could help those children. What was wrong with her? She gave up her baby for adoption because she couldn't care for her. Why would she think she could help any other kids?

"God, I am so ignorant and stupid!" she shouted.

"No, you're not. You're not ignorant." Addy stood in front of the sobbing CC. "Please don't think that. I should have told you about Star."

CC tried to hide her face as she wiped away the tears. Standing up, she avoided Addy's eyes and managed a weak, "Let's just go. I want to get out of here and go home."

They started for the truck and Addy tried to resume a half-hearted cheerful attitude again. "CC, it's okay. Star is having trouble reading and she's embarrassed, but we'll keep working with her."

CC just shook her head and managed not to yell at Addy. "Let's talk about something else. I don't want to talk about Star. She's got a lot of problems if she can't read and I can't do anything about it. I have enough problems of my own, Addy. Just drop it."

They climbed in the truck and CC prepared herself for an awful silence on the ride home, but was relieved when she heard Addy humming along to "Treat Me Nice" on the radio. She put her head back on the seat and closed her eyes, but she couldn't get Star's face out of her head.

CHAPTER 19

CC leaned back against the seat and listened to Addy hum along to "Lonely Teardrops." CC wanted to keep the conversation light. "Addy, what else do you do around here? You into anything besides teaching reading and hanging out with Miss Jessica?"

Addy acknowledged CC's question with another big grin. "Funny you should ask that. I was just thinking about something. Remember I told you we have a swimming pool. I'm gonna give a July fourth pool party tomorrow night and I want you to come and meet some of the kids. You can bring Johnny. It'll be a blast!"

Blood rushed to CC's face as she turned to look out the window. Thinking about being around other kids and wearing a bathing suit so soon after the pregnancy made her feel uncomfortable. She squirmed in her seat and avoided Addy's questioning look. It was just hard to imagine hanging out in a swimsuit acting like a normal high school kid.

CC turned and faced Addy's arched eyebrow. She tried to answer by teasing. "You want me or you want Johnny?"

"I want both. How about it?"

CC shifted in the seat and drew a deep breath. "I'll ask Gran. You know I should check everything with them. I don't know about Johnny."

"What's up? You think they'll say no? Like your grandparents know me and all. Should be a slam dunk."

CC countered, "Addy, I'm just being polite, you know."

"Just asking. Well, call me later tonight and I'll check around with the kids."

CC shifted around in the seat. Addy was getting on her nerves, and she wanted to be alone for a while. She was relieved the farm's gate was in view. "You know, Addy, you can let me out by the gate. I'll walk in."

Addy was not one to give up. "CC, I want both of you to come. Johnny can check out the pond. See the damage I was talking about. Come early. It doesn't get dark until eight or eight thirty." Addy brightened again. "You can meet some of the kids. They're fun. Tell us about the big city. What do you think? Wanna come?"

CC let her suffer for a few minutes, but she did like the idea of getting away from the farm and going out. She could think about the swimsuit later. Come up with something.

"Yeah. Sounds fun. I'll talk to Johnny. Look. Addy, I'm sorry I was so upset over Star. I've had a bad few days - I'll call you later." She hopped out of the truck and started down the gravel driveway.

The daytime crickets chirped as loud as ever and served as background noise as CC ambled along. Her feet hurt from the crush of the stones so she moved over to the grass. She stopped and kneeled to run her hand over a patch of purple wildflowers. Balancing on her bent knees, she watched as a wasp buzzed around the flowers. A butterfly fluttered over the patch and she instinctively leaned over to hold her hand near the leaf where it perched. Her patience paid off and her new friend crawled on top of her hand and quivered its wings. Smiling at her accomplishment, she thought of Uncle Bud and remembered how he coaxed bees to land on his hand.

CC pulled herself up and looked at the indentation she made in the grass. The butterfly still quivered and she hated to leave, but she needed to talk to Gran. She wished she could talk to her about Eric. There must be something wrong with her. Eric tied to hit on her after just seeing her with Uncle Bud. It was weird.

And then there was Star. The little girl upset her and reminded CC of what it could be like for her baby. She hadn't thought about her own little girl much or how people might treat her.

Distracted by her thoughts, CC wandered following the driveway and practically ran into Gran working a flowerbed close to the house. She peeked up at CC from under her large-brimmed straw hat. CC noticed she wore her gardening gloves and a long sleeve floral blouse with long pants.

"Geez, Gran, you get hot in the kitchen and I know you're burning up out here with those clothes."

Gran's wide smile was welcoming. "Yep. I suppose. But it protects me from getting too burned. I'm getting' older you know. Gotta protect my skin." She shifted her weight and settled on her little wooden bench. "How was your time with Adelaide?"

CC snickered. "You better call her Addy. She gets riled up with her real name."

She ignored the comment and kept puttering with her flowers. "So, what did y'all do?"

CC picked a daisy and whirled it between her fingers. "I tried to help a young girl named Star with her reading," as she looked down at the ground. "But I guess I screwed it up."

"Why did you say that? If you tried, I'm sure it was worth a lot."

She hesitated answering. She wanted to talk to Gran but could she understand what the incident with Star meant to her? She looked up at her grandmother's face and saw a soft understanding look in her eyes.

CC bowed her head and twirled the flower. After pausing, Gran put her hand on CC's shoulder and rubbed lightly. She thought she might tear up if she talked about it, but she did want to tell her grandmother what bothered her so much.

"Gran, she was the prettiest little thing. All small and helpless, but strong at the same time. She made you just want to scoop her up like a doll. I thought she could read some, but she couldn't and I embarrassed her and myself."

Gran leaned over and cupped CC's chin in her fingers. "So, you feel sorry for her? That's understandable." Gran waited for her to answer.

"I thought about my baby when I was reading to Star. Wondering if anyone would take time with her. If anyone would care about her. What if she can't read either?" CC rested her upper body over her knees and buried her face in her hands. "I wish I could start over."

Gran pushed a strand of hair away from CC's face. "We can pray she learns to read, CC. It's terrible not being able to. I see it all the time around here with both colored and white folks. That's why I tried to help last year. Still do."

"What did you do last year?"

Gran sat up straight and stretched. "I ran for the school board. Tried to talk about equal education for all the children. Giving books and supplies to the Negro schools as well as the white ones." Her face clouded over. "It got ugly. Some folks called me names and gave your Gramps a bad time. But some people agreed with me."

"Why didn't they speak up? I wish I had been here to help you." CC beamed with pride at Gran.

"It was a rough time. But I'm glad I did it. Things will change for the children. But it's slow here in North Louisiana. We must keep pushing for these children. All of them." Gran shifted again. "Now back to you. What else is worrying you?"

"She is half colored. Will even want to teach her. Will anyone care? What's going to happen to her?" At that CC leaned into Gran's side and lay her head down. She wanted to let her worries tumble out, but she worried how to say it all.

"Should I have thought about all of this before I agreed to let her go? What else could I do?" Looking up into Gran's eyes, she blurted out, "I'm ashamed. I didn't think about her. I just wanted to get it over with. Is that horrible, Gran?"

Gran brushed CC's hair back from her face and leaned her forehead into her granddaughter's and declared, "CC, it's called surviving. You did what you had to do at that time. And it took bravery. You had to put up with the pregnancy and childbirth and all that pain by yourself, and then face coming here and getting on with life. None of that is easy, child. You did it!"

"But Gran, what about my little girl? She's not white. Or at least not all white. What will happen to her?"

"I remember your Mama telling me they will look for a home that will take care of her. There are mixed families."

"I went to Shreveport because I didn't want to marry Marcus. But we couldn't get married anyway. Marcus checked when I got pregnant. Did you know it's the law, Gran? Whites can't marry Negroes in the South. Maybe not anywhere. So, I went along with the unwed mother's home and then giving up the baby, but I never thought about her being mixed race until she was born. How will she be treated?"

CC pulled back and looked into Gran's eyes, "Oh God, what's wrong with me?"

"Child, please let me hold you a little longer." Gran held her and started a gentle rocking motion. After a little bit, Gran pulled a hanky from her pocket and handed it to CC.

CC noticed the hanky smelled like Gran's soap, too, and she couldn't help but let out a slight chuckle. "Gran, do you always have a hanky nearby?"

Smiling, Gran nodded. "Yep, guess I do. Comes in handy. You know there may be a way to consider what happened to your baby, but we need to talk about that another time. It will take some doing. Now, what else is going on? Anything else happening I should know about?"

CC wiped her face and blew her nose. She thought Gran was hinting about Eric and she sure didn't want to talk about him now. Did she know what happened? She decided to change the subject.

"Addy wants me to go to some dumb swimming party at her house. I don't have a suit and I don't think I can wear one anyway. And what am I going to say to her friends? All those juniors and seniors from the high school?"

Gran laughed and leaned back on her stool. "Have you looked in the mirror the last few days? You are already tanned and your hair has some pretty gold streaks. You always had a cute figure and you still do. Nothing to worry about there. I bet you could be a knockout in the right swimsuit. How about I take you into town tomorrow and buy you one? Your pick. My treat."

CC seemed to be thinking about it too long, so Gran added, "You know I could give you another driving lesson on that road from town. We can go the back way this time. Hardly any cars."

With that CC perked up and whooped, "That would be so fab." CC jumped up and grabbed Gran to give her a hug. Gran squeezed her just as hard, and, putting her arm around CC, they started for the house.

The next morning, they took off for town. Gran was so cool about the shopping. They walked in the Ruston department store, and she knew the saleslady, Marie. The girl called her by name and they seemed to know each other well. Gran just pointed to CC and said, "My granddaughter, CC, needs a swimsuit. Would you help her find one? I'm going to go over here and look at the dresses for me."

Gran stuck to her word and CC came out of the dressing room feeling like she didn't have any clothes on. She hadn't posed for anyone since she was a little kid. Her legs felt rubbery and she could swear she blushed. But she managed to stand there waiting for Gran to pass judgment. She didn't have to wait. Gran walked over and had the biggest smile on her face.

Gran stood there and folded her arms over her stomach and CC heard her exclaim, "Wow." She wasn't the only one. Marie held on to a nearby rack and managed a little whistle. From out of nowhere another sales lady appeared and said, "That is definitely your color. Perfect!"

CC knew she was blushing now and couldn't resist asking, "You think red is OK, Gran? It's not like too much or something?"

"It is absolutely perfect, especially with that black trim across the top. And the one piece sets off your figure. Is that what you want?"

"Oh, yes. Yes. I love it!"

"Then it's yours."

CC practically knocked Gran over giving her the tightest hug she could muster, and kept saying, "Oh, thank you. Thank you. I love it."

The swimsuit made her feel special, like a normal girl. She almost forgot about the driving lesson but not for long. Gran started home a different way and CC sensed this was the lonely road she mentioned earlier. Gran pulled over and turned to CC. "Now, here we go. I want you to practice shifting again and finding the brakes. This is an old car, but it can get away from you. Watch me for a minute."

Gran went over the clutch again and slowly released the clutch to shift from first to second to third. "Let's just focus on that for now. We'll do reverse later at home. Wanna try?"

CC jumped into the driver's seat anxious to start. Her confidence soon faltered when she released the clutch and the old Ford leaped forward. The motor died without sputtering. Gran laughed and CC started giggling so hard, she had to wait to start the motor and try again.

"Don't worry, Honey. It happens to everyone in the beginning. Takes practice to release the pedal evenly."

After a few more tries, CC could get the car moving without stopping. It helped that Gran was so patient with her. "Now when we get home, we'll park in that circular driveway in front of the house, and you can practice until your heart's content shifting and driving around in a circle. That way you can learn and I can listen to make sure you're not stripping the gears."

Thrilled at her second driving lesson, CC was ecstatic to get home. But before she did anymore practice, she ran upstairs to try on the red suit and model it by herself in front of the mirror. *I hope I look as good as Marie said. A party. Wow! A party.*

CHAPTER 20

CC couldn't wait until Johnny came in from the field that evening so she could talk to him about the party She paced back and forth, wondering if she would be able to convince him to go. She didn't want to go without him.

"Johnny, you have to go. July fourth is next week so she's having her swim party this weekend. If you don't go, I can't go either." CC had pleaded with her cousin until he relented, but only after she persuaded him she would look at dead fish with him in Addy's pond.

"You know you want to investigate what's going on there. We've been checking on these birds. Don't you want to know what's going on at Addy's farm?"

He had looked at her with a blank stare and then popped out laughing. "You aren't interested in those fish. You just want to go to that party."

"Well, Addy's been nice to me and I think we ought to go." At that she popped out laughing, too, and they agreed they both wanted to check it out for different reasons.

CC ran into the kitchen the next afternoon to help Gran before she got ready for the party. Gran asked her if she needed any help with her outfit.

"What outfit? Oh, you mean what I'll wear. Thought I'd wear my shorts and bring the suit in a towel. Should be able to change at Addy's. We're going early cause Addy wants to show something to Johnny." She was surprised Gran didn't ask what that something could be and CC"s admiration for Gran showed in her humming and skipping up the stairs.

CC took her time getting ready up in her room. She closed her door and studied herself in the mirror. The bathing suit had black trim across the top which looked sophisticated against the red. She was pleased with how she looked, but she couldn't decide on her hair and brushed it several different ways, even trying a ponytail. She settled on just brushing it and letting it hang loose down her back. Gran was right. She had these pretty gold sun streaks.

She turned several ways in the mirror to check her figure and decided no one could tell she just had a baby. She had a lingering thought from her talk with Gran yesterday. She remembered that Marcus was very smart. The baby might be like him and be real smart in school. That would be cool if she could read and write like him.

CC bounced down the stairs and walked in the kitchen. Gramps did a double take and let out a "wow."

Gran turned from the stove and gave CC the biggest smile. "I guess I look OK?"

Gran folded her arms over her middle and Gramps offered the first verdict. "You look more than OK, CC. You look very nice."

CC knew this was a big compliment coming from Gramps and it was easy to throw her arms around him. Then, with a peck on the cheek for Gran, she circled to show them her outfit and held up the folded towel with her swimsuit. "Guess I'm all ready to go."

In unison, her grandparents said, "Have a good time."

She departed from the kitchen as she teared up. This felt so different for her. She wasn't used to having family tell her to have fun or good night, much less help her get an outfit together or anything for that matter. She wiped at her eyes and intentionally did not dwell on thinking about what it was like with Mama. She didn't want to spoil the evening and hurried to the barn to find Johnny.

Johnny came walking around the corner of the barn and she could tell by the look on his face he thought she looked good. "Hey, Cousin. You sure clean up nice."

With that, CC smiled at him. He flipped his keys in the air and motioned for her to follow. "Let's go before it gets dark. I want to see this pond y'all are talking about, CC."

Johnny's old Ford truck rumbled along on the country road. The windows were rolled down and the early evening breeze on CC's face felt refreshing. She had put on some light peachy lipstick earlier and was glad she put the tube in her pocket to apply some later.

They drove up to Addy's gate and CC let out a low whistle. It was a large ornate entrance much bigger than her grandparents and had been painted with a glistening white finish. It didn't look like a farm. There were fully grown oak trees inside the fence and the smell from the freshly cut emerald green grass floated inside the truck.

CC couldn't believe it. Addy was sitting in her red truck just inside the gate, and when she saw them, she put her arm out the window and started waving. She heard herself say, "I wonder if she's been sitting here all afternoon waiting for you. For us, I mean." She heard Johnny laugh.

Addy walked to the gate and opened it motioning them to drive in. When they reached her, Addy leaned into Johnny's window. "Hey, follow me. I'll take y'all to the pond first."

They drove on the grass and over a small hill. CC could see a large pond that butted up to a fence. It looked normal enough to CC, but she wasn't sure what she was supposed to be looking at. Johnny seemed absorbed in parking his truck and scanning the water so she waited to see what they were going to do.

Johnny hopped out and Addy walked over to him. As they got nearer, CC noticed a funny smell. It wasn't too bad, but she wondered if that had anything to do with the fish dying. Addy motioned to Johnny to follow her to the other side of the pond. They seemed to be looking around, so CC stood nearby where she could hear what they were saying.

"My dad says the fish aren't hatching much anymore and he doesn't know why. There is kind of a putrid smell but we don't know if that has anything to do with it. A few bass drifted up last month." Addy was concentrating on Johnny so CC just watched them.

Johnny was interested. "Anything happen recently?"

"Just that the bass aren't hatching very much. This pond used to be filled with them and the workers would fish after work."

"Any chance they fished it out? You know you hear about men, temporary hires, working for a little while and hunting and fishing all the wildlife out or at least a lot of it. Don't leave much for the families or the regular workers."

Addy put her hands in her front pockets and stood a little closer to Johnny. "I know, but we have full time people. If they did that, my dad would let them go. He keeps a close eye on everything."

Johnny walked around the edge of the pond. CC thought the water looked dirty, but she didn't know what it should look like. He kneeled and ran his hands over the weeds near the edge. Then she noticed he looked out at the field. "Who's on the other side of this fence, Addy?"

"Oh, that's Mr. Gibbs. His property butts up to us and to your Gramps' land. And that water on his side is part of the lake that goes into the state land."

CC noticed Johnny perked up when Addy told him about the lake. Standing up he asked her, "You mean Gibbs land horseshoes around both properties?"

Addy looked back at CC and her eyebrows raised in a questioning look. "I don't know what you mean, but yes, his land is on both boundaries."

The three of them stood for a minute taking the conversation in. CC wasn't sure what any of it meant, but she was getting impatient and wanted to get on with the party. She hadn't felt nervous on the ride over with Johnny. But now that they were here, her stomach felt queasy and her throat went a little dry. Honestly, Addy was milking this pond thing with Johnny.

They turned to walk back to the trucks and Johnny flashed a big smile at CC. Addy asked her if she was ready to go, and CC couldn't resist a curt response of "I've been ready since I got here."

She felt bad when Johnny's look changed to a frown. "I thought you wanted me to come with you and look at the pond."

CC picked up his hint immediately. "I did. Just thought Addy might want to get to the pool. I heard cars driving in."

Addy's smile was plastered on her face. "Oh, that's okay. They'll pull up and wait for me before they get in the pool. But let's go. Just follow me."

The drive to the house proved to be just as impressive. It was a large two-story red brick with posts on the large front porch. CC guessed some people would call it a mansion, but coming from New Orleans, she was accustomed to seeing huge mansions on St. Charles Avenue.

It was as though Johnny knew what she was thinking when he asked her, "Pretty place, huh? Looks big."

"I've seen bigger." CC immediately regretted her comment. She knew it sounded petty, but fortunately Johnny didn't respond. He followed Addy into the circular drive in front of the porch. CC noticed the others were pulling into the long driveway on the side of the house. There were more trucks and old cars than she thought would show up.

She turned to Johnny and he was smiling at her again. "Are you getting out of the truck? Addy is standing there waiting for us."

CC didn't say anything as she swung the door open and slid out of the seat. She remembered to get her towel and swimsuit. She felt like she was moving in slow motion. Her instinct was to grab Johnny's arm and drag him back inside the truck, but she managed to put one foot in front of the other. She knew if she turned around, there would be no turning back. She might break down from her nervousness, go back to the farm and shelter down in Mama's room.

Honestly, she didn't know what she was afraid of, but she knew to keep walking. She could feel Johnny behind her. She turned slightly and heard him whisper, "Keep walking." What did he know? She felt her stomach tighten and tried to swallow. Her throat was so dry.

At that moment, she turned the corner of the house and instinctively took a deep breath. Before her was a picture she used to run from at school. In the cafeteria, in the gym, in crowded classrooms. It was the collection of happy, attractive teenagers, lost in their ability to drown out all the problems or sadness that didn't exist in their worlds.

If you mentioned the problems or sadness, they did not let you in. There was some secret code that helped you to know what to say or how to look when you were around them. CC had never discovered it and given up trying to figure it out, instead staying alone or with kids like Marcus.

CC could turn and run back to the truck, feigning sickness which would be close to the truth. She could don her sarcastic tone, telling Johnny they were above it all. What did it matter?

But it did. Gran had taken her to the store, Addy was excited they came, and mostly CC knew she wanted to try to act normal.

CC took another deep breath and plunged, not into the swimming pool, but into the action. With the slightest grin plastered on her face, she mumbled, "I can do this."

CHAPTER 21

As soon as she walked into the pool area, she heard Elvis crooning "Don't be Cruel" through speakers and then a groan from the group, "Not Elvis again. How about that record by the long-haired boys? The guys from England."

CC smiled at that last request. But the next song coming through the speakers was, "Surfing USA," and she knew that had to be Addy's pick.

Addy stood near a table talking to a couple of girls. She looked up and saw Johnny and CC and waved, motioning them to come on over. She was already wearing her suit and CC noticed it was a newer two-piece version with large polka dots and a little skirt on the bottom piece. She thought it looked cute, if you want to do cute.

Addy didn't wait for them and came rushing over. "Hey, come on in. You can put your suits on, if you want, in the pool house over there. I want you to meet my friends."

CC noticed a door marked 'lassies' and mumbled, "Good grief. Who calls a lady's room that?" She easily slipped into her suit and double checked herself again in the tall mirror for any signs of a pooch left over by the pregnancy. "I guess I look OK. No big stomach and my breasts are not swollen."

She thought about putting her shorts over the swim suit but left them hanging in the room. "Oh, damn it. No one will notice me anyway. I'll just go out like the other girls in my suit and sneakers without socks. Should look OK."

Leaving the bath house, she felt that blast of cold air. She didn't see Johnny so she took a deep breath again, opened the door, and peeked out to see if she could see Addy.

Addy was standing across the pool with Johnny and a couple of other girls. He must have said something hilarious cause they were all laughing. She took a few steps out and stood on the small landing with her hand resting on one of the columns looking out over the crowd.

Someone must have seen something because she heard a whistle and then another. But the second one was a wolf whistle. She looked around to see who they were whistling at and she noticed Johnny staring at her with a big grin. Addy was standing next to him and CC could tell from her smile she looked fine.

"What are they whistling at," she wondered. CC was still in the dark. And then she saw everyone looking at her, even the girls. The guys were all smiling, and one of the short ones made a mad dash for her, stumbling over an ice chest. He recovered right away and before the boy next to him could make it to CC, the short one pounced in front of him.

"Hey, I don't know who you are, but I'm Shorty. I guess you can tell that, but I'm a good dancer. Wanna twist?"

CC just stared at him, not sure what to make of it all. But a small group of boys were laughing and one of them shouted, "He's harmless."

Another one shouted, "But I'm not harmless. I want the next slow dance." They all laughed at his remark.

Shorty got even closer. "They're not playing Chubby Checker yet, but you want to get a coke? Addy filled up the cooler. Or how about a hot dog? Anything you want."

She felt someone pulling her arm and turned to see Addy beaming at her. "You sure turned heads. That's a great suit."

CC could feel her face turning red. She never imagined the boys would think she looked good. She felt kind of stupid standing there with just a suit and sneakers on, but she managed to say, "Addy, I think you look great in your suit. It's new, isn't it? I mean I've seen suits like yours in Seventeen." CC wished she could think of something more inspired to say, but Addy seemed grateful.

"Thanks, CC. Don't be nervous. Some of the girls look jealous, but my close buddies are nice. Come on, I'll introduce you. Shorty, we'll get back to you."

When Shorty rubbed his eyes and pretended to cry, CC laughed and followed Addy. She spent some time answering questions from Addy's friends. "Where are you from? What's New Orleans like? How long are you staying? Where are you staying?" It was easy to say she was spending time with her grandparents. Everyone seemed to know them and the farm.

The sun was going down so Addy flipped through the records and yelled, "Hey, I'm playing that new record by the guys from England." CC was relieved to hear "I Wanna Hold Your Hand." That was some cool music.

Three boys made a bee line for CC, including Shorty. He wasn't her favorite, but he had already asked her to dance, so she took his hand. A few of the kids applauded at his success and she hoped she could follow his lead. She didn't have too much experience dancing, but she didn't have to worry. He was clumsy and she did her best to stay away from his feet. She laughed when he told her he was better at twisting. "I've got that down pretty good."

She didn't know if she felt awkward being in a swimsuit dancing or if she couldn't shake the fact she had a baby a few months before. It was always in the back of her mind. She couldn't help it. She felt different from the girls at the party. She also wondered if they knew something was different about her. Girls had a way of knowing things.

As the song ended, CC told Shorty she needed to find someone. She found a lawn chair near the pool and looked around. Addy and Johnny were nowhere in sight, so she decided to try the pool out since no one seemed to be swimming. There were two couples hanging out at one edge and a girl was paddling around in the shallow end. She checked the depth number, kicked off her shoes and did a sleek dive from the poolside.

She swam the length of the pool and back effortlessly like she used to do at the YMCA in New Orleans. When she got to the ledge, she realized she didn't bring her towel so she yelled at Addy. The music drowned her out, but CC didn't have to worry. A couple of boys ran over, towels in hand. The taller one with a blond crew cut leaned over and offered to help her out.

"No, I'm perfectly capable." She easily lifted herself up and sat on the ledge.

"So, you're CC. Where you from? You're new around here," asked the tall one.

CC couldn't help but laugh at the rapid fire of questions. The taller, blond guy had a crazy looking shirt open at the chest and a pair of white and black trunks. He settled down next to her. "Hi, I'm Jimmy and the goofy looking guy with me is Tyler. Are you staying here all summer?"

The closer Jimmy got to her; the more uncomfortable CC felt. Tyler stood too close and she couldn't see his face. She looked around for Johnny and Addy, but didn't see them. She thought she might get up and find Shorty since he seemed harmless.

Jimmy blurted, "Hey, look at Marilyn Monroe coming in."

When CC looked in Jimmy's direction, she saw a couple standing by the entrance who seemed to have everyone's attention. A blonde hung on the boy's shoulder, and CC thought she looked older than the other girls at the party. She had a lot of make-up on which made her look like she was twenty something. Her long blonde hair was all teased and flipped up at the ends. CC couldn't see all of her make up but she obviously had on eye color and bright pink lipstick.

It was her bathing suit which CC knew got the attention. It was a shiny two-piece lime green swimsuit and even from CC's vantage point, she could tell the girl had very big boobs and they stuck out over the low-cut top. She had a tiny waistline and CC could have sworn she was wearing high heels. She murmured, "Maybe she is Marilyn Monroe."

Jimmy heard her and laughed. "No, she's just Stella. We tease her about looking like Marilyn." He looked sideways at CC and snickered, "It's the hair."

Tyler moved closer to another group of guys who were gawking at Stella and seemed speechless. One of them let out a low whistle and CC heard Tyler say, "Man, would you look at that green bathing suit!"

The other guys started laughing at him. "Yeah, that is a green suit all right! What else do you see?"

Jimmy asked, "I wonder who that guy is with Stella.?"

CC let out a long sigh before answering, "That's Eric. Eric Ralston."

CHAPTER 22

The party was in full swing when CC spotted Eric walking in with the flashy blonde.

CC also noticed the music was much louder and wondered if Addy upped it to draw attention away from the new couple. She turned back to Jimmy but he was already gone. For the first time since she came out of the dressing room, CC felt out of place. She looked around to see if there was anyone she could talk to. There was a tap on her shoulder and when she turned, there was Shorty.

"Hey want to dance? Addy played a twist," Shorty yelled, "That's what I like. Everyone knows how to twist or they can pretend and look OK."

CC just nodded. It was too loud to try to talk over the music. She noticed out of the corner of her eye, Eric was looking in their direction and, of course, he was smirking. A couple bumped into them and she heard the girl say, "Sorry, can't take my eyes off that guy who just came in."

As the next song came up, Eric walked CC's way. "I didn't figure Miss *New Orleens* for a twister. You more of a slow dance kinda gal. How about it?"

A Johnny Mathis tune came up. She was surprised how gently he turned her as he reached for her arm, and before she could protest, his arms were around her. Those dark piercing eyes bore down on hers and she felt hypnotized as he led her expertly into a slow dance. Their bodies touched, but he did not push into her as he had done at the farm.

As the song ended, CC didn't realize she had closed her eyes during the dance. As she opened them, Eric stared into her and his lips spread into a soft smile. "CC, wanted to say sorry about..."

Before he could finish his sentence, Eric's date slinked over. "Well, Honey, there you are. I caught up with you. Why don't you introduce me to this new gal?"

CC felt a slight push and Stella managed to wedge herself next to Eric and her arm was around his shoulders just like when they came in. CC stood there waiting for Eric to say something to her, but he looked at Stella and said, "This is CC. From *New Orleens.*"

"It's New Orleans, Eric. Oh, never mind," as she walked away.

CC made it to the dressing room and collapsed on the first bench by the door. "God, what is wrong with those people? What's wrong with me? Why did I dance with that creep?"

Despite her anger, CC started crying like she was mad at first. She wasn't sure she would be able to stop if she started, but she broke loose anyway. Sitting alone in the room, she let it out. She was not sure why she was blubbering, but did it anyway and felt herself starting to tremble. She tried to stop but couldn't.

There was a soft touch on her back and she could hear Addy whisper, "It's Okay, CC. I'm here."

CC leaned over and held her stomach. She wasn't sure what to do so she turned around and faced Addy. She managed to say between sobs, "Don't know what's wrong with me. Crying like an idiot. Why am I crying? I should be angry."

"CC, I don't know why she brought him. Stella comes to our parties, but I didn't think she knew him." Addy sat next to CC and her big eyes were filled with concern. "Here, use this towel. Don't have Kleenex."

CC could hear a song in the background, and she let out a little laugh as she wiped her face. "This is so stupid. I'm at a party and I'm sitting in this room crying like a little girl. I am just done with boys. Nice ones or creeps. How do you even know the difference?"

Addy's eyes grew even bigger and with a serious tone she said, "Gosh, I wish I had that problem."

CC put the towel in her lap and just stared at Addy. They broke out laughing. After a few minutes of giggling, CC managed to counter with,

"Don't say that. You don't want to be chased by just any boy. And it can end up bad too. It can end up terrible and you won't be able to change it."

Addy waited to hear what else CC wanted to say. Before they could continue, there was banging on the door and a girl's loud voice. "Addy, I know you're in there. Come on. We need you out here. Somebody must've snuck liquor in and some kids are getting crazy."

The two girls looked at each other and Addy told her friend, "You can stay. I've got to stop this before my dad hears about it."

"I'm coming. I'm going to throw my clothes on first." CC rushed to the changing area and put her top on. She didn't have time to worry about what she almost blurted out to Addy. Hurrying out to the pool, she could see Addy trying to push Brad away. She recognized him as one of the boys who tried to talk to her earlier. Shorty was leaning against a trash can and looked like he wasn't too steady.

When he saw her, he waved and stumbled towards her. "Hey, CC. Remember me. I'm the twist guy. He made a hip movement and turned and almost fell. He started laughing hysterically so anyone could tell he had a few drinks.

"Hey, Shorty. That's the chick you were dancing with," Brad yelled across the pool so everyone could hear him.

Oh, shut up, Brad." Addy warned him. "Where did you get the alcohol? Did you bring it?" She pulled back from the smell when Brad tried to get into her face. "Get back, idiot."

"Oh, come on. Don't be so stuck up, Addy."

Addy pushed him and tried to break away from his grasp. "Ow. That hurts. Let go of me."

"You heard her. Take your hand away." Johnny stood next to Addy. He was taller than Brad but that didn't stop Brad from acting like a big shot.

"Who the hell are you? Another punk from nowhere. Get away from my girl."

Addy was quick to respond. "I am not your girl, Brad. You better go before you end up in a lot of trouble."

"What trouble? Who's gonna give it to me?"

Before anyone could make another move, CC saw Johnny grab him by the neck and kick the back of his knee. Brad yelped and went down. "You stay there. Who brought the liquor?"

CC spoke up. "Someone must've brought it in after the party started. There wasn't any sign of it before."

Everyone turned and looked around, settling on Eric and Stella. She put her hand on her hip and gave everyone a dirty look. "Don't look at us. I wouldn't sneak it in to this dumb party. Y'all are a bunch of kids. You don't even know how to drink. Ha!"

CC watched Eric standing behind Stella. He never said a word. Just leered at everyone. Johnny started towards him with his fists clenched at his side. The drinking was bad enough. Addy would get in a lot of trouble if a fight broke out and, with these idiots, anything might happen.

Eric raised himself up to full height and pushed Stella's arm to get her out of the way. Johnny continued to approach until the two of them stood within inches of each other. CC could feel the tension, and just as Johnny began to say something, Addy ran over and whispered in his ear. Johnny turned to her and CC heard him say, "You've got to be kidding. It's that Brad guy. He brought it in and got drunk too. Why didn't anyone say anything?"

CC was relieved there wasn't going to be a fight. She didn't understand why, but she was also relieved it wasn't Eric who snuck in the alcohol. Before she could ask Johnny to leave, Eric stormed at Johnny. "This is the second time you've gotten in my face. Don't make the mistake of doing it again."

"Back off. I didn't accuse you of anything." He turned back to Addy. "Are Brad and his friends leaving?"

"Yep. They have rides home. I'm going to put some music on. Why don't you come on over to the table and get something to eat?"

CC spoke up before Johnny could say anything else. "Addy, I'm leaving. Time to go home. Johnny, are you ready?" She was frayed from all the skirmishes tonight. She looked over and Eric was staring at her and for once he didn't have that sneer on his lips. Their eyes met briefly and she saw Stella move in to whisper something in his ear. He didn't react at first and continued to stare at CC. After Stella pulled him away, he turned and said something to her and they walked off.

Between the short talk and crying spell and then all the uproar over the drinking, CC had enough. She didn't wait for Johnny to answer and started walking to the front of the house. Johnny followed her but didn't say anything. When they got to the truck, she climbed in and rested her head on the seat. Johnny put the keys in the ignition, but before starting the motor, he asked, "CC, you OK?"

For a minute, she thought she might scream at him. CC didn't understand her emotions at all. She let out a deep sigh instead. "Fine. I'm fine. But I hope Addy doesn't get into any trouble."

CHAPTER 23

"Hey, CC. Are you in the front?"

CC heard Johnny and threw her book down. She had been sitting on the couch in the living room for a change. Ever since the party, she spent time reading her book and riding Lady. She hadn't talked much to Johnny for a couple of days. He had been working on the tractor in the back field.

Walking in the kitchen, she saw him standing near the sink. "Hey, Johnny, are you through in the barn already?"

"There wasn't much to do. I cleaned Lady's stall and put some hay out. That's all Clay wanted me to do for now. Are you okay? You seemed kind of upset after the party the other night."

CC let out a kind of bitter laugh. "Well, yeah. It wasn't what I expected. I guess I thought it would be a bunch of country kids hopping around to some bubble gum music. Instead, well you know." She paused trying to figure out how to describe them.

"Yep. Not a lay back bunch. But most of them were regular kids." He filled a jelly glass with water.

"What's a regular kid?' Johnny laughed and she remembered she wanted to ask him something. "Johnny. Did you say anything to Gran about the party and the drinking?"

A look of surprise crossed his face and then he grinned. 'You're kidding, right? Gran would be cool about it, but if Gramps found out about the drinking, that would, well, you know. Anyway, we didn't do anything wrong. Why did you ask me that?"

"Just wondering. I spent this morning sitting with Gran listening to a bunch of stuff about civil rights and the schools. Forget about it."

Johnny smoothed his hair back. "What brought that up? I know Gran is steamed about the situation with the schools here. She wants the colored kids going to the same schools as the white kids." Johnny put the glass in the sink. "In Waco where I come from, they're still fighting it out, but I think they need to make it all equal."

She didn't say anything about that comment. *I wonder what Johnny would think about my mixed baby. As nice as he is, I just don't know what he'd say."*

CC turned and walked over to the coffee pot. It was empty so she stood for a minute with her arms spread out on the counter. "I guess so. You know, we had a lot of problems in New Orleans with mixing the schools, but it's moving along. I even have a couple of Negro friends." She waited for his reaction. He just shrugged so she dropped it. "What's up? What're you going to do now?"

"I've been thinking about what we saw over at Addy's pond. The fish are not hatching normally." Johnny took a long breath. He still had sweat on his shirt, and a dark furrow formed across his brow. "And here on our farm. There's something about the way the leaves on those trees look and the fact there's no fruit near Gibbs' fence. And the dead birds and dead fish over at Addy's."

CC remembered how the peach trees looked. "But I thought Gramps was going to figure all that out. Why not leave it up to him, right?"

CC stared at him. He seemed so serious. "I don't expect you to get involved, but I want you to know what I'm up to, just in case."

"In case of what?" An alarm went off in her head. "What are you up to?"

Johnny put his glass down and rested his forearms on the counter. "After Clay left, I looked over that clump of shrubs near the back fence. I wanted to see if there was anything going on by Gibbs' shed. It's near the back of his property, kind of hidden by the brush. I saw Gibbs and one of his guys carrying a sprayer."

"So, what? What are you talking about? What difference does that make?" Johnny was snooping around on a neighbor's property like an investigator, but CC didn't understand what he wanted to investigate.

Johnny pulled his lanky frame to its full height. "I'm going over to check out what he's keeping in the shed. I'm not sure yet, but I think this may have something to do with the chemicals I read about. Have you seen Gran and Dad?"

CC spit out the words. "You're going back on that property? We just had that talk with Gramps. For what?"

"I have a feeling they're doing something to hurt Gramps' land. That's why there's a hole in the fence and why they're starting those brush fires. The fires are hiding something."

CC felt like this was something that had nothing to do with her. "This is crazy. That's what. Is that why you didn't tell Gramps about the hole in the fence and the brush fires? You have your own suspicions and you want to figure it out yourself?"

Now Johnny couldn't hide his feelings. He shouted, "Look, Gramps and Gran have taken care of my dad all these years. I told you I want to help them. Whatever it takes. I think I'm on to something."

CC stared at him. She thought about the summers they ran around on the farm, riding Lady and playing tag. Instead, here they stood in the kitchen and she didn't understand why Johnny was determined to go looking for trouble.

Johnny turned and rinsed out his glass. "I'm going over there. They finished working for the day and I'm just gonna peek in the shed."

He headed for the back door and CC stood glued to the kitchen linoleum. It was like everything stood still as she watched him go. He's being an idiot she thought. Nothing is ever peaceful around here. Why can't everyone mind their own business!

Despite her doubts, she heard herself saying, "Wait up! I'll keep a watch out for you if you are set on doing this," and followed him across the back yard.

Johnny tuned back to her "Are you sure? I don't wanna get you in any trouble."

"I'll just keep watch. I don't have a clue what you're thinking, but I can't get in trouble for just keeping watch, right?"

Johnny gave her another chance to turn back. "You sure, CC? You don't have to go with me."

"I'm just keeping watch, that's all. Just don't want you going alone." She put her head down and got in step with him.

They rounded the back of the barn and headed for Gibbs' fence. Johnny was like a person on an important mission and CC rushed to keep up with him. Her heart raced and by the time she reached the fence, she was panting. Johnny didn't hesitate, lifted, and sailed over in a split second. CC hoisted herself and climbed awkwardly over the top. "Glad it's not any higher," she whispered to herself as she landed on her feet.

"C'mon, CC. I want to try the door on the front of the shed."

She felt some sweat trickle down her neck and wished she had taken a little time to put on a lighter shirt and tie her hair up. "Johnny, are you sure about this?"

"Why ask me that now? Don't worry. We'll just be a few minutes." He didn't answer her question, but CC was too busy making sure no one was following them to demand one.

Johnny crept to the shed door and crouched at the entrance, looking around to make sure no one was on the other side of the small building. She heard him murmur. "Damn. It's padlocked."

CC lowered her head and whispered. "Whew." She wanted to mop the sweat off her forehead, but didn't have a bandana. She leaned over and put her hands on her knees, but her relief at Johnny's discovering the padlocked door was short lived.

He was already looking around the perimeter of the building. "CC, give me a hand. There's a window on this side. Need to look inside but can't reach it. You see anything to stand on?" Even though there wasn't anyone around, they both whispered.

CC saw a few tools lying around. "Wait, there's a wheelbarrow. I'll drag it to you."

"That should work. I can turn it over and stand on the bottom. Should give me enough height. Thanks."

"Don't take too long. If someone sees us, they'll think we're trying to break in'"

"It's OK. Just gonna take a little look. Give me a sec." Johnny stood on the flat surface and peered in the shed. "There! I think I can make out something on the shelves close to me." She saw him wipe the window with his bandana.

"Johnny, hurry up. We can't take too long."

"Not yet. I can see four canisters lined up on that shelf. Their labels are facing this way."

CC couldn't help herself. "What is it? What's so important we had to creep over here?"

"Damn. I was afraid of this," Johnny said out loud. His face was pressed against the window, and he held himself up with his hands on the top of the window frame. "I didn't know farmers still used this stuff."

"Afraid of what? What are you talking about?" She tried not to yell, but was getting totally exasperated. She didn't know what he was talking about.

Johnny stepped off the wheelbarrow and wiped his brow with his bandana. CC faced him. "What is it? What did you see?"

"DDT. Like poison. It hurts animals and plants, And streams, ponds." He looked at CC like he was going to say more, but stopped. "I'll tell you about it back on the farm, but let's..." He didn't get to finish that sentence.

They both jumped when a familiar voice yelled, "What are you kids up to now? Been watching you from that tree over there and you're up to no good."

CC watched Mr. Gibbs charge towards them. "Oh great. We were sitting ducks, Johnny." CC felt her heart pump faster. "What do we do now?"

CHAPTER 24

Johnny didn't have time to answer. Mr. Gibbs kept yelling, "What are you doing on my property again, and why are you lookin' in my shed? Whatta you want? Were you gonna take something?"

Johnny stuttered and then managed, "We're trying to find some tools Gramps is looking for. We thought maybe…"

He didn't get to finish. Mr. Gibbs walked closer to Johnny and for a minute, CC thought he would hit him. Instead he got between them, grabbed them up by the arms and pulled. "I'm taking both of you back to my house, and we'll find out exactly what you're up to."

He started dragging then away from the shed, and CC felt his firm grip on her arm. "Ow! You're hurting me. Let me go!" His grip tightened instead and she managed to turn and kick him in the shin.

Johnny pulled away. Gibbs let go of her and rubbed his leg. "You are going to pay for this big time, Missy. Wait till your Grandpa gets ahold of you."

"Wait till I tell him you hurt my arm, Mister. You are going to…" She didn't get to finish her sentence either. Heavy footsteps thumped behind them. Before she could turn to see who it was, someone pushed her on the side and she fell to the ground.

"No! Hands off. No." From the strength of the push, CC knew it was Uncle Bud, yelling and charging at Mr. Gibbs.

CC watched in shock as Uncle Bud pushed and slapped the old man. Mr. Gibbs held up both hands in front of his face to protect his head from Bud's assault, but the big man threw punches and slaps continuously at the older man's body. He landed a hard punch on Mr. Gibb's middle and CC heard 'Oomph!' as the old man gagged and clutched his stomach.

CC was glued to her spot on the ground. "Johnny, you better stop your dad. You should do something. Help Mr. Gibbs. Bud will kill him!"

Johnny sprang up and yelled, "Dad, stop. Stop! You're gonna hurt him. Stop!"

CC knew she had to do something. Somehow the adrenalin in her body got her legs to move and she took off for her grandparents' farm. Jumping over the fence in a split second this time, she ignored the scratch from the wire on her leg and ran like a streak of lightning. *I've got to get some help. Please let Gramps be home.*

She was in luck. Gramps was driving up to the barn in his pickup. "Gramps, help!" She yelled so loud he stopped his truck and tried to yell back from the window. She couldn't hear him and she didn't wait. She ran up to the passenger seat and jumped in the cab. "We have to get over to Gibbs' shed. Uncle Bud is over there laying a beating on Mr. Gibbs. We've got to stop him."

"What's going on? What happened?" Gramps asked as he shifted gears and started driving though the grass for his neighbor's land.

"Uncle Bud saw Mr. Gibbs grab Johnny and me by the arms, and he started clobbering him. Johnny tried to break it up, but he needs help."

"Johnny can't stop him once Bud starts. He must've gotten real mad about something," as he gunned the accelerator. When they reached the fence, CC could see Johnny trying to hold Bud back, but her uncle didn't stop. His arms flailed in the air and she could see that he was still yelling. She heard Gramps swear as he pulled right up to the fence and jumped out the creaky truck door, shouting as he ran, "Stay over here, Cicely. I mean it."

Gramps climbed over the fence. It seemed like forever to CC. She heard him yell, "Johnny! Bud! What are you doing? Stop it! Back off!" He pulled Johnny away and swung Uncle Bud around by the arms. For a minute, it looked like Bud was going to swing at Gramps but fortunately, he dropped his arm.

CC gawked back and forth at all three of them and decided she couldn't just stay where she was and watch. No matter what Gramps said, she was part of this now and she started for the fence. She jumped over again ignoring the cut on her leg. She could hear Mr. Gibbs hollering.

"Scott, I said you needed to keep these kids off my land. He was trespassing again," as he pointed at Johnny. "Look what happened cause they didn't listen. Your idiot son attacked me and walloped me in the gut and your grandson is no better." CC could hear him wheezing as he leaned over and held his stomach and tried to talk.

"Now hold on Gibbs. There must be an explanation for this. Slow down. Can you tell me what happened?"

"That crazy nut case of yours smacked me in the face and punched me in the gut. I told you a while back he's trouble. You need to put him away. He's crazy!"

"Stop it! Don't say that. You can yell at me and call me names, but don't call my dad that name." Johnny was crying and shouting at the same time as he held his dad back.

When CC heard Johnny, she couldn't let him handle this alone. "Uncle Bud was protecting me. He saw Gibbs dragging me and hurting my arm."

"And she, that girl, kicked me in the shin! You better keep her away from these two."

She couldn't believe Mr. Gibbs was saying all these things. "But, Gramps, he started it by dragging me. My arm hurts. Look."

Gramps gave CC a warning look and stepped in front of Johnny and Uncle Bud to keep them back. "Listen. Gibbs. Just tell me what happened? What started this? What set Bud off? He's usually provoked. He doesn't go around just attacking people."

Mr. Gibbs leaned over holding his middle. His face was red and quenched up like he was in a lot of pain. He struggled to talk but he got some words out. "Your grandson, over here again. Tried to break into my shed. Your granddaughter watched him. She jumped over here too."

Gramps turned and looked at her. As CC watched, she saw Uncle Bud pacing and shaking his fists, talking to himself. She rubbed her face. She felt like she was watching a movie and Uncle Bud wasn't making any sense.

"I'm callin' the sheriff. Telling him to come get your crazy son and pick him up." Gramps held his hand up to stop Johnny from jumping in. "I'm gonna have your boy arrested for this. And your grandson too."

Gramps didn't move. He just looked back and forth at Johnny first and then Uncle Bud. He ran his fingers through his hair before asking Gibbs, "Can my family and me meet at the house first? You call Sheriff Jack. Tell him we'll be at the farm. You know I'll have them there." He motioned to Johnny and Bud. "We'll straighten this out. We been neighbors for too many years. You know I'm a man of my word, Harold."

"Is there an explanation for your son pouncing on me and beating me?" Still holding his middle and sputtering, "Can't let your son run around the fields actin' up and attacking people."

Gramps gazed down at his feet first and then back at Mr. Gibbs. "I'm asking you to let us go back to my farm. Let me settle them down and talk to them about what set Bud off. We'll be in my kitchen waiting for you and Sheriff Jack. You got my word on that, Harold."

Gramps held his hand out for a handshake, but Mr. Gibbs turned away and muttered, "We'll be there. You keep your crazy son over there. Don't want him on my land."

CC saw Johnny make a move towards Mr. Gibbs again, but Gramps motioned him back. They headed for the fence. When CC turned back, she was shocked to see Eric standing over by the gate. She had forgotten he worked for the Gibbs farm and almost tripped over her feet when she saw him. He didn't move. Just held the gate open. She couldn't tell anything by the look on his face. Normally, he had this sneer, but his blank stare didn't reveal anything.

As the group walked through, she heard Johnny say, "What are you doing here?"

Eric was quick to answer him. "You were told to stay off Mr. Gibbs' land. I work here, that's why I'm standing here."

Gramps had his arm over Bud's shoulder and was talking in his ear, but he stopped. "Johnny, keep moving. Let's get home."

CC knew Gramps could keep Uncle Bud calm. Johnny walked slightly behind them, but he looked back at Eric one last time.

CC didn't say anything else. She didn't want a confrontation with Eric after everything that just happened and her arm was already throbbing. Behind her, she heard Eric shout, "CC, you better put something on that cut on your leg." She decided to ignore him.

When they got to the truck, Gramps motioned for CC to hop in the back. He held the side door for Bud and guided him on the seat. Johnny started to climb on with CC, but Gramps uttered, "Uh-huh," and Johnny slid on the front seat next to Uncle Bud.

Gramps walked around the back of the truck where he could look at CC. His face sank with disappointment, but he said. "Let's fix that leg up as soon as we get back. Here, put some pressure on it with my handkerchief."

CC dreaded the ride home and facing her grandparents at the farm. Mostly she thought about Uncle Bud and what might happen to him. *What will the sheriff do? What will Mr. Gibbs do? Will Uncle Bud go to jail? Will Johnny be arrested for trespassing?*

As CC stared through the dirty back window into the cab, she wilted as she had another thought. *What about me? I was trespassing too. Gran is expecting more from me. I don't need any more trouble. Why did I follow Johnny? That was stupid!*

CHAPTER 25

CC trudged to the back door. She faced a rush of hot air and bright sunlight as she entered the kitchen. CC thought all the sunlight in the world couldn't brighten this day.

"Where have y'all been all afternoon? I thought you were upstairs reading, but when I went up..." Gran's voice trailed off when she saw CC standing at the corner of the table with her head bent. "Why don't you sit down? I'll get you a glass of water. Is Johnny with you?"

Before CC could answer, Johnny walked in followed by Uncle Bud and Gramps. CC thought it was easy for Gran to see something was wrong. Johnny's hair was tousled, his shirt was half out of his jeans, and his knees had grass stains.

Gran's attention turned back to CC, and she grabbed a bottle from the cabinet and a wet rag. "Sit down. I'll wipe the blood off your leg and put this antiseptic on it. How did you get this cut? Never mind. I guess I'm about to hear the whole story."

As Gran wiped her leg, CC kept her eyes peeled on Uncle Bud. He mumbled what sounded like gibberish and started pacing in front of the sink. Gramps took him gently by the arm and in a very soft tone told him, "Son, it's all right. Come on over by your stool and I'll get you some water."

Uncle Bud sat down but he started rocking and babbling, "Not crazy. Mean. Mean. Not crazy."

Johnny started for his father but Gramps motioned for him to sit down. "You sit and cool off, Johnny. Your grandmother will take care of your father."

Gran finished working on her leg and went over to Uncle Bud. She talked softly to him and handed him pills to take. CC still felt like she was watching a movie.

As she looked at Johnny, she thought he was seething and about to explode.

Gramps pulled his chair in front of him. "What happened out there, Son? Why were you and CC on Gibbs' land after I told you to steer clear? And Bud? What happened to rile him up?"

Johnny pounded his fists on the table. Uncle Bud jumped up when he heard the sound, but Gran eased him back down. "I tried to protect your land, Gramps." Johnny hollered. Gramps motioned for him to hold it down, so Johnny leaned back in his chair and started over in a reasonable tone.

"I wanted to find out what Mr. Gibbs had in his shed and I was right. He's got dangerous chemicals out there."

"So, you snuck over there without coming to me? You trespassed on his property. You grew up on farms. You know you can't do that."

"I was thinking about you and Gran and the farm. I wanted to figure out what was causing the birds to die and the trees to look so sick. Gramps, I found canisters of DDT. That stuff is ruining farmers' land and killing wildlife."

It seemed to CC like the whole family was in slow motion. Gramps stood up slowly and turned away from Johnny. CC heard him swear under his breath. Uncle Bud stared calmly into space from his stool as Gran hovered near him. Johnny bent over with his hands clasped.

What a mess. Everywhere I go it's a mess! She rubbed her arm as it started to throb. She started to speak up and tell Gramps how she was dragged away by Mr. Gibbs, but before she could, CC heard heavy footsteps on the back porch.

The screen door creaked and in walked the tallest man CC had ever seen. His huge frame filled the doorway and blocked the sun. As he stepped in, Sheriff Jack took off his hat and twirled it in his hands. "Evening, Mrs. Scott."

CC knew her mouth was still open, but she couldn't help it. She watched as Gramps went over and shook the sheriff's hand. Seeing them side by side made Gramps seem very small. She watched Johnny gawk at the big man, and then turn to her. His expression said it all. They were really in trouble.

Gran recovered and sprung into motion. "Good evening, Sheriff. Jack. How about a cup of coffee? I can make fresh."

"No, Ma'am. Believe we need to figure out what happened at Gibbs' place today. There seems to have been some trouble." CC noticed the whole time he spoke he never took his eyes off Uncle Bud.

Johnny cleared his throat as though to speak, but Gramps jumped in. "Sheriff, I think the kids went over investigating without permission and things got out of hand."

"Who went over without permission?" His eyes scanned the room.

"I did, Sir." Johnny stood up as he spoke. His face was pale but his voice seemed steady. I wanted to look for something."

The sheriff's eyes seemed steely as he stared at Johnny. "That right? Did you ask your Grandpa about it first?"

"No, Sir. I went on my own." CC started to say something, but the sheriff asked another question.

"Let's move on, Son. How did the fight start?"

Johnny glanced at Gramps who motioned for him to keep talking. "Mr. Gibbs shouted at us and then started dragging us by the arms. I'm OK, but CC got bruised up."

CC knew it was her chance to help. "My arm is bruised. I started kicking him to make him let me go and that's when Uncle Bud jumped in and tried to help us. He pushed and shoved Mr. Gibbs." She held her arm so the sheriff could see it and he nodded that he saw it.

The sheriff asked, "Did your uncle stop punching when you yelled at him?"

CC felt her heart racing as she tried to figure out how to answer the question, but there was no way out now. "He punched Mr. Gibbs in the stomach. So, I ran to get Gramps."

The sheriff looked at both Johnny and CC, and then turned to Gramps. "Let's talk on the porch, Ethan."

The kitchen was quiet except for the constant dripping of the faucet. CC jumped as the clock chimed six o'clock and was surprised it was so late. Johnny slumped over in his chair. CC started to speak to him but thought better of it.

It seemed like just seconds before the sheriff and Gramps came back. Gran didn't seem surprised when Gramps asked her if she gave Uncle Bud any medicine. "Yes. I gave it to him as soon as he came in."

CC noticed Sheriff Jack put his hat back on. "Mrs. Scott, I have to take Bud in. Gibbs issued a complaint and I am following through. Would you get him a bag with pajamas and robe and so forth?"

Johnny sprang from his chair. "You can't do this. It's my fault. Don't arrest him. Take me."

CC grabbed the back of a chair. "It's not fair. He was trying to protect us. Please, don't."

Gran spoke up. "Both of you be quiet. The sheriff is doing his job. Gramps will handle this. There has been trouble before with Bud."

Gramps held Bud by the elbow and said, "Come on, Bud. We're going for a ride." Uncle Bud shuffled out the back door and CC could see the sheriff holding the back door of his police car open. Johnny cussed under his breath and ran out the door.

Johnny pleaded with Gramps to follow them in his truck but Gramps turned and shouted, "Get back in the house."

The sheriff started up the gravel driveway as Gramps rumbled across the yard and angled behind the sheriff. As they passed the back porch, CC could see Uncle Bud in the sheriff's back seat. He looked at her and CC could see that sweet smile of his as he lifted his hand and waved to her.

Fighting back angry tears, CC stormed into the house and to the living room. She fell on the old velvet couch and wiped her eyes with the back of her hands. *What's going to happen to him? Now what?*

CC curled up on the couch. Gran came in and stood above her.

"I know you want to lie down and hope it will all go away, but it's not. Sit up and let's talk," as she sat down and patted the center of the couch.

"CC, what possessed you to go to Gibbs this afternoon?"

CC looked at the old black and white television sitting on the opposite wall and tried to come up with a reasonable answer. There was none. "I guess I wanted to help Johnny. He told me there was something he wanted to look at and I went along to keep a watch for him."

"So, you knew there might be trouble? Keeping a watch, I mean."

She sighed and hung her head. "Gran, I didn't think. I just went along with him." CC felt Gran moving closer to her. "I'm sorry. I messed up. Mr. Gibbs is trying to put us all in jail."

"Yes, there's a lot of trouble because of what happened, more for Bud than anyone else, but you're not going to jail.

CC stared at the floor.

"And you have other things you can do around here besides following Johnny around."

CC raised her head and looked into Gran's eyes. "Yes, you're right. I'm going to call Addy tonight if that's OK." She had to ask, "What are they going to do to Uncle Bud?"

Gran leaned back on the old couch and stroked her forehead. "They'll keep him medicated. See what they can do to settle him down. We've been through this before. Bud has acted out before, but not this bad."

She didn't know what else to say to Gran. "It's almost dark. Is it Ok if I go for a walk? Just by the back and the barn. I'd like to see Lady."

"Sure. We're just having pot luck when your Gramps gets home. Stay nearby."

CC walked out the front door of the house. No one ever used that door and it stuck when she tried to open it, but it gave way after a couple of tugs. She could already hear the crickets warming up for the night. Leaning against the small front columns, she looked at the front yard. She had forgotten how Uncle Bud kept these flower beds up. The daisies were in full bloom and his rose bush was full of small red flowers.

She thought she might cry thinking about Uncle Bud and his flowers so she hurried to the back of the house towards the barn. Lady signaled with a loud whiny letting CC know she wanted to see her.

When she got to the barn door, it was already getting dark inside so she found the lantern and struck one of the long matches in the box next to the door. She ambled over to the horse but put the light down on the outside of Lady's stable so she wouldn't frighten her.

CC leaned into Lady and stroked her neck. As she patted the horse, she whispered into her big ear, "Sorry I didn't bring an apple. Let me brush your mane."

When she turned to get the brush from a nearby basket, she was startled by a lone figure near the door. He was blocking any light, but CC recognized the voice. "She knew you were nearby. I heard her from the field."

Eric stood a few feet away. CC smelled a woodsy kind of fragrance, and she recognized it as the same fragrance as the one he wore to the party. "What are you doing here?"

He moved nearer but kept his distance from her. "My dad works here, remember? I also wanted to find out how you're doing. How's your leg?"

CC held the lantern between them. "It's OK. Gran fixed it up."

Eric's face looked surprised. "What's that on your arm? What happened?"

CC had forgotten about the bruising when Mr. Gibbs' yanked her. but when she looked down, the memory of that incident made her angry. "The man you work for dragged me away from the shed. Guess he thought he had the right. But that's when Uncle Bud walloped him."

Eric leaned against the stall door. "Didn't know he got that rough with you. I was in the field when all that happened. Anything happen to your uncle?"

CC put the lantern down on the ledge and shoved her hands in her front pockets. "The sheriff picked him up and took him to the hospital. I'm worried about him."

They stood facing each other. Eric spoke first. "You wanna take a walk? There's still some light."

CC straightened up. "Let me ask you something. What were you going to say at the party when we were dancing? You know, before your date cut in?"

She could have sworn Eric's face turned red. "Oh, you know."

"Know what?"

It took a minute. "I was going to say I was sorry for kinda pushing you the other day in the back here. You know. When I tried to kiss you." Then he mumbled, "And so forth."

"And so forth what?" Before he could answer, she heard Gramps truck rumbling through the gravel and stopping in the yard.

"I've got to go in. Gramps is home."

As she walked out, she brushed against Eric. Their faces almost touched and when she looked up at him, he smiled down at her. His typical steely expression softened as he said, "Hope I see you soon. We can take that ride."

CC kept walking but she smiled for the first time that day.

CHAPTER 26

CC nestled her head against her pillow and enjoyed the fresh outdoorsy smell of the pillow case. When she arrived at the farm and spent the first night, she didn't notice all the nice touches from Gran. She didn't remember ever having such nice bed sheets, much less freshly washed ones. She used to watch Gran hanging the sheets on the clothesline and didn't think anything about it. Now she realized the wonderful scent and feel of the things Gran did... well, not to be taken for granted.

She thought of Eric when she opened her eyes. When she first met him, he intimidated her. But the other night he seemed different and she couldn't help feeling tingly standing near him. She got a rush when she thought of him, the way his black hair fell over his eye, and that cool looking belt buckle he wore. She was sure he wanted to kiss her and she might not have pulled back this time, only the rumbling of Gramps' truck stopped her.

She stretched her long legs and touched the bottom of the wooden bed frame. The old rooster, Buster, crowed and CC laughed out loud realizing she beat him by waking up before he sounded his alarm. The thoughts of the fight at Gibbs shed ran through her mind. Her eyelids shut tight as she remembered the fight, and she wondered if he had cooled off.

"He can't still be mad at Uncle Bud." CC shot up as she had another thought. *Did*

Mr. Gibbs have trouble with him before? It sounded like he did. Is that why he is so mean to him. Will Gramps be able to bring him home today?

But the look on Uncle Bud's face when they drove away lingered the most. It hurt to think about how lost he might feel locked up without any family. She covered her face from memory.

"I've got to do something. He's been gone two days. He must be so lonely."

She called Addy last night to pick her up to go to the bible school to help the kids, but she had another thought. CC threw on her shorts and top and ran downstairs to the phone in the hallway. She looked around to make sure the coast was clear and no one could hear her. She tried to dial slowly so it wouldn't make noise.

"Hey, Addy. It's me."

She could tell her friend was groggy. "CC, is that you? What time is it? I'm still in bed," as CC heard her yawn.

CC groaned to herself, thinking Addy was usually all jazzed up. "Listen, wake up and pick me up in an hour. OK?"

"Thought you said about noon. What's up?"

"I'll explain when I see you. But it's real important or I wouldn't ask. OK?"

She didn't wait for an answer and bounded up the stairs to get ready. She had an outfit in mind that would make her look older and wanted to put a little make-up on, too.

She heard someone in the kitchen rattling around, and tried to think of a way to leave without being seen, but decided on an alternate plan She grabbed the purse she hadn't used since she got to the farm and loaded it with powder and lipstick and a dressy blouse. She looked around her room and decided to squeeze in a pair of flats to replace her sneakers. "These will make me look older too."

Taking a deep breath, she stood up straight and walked calmly down the stairs. When she turned the corner into the kitchen, she saw Johnny standing at the counter blowing into a cup of coffee. As usual, Gran was at the sink washing dishes.

"Morning. I'm gonna have a quick cup before I leave."

Johnny gave her a side glance. "What are you off to this early?"

Gran turned around and started wiping her hands. "You called Addy last night? Going off with her?"

CC picked up her favorite mug and poured a cup from the stove. "Yep. We're going to the bible school." She turned and stared at Johnny while she took a sip of the strong stuff.

Johnny continued to look at her with suspicion. "Aren't you gonna wait to see if Gramps has any news?"

Gran cocked an eyebrow and answered for CC. "She can find out when she gets home. Be a good idea to spend time with Addy and help those kids. Right, CC?"

"Yes'm. I think so," as she avoided looking at Johnny again. She put the cup in the sink and grabbed a piece of toast from Gran as she hurried out the door. As nervous as CC felt, she managed to gulp down the buttered bread and wish she had brought the cup with her to wash it down. She wasn't too surprised when she heard the screen door screech in back of her.

She turned to face Johnny and waited for him to comment.

"I thought I might catch a ride with you and Addy. My truck had been acting up."

CC snickered before countering with her own thoughts. "You mean you want to find out what we're up to, right?' Johnny cocked an eyebrow in anticipation of any explanation. "We're going to the bible school and I want to talk to Addy about the party the other night. I haven't had a chance. You know - girl stuff. You sure you want to ride with us and hear us talk about you some?"

CC knew she was biting her lip and scrunching up her face. Johnny watched her closely, and started laughing. "OK, you got me. Y'all go ahead." She heard Lady's neigh getting louder and made a mental note to spend time with her when she got home later.

As though on cue, CC heard Addy's truck coming up behind them on the gravel driveway. As usual there was the familiar radio blaring away, but CC only recognized a twangy country sound, no Elvis this morning.

Johnny turned and CC thought he was walking to the barn but instead he headed for Uncle Bud's garden.

Johnny just waved his arm as though to say yes and kept walking. CC realized he must have felt hurt that she didn't say any more about his dad, but she wanted to get her plan in action without having to explain it to him or anyone else.

Addy spun a little as she pulled around to stop. "Morning. Is that Johnny? Sure would like to talk to him."

Before Addy could ask anything else, CC opened the truck door and slid into the passenger seat. "Morning. Thanks for getting here early"

Addy didn't respond but pulled away and headed for the main road away from the farm. She reached over and turned the dial off. "Wanna tell me what's going on, or keep me in suspense?"

CC glanced sideways at her friend and wondered how much she could trust her. She hadn't known Addy that long, but after a moment's thought, she decided Addy was the only friend she had. "Take me to the hospital. There's only one, right?"

Addy almost veered off the road. "Oh my god! Are you sick or something? What's wrong?"

CC couldn't help but laugh. "I'm fine. I want to see my Uncle Bud. He's in the mental unit there or whatever they call it. I need to see him and see if he's okay, see if they're treating him right."

There was a long pause. Addy didn't say anything. CC thought she might turn around, but then she said, "That sweet man. Why's he in a nut ward?" Addy must have felt CC bristle, so she corrected and said, "Sorry. I mean a mental unit?"

CC let out a long sigh before continuing. "There were some problems on the farm next door. I don't want to get into it, but I feel responsible, and I just want to make sure he's okay. I feel like it's my fault." She was afraid she might start crying, so CC stopped talking.

Addy must have realized her sadness and just kept driving into town. It was easy to spot the hospital right off the main road into town. A couple of red brick buildings and a larger one were surrounded by large trees, and a big parking lot. A circular drive was in front of one of the largest buildings. CC saw an emergency sign on the right side and wondered if they had taken her uncle in that way last night.

"Where do you want to park, CC?"

CC looked around and told her to pull into the large lot. She grabbed her purse and started for the large building. There was a lady's room in the lobby and CC slipped in and started her transformation. Addy stood next to her in the mirror with her mouth wide open but didn't say anything. CC proceeded to put powder and lipstick on and reached for her flats. She flipped off her sneakers and slipped into the flats. Standing back, she surveyed herself in the mirror, asking Addy, do I look like I'm eighteen?'

Addy popped out laughing. "Is that what you're going for? It works. You look twenty-one to me. What are you doing?"

"I don't want to look like a kid. Need to get in. I think you have to be eighteen."

CC put her sneakers in her purse, took a final look in the mirror and started for the swinging restroom door. She motioned for Addy to sit in one of the chairs in the lobby and whispered she would be back soon. She was on a mission.

As she approached the information desk, she donned a friendly smile and headed for the lady in the back of the desk. "Good morning, I'm Cicely Scott. My uncle was admitted last night in somewhat of a crisis, and I want to see him for a few minutes."

The plump lady looked up and CC stared at the cat's eyes framed glasses staring back at her. CC was relieved to see her return a friendly smile. "What is his name, please?" as she removed her glasses.

CC cleared her throat before saying, "Bud Scott."

The plump lady smiled even wider. "Oh, I know Bud. Everyone knows him. He lives on the Scott farm." Giggles followed as she countered with, "Of course he's on the Scott farm. His name is Scott." She rebounded and put her cat's eye framed glasses back on.

"Let me see if I can find him," as she shuffled through some papers on her desk. "Oh. Oh. I see." She looked at her with a sympathetic expression before leaning over the desk to tell her, "He's in a special unit in the other building. You know, until they can help him. I mean, you know. Listen, just walk over there. You'll have to talk to the charge nurse, but I'm sure she'll give you a few minutes with him. Family, you know."

She turned and explained to Addy she was going to the building next door. "Why don't you wait here?"

"Oh no. Not on your life. We're in this together, but I'll hang back. You might need me."

CC couldn't figure out what in the world she might need her for, but she didn't have time to argue, so she took off for the exit door. The rushed along the sidewalk leading to the other building. When they got to the main door, CC turned to Addy. "Listen, please stay back. Sit in a chair nearby, but let me handle this. I don't want them thinking we're a couple of nosey kids."

She didn't wait for an answer, but hurried inside to look for the unit. It was easy. There was no one at the service desk so she followed a sign announcing "Mental Health Unit." She realized Addy wasn't following her and was relieved. She needed to do this on her own.

CC took a deep breath and entered the glass door. There was a nurse sitting at a counter in a white uniform who looked up as she entered. "Can I help you?"

CC dove in before she lost her nerve. "Yes, please. I'm Cicely Scott. My uncle is a patient here. Admitted two nights ago. Bud Scott. I would like to see him for a few minutes. I brought a couple of shirts with me," and she held up the paper bag. She remembered to get them from the clothes line before she left.

"Wait here, I'll check."

CC tried to swallow. Her throat was dry and she felt her hands getting clammy. She wasn't sure if this was a good idea, but it was too late now. She didn't have to wait long; the nurse returned right away.

"You can see him for fifteen minutes. He's in the day room, but you need to sign in first," as she turned a book around on the counter.

CC was sure her hands shook a little, but she managed to write her name.

The nurse looked at the signature and said, "Your address too, please."

CC had to think for a minute. It was always the farm and she couldn't remember the actual address, so wrote, Spring Road, Scott family farm.

"Are you Mrs. Bess Scott's granddaughter? I thought you were younger"

Before CC could answer, she asked, "When is your birthday?"

CC mumbled," Uh."

"It's usually an easy question, Miss. Are you at least seventeen?"

"Yes, Ma'am."

An obvious sly grin crossed the nurse's mouth. "Make sure you tell Bess hello for me. I see her every month at the board meeting."

The nurse stood and led her through the door and then into another locked door. CC started to say something about the lock, but remembered where she was. She walked in and was surprised at how bright the room was. It was sunny with a few plain white tables and chairs. There weren't many patients at all. She only saw three at first, and then she spotted Uncle Bud sitting by himself in a chair by the window.

She walked over to him and whispered, "Uncle Bud. It's me, CC."

He turned and she saw a blank look on his face. After a moment his expression changed to what she called his sweet look, and he said, "Sis."

He sat and didn't move staring at her with that sweet expression of his. She wanted to hug him and tell him how sorry she was. She knew he was only trying to help. She felt the welts on her arm throb from the memory of being grabbed by Mr. Gibbs, and she could hear the yelling and the smacking sounds as her uncle hit the old man.

CC wished she could go back and keep Uncle Bud safe, but it was too late. She pulled a chair over to the window and sat next to him. All she could think to say was, "How are you, Uncle Bud. You OK? Did you eat this morning?"

She jumped from a screeching sound behind her. As she turned to look, she saw another man rocking in a chair at a nearby table and moaning to himself. She looked around the room again and realized it was bare except for tables and chairs. There were no curtains on the windows. She was relieved there was a tree outside of Bud's window, and she hoped there were birds, but she didn't see any now. She leaned back and sat with him for a few minutes.

"Sis, Johnny. Tell him sorry. Sorry. Didn't mean to hit."

CC took a deep breath hoping to hold back tears, and was almost relieved when a nurse came in with a cart. She walked over and whispered in CC's ear, "We have to give medications now. You'll have to leave."

CC leaned in to Uncle Bud and told him softly, "It's all right. Johnny knows you didn't mean to hit anyone. You'll be home soon and you can tell him yourself."

He just looked at her with the same sweet expression and CC felt the nurse gently nudge her arm. She got up and walked out of the room while everything spun around her. The walls were so white she thought she might bump into them, but mercifully found the exit door and just kept walking briskly almost running and bumped into Addy.

"Hey, slow down. You all right?" CC nodded and held back the tears. Addy led her by the arm and together they marched to the truck.

The drive to the bible school was quiet. CC didn't notice Addy kept the radio off until they were almost there. "Hey, you could have turned on the music."

Addy glanced at her before saying, "Thought I would give you some time. How was your uncle?"

"He looked doped up but okay, I guess. I wish I'd asked Johnny to come with us, but I'm glad I went." CC shifted in her seat and turned the radio knob. Strains of "Blue Moon'" floated through the truck cab.

Changing the subject, she asked, "What are we gonna do at the bible school?"

"Just visit and I want to check to see if they still want to come to my house tomorrow for the picnic. You still going with us?"

"I guess." CC was glad to see the grove of trees since she wasn't in the mood for talking, but she wondered how Star would react to seeing her.

She didn't have to worry. When they entered the red door, the children bounced up and down. Star was at the back of the pack, but CC spotted her immediately.

She seemed prettier than before. Those big almond eyes stared back at her and slowly a smile spread across the little girl's mouth. CC walked over to Star. At first CC thought she was running from her, but Star was back in a jiffy and held up a pretty flower, a red one with a long stem.

"Is that for me?'

She shook her head up and down, and CC couldn't resist. She leaned over giving Star a big hug and realized she needed the embrace for herself. She missed Uncle Bud more than ever after seeing him in that place. As though Star could tell without looking, she squeezed a little tighter. When she opened her eyes, CC saw Addy smiling down at them and it all seemed perfect for just that moment.

CHAPTER 27

They spent less time at the bible school, but CC enjoyed the time with Star. They were back in the truck as Addy started talking about the children's party. Addy scratched her nose. "Yep, I wanted to tell you I better make it early. We have to pick up cola and chips unless Mom gets it."

They were both excited about taking the children to Addy's house. CC was excited about another July 4th party. It was going to be the week after the fourth, but at least the children could celebrate. They had talked about the importance of the holiday with the children.

She jumped out and waved to her friend. She wanted to talk to Johnny. She knew he must feel terrible about what was happening with his dad. What should she tell him about her visit to the hospital?

Johnny walked over to her. "You're back. Heard you saw Dad. How is he?"

CC raised her eyebrows. "How did you know I went?"

"Some nurse called Gran. How is he?"

"They're taking care of him and at least he's not locked up in jail."

"But is he doped up? I know they must've given him drugs to keep him calm while he's there. Did he look OK? Was he clean?"

CC felt bad for her cousin and for Uncle Bud. She didn't want to tell him everything, but she had to give him some of the news. "He's in pretty good shape, but you're right. They gave him a lot of medicine. I left after a few minutes since they told me he needed medication."

Johnny leaned back against the garden fence. Pushing back his hat, he rubbed his eyes. "I wanted to see him too, but Gramps said I should stay away today. Give everything a chance to calm down. I don't know, I still think..."

He struggled with what else to say, but added, "Maybe he's right."

"What about Gran? Is she going?"

Johnny said, "She wants to try to get him out. She's been on the phone."

"How's she gonna do that? Doesn't old man Gibbs want to keep him in custody?"

"I think Gramps has talked to Sheriff Jack and they seem to think there's a way to get him out."

"I hope so, too." CC threw her purse over her shoulder. She heard the back-door screech and Gran whistle for Champ. Before she could say anything, Gran called out to her. She walked over to the back porch and looked at her grandmother. "What's up, child? You feel all right or is it your visit with Bud that has you down?"

CC shook her head and marveled at Gran. "I should've known you knew about that already. That nurse called you? The admit nurse?"

"Doesn't matter. How'd you find him? Is he eating?"

"And I should've known you would want to know whether he is eating or not. He was staring out the window when I got there. I thought I might have trouble getting in to see him, but it was easy."

"Did your clothes and those shoes in your pocketbook help?" CC heard Johnny laughing behind her and when she looked down, she saw her flats sticking out of her purse.

CC glanced at Uncle Bud's garden. It already seemed overgrown. "Gran, he seemed to be in good shape and they were taking care of him." She got closer to Gran and spoke softly so Johnny couldn't hear. "He seemed sad, like depressed. I guess he hasn't been away from home much, huh?"

Gran touched the side of her face and pushed a loose strand of hair back. "I'm glad you saw him. Sure, it gave him hope, you know? But next time, tell me. Trust me."

"I think I'm gonna go upstairs for a while. I'm tired." She wanted to be by herself and wished she had brought her record player and records from home.

"Wait. Let me look at your arm." Gran turned her wrist over so she could see the bruise. "Looks like it's changing color. Good sign. Does it hurt?"

"Nah. Forgot it was there. I'm going up for a while. I'll come down later to help you.

Gran's face shadowed with that look of concern, but CC turned and ran up the stairs. She wasn't in the mood to answer any more questions and just wanted to be alone. Sometimes as nice as Gran was, it was irritating to answer so many questions.

Opening the door to her room, or Mama's room, she took in the light beaming from the afternoon sun. She hadn't noticed how bright it was here. The bed was made up, of course thanks to Gran, and her things were picked up from the floor.

Note to self – pick up my stuff so no one looks through my things. She didn't think there was anything too secretive, but you never know. CC congratulated herself on not keeping a diary.

She plopped down on the side of the bed and for the first time in a while, thought about Marcus. Sometimes she felt guilty because she didn't think of him too much. He fell for her when they were in science class together, or at least she thought so. She liked him as a friend, but that was all. When she found out he lived across Fontainebleau in the colored neighborhood, she walked over and they listened to Motown records. He was fun and knew music. She wondered if he was looking forward to school this year. Did he think about her?

That night just happened, and CC knew it meant more to him. They talked once about getting married but it was against the law. And the odds of being accepted with a colored baby. She just couldn't keep the baby. She was too young and didn't know how she could handle a baby. Going to the maternity home seemed like the only option.

"I have to think about the picnic tomorrow and take my mind off this other stuff." She hurried downstairs and spotted Gran who was just coming in from the porch.

"So, what do you think? I'd like to help her take the kids."

CC filled her in and Gran arched the famous eyebrow. "Yes, but we'll both help. I'll meet you there with some cookies and treats for after."

Bounding back up the stairs, she chuckled to herself. Gran could always get her point across with that eyebrow, but CC remembered her commitment to doing school work. She kicked her shoes off and checked the novel's dog-eared spot where she left off which was only a couple of pages.

She nestled into her propped-up pillows and told herself to read and not fall asleep.

The next day as she waited for Addy, CC thought about Scout, the young girl telling the story in her book. She thought that Boo was like Uncle Bud and that caught her attention. She had to admit, it was getting interesting.

On the way to pick up the children at the vacation bible school, she decided to tell Addy about it.

"What's the name of the book?"

"It's called *To Kill A Mockingbird.* Isn't that weird? But the name of a person in it is called Boo. Almost like Uncle Bud. Doesn't say much."

"That is weird."

CC didn't know what else to say about it and she had only read the first few chapters. "I'll tell you more later if you want."

"Yeah. Miss Jessica is nice to help you catch up, don't you think?"

CC scrunched in her seat. She hasn't thought much about her since the day at the high school, but Miss Jessica had been nice to her. "Yep. She was nice. I need to start catching up on my work. I would like to go on to eleventh next year."

Addy snorted. "Yep. School's fun."

CC just looked at her and thought she liked school because she was popular. CC was a loner and didn't get much attention which was fine with her. They entered the drive at the church and CC wondered if Star was waiting for her. She wanted to help her have a good time, but she felt a little nervous about the picnic. Since the little girl was a loner, she'd have to find a way to bring Star out.

Addy rushed ahead of CC. "Come on. We want to get to my house as soon as we can to make a day of it."

The kids were as rambunctious as ever, but they looked cute in their summer clothes. CC was glad she remembered to bring her bathing suit in case Star wanted to get in the swimming pool. As usual it was a hot day so that should motivate the kids to jump in.

The girls didn't have any trouble loading everyone in the truck. Miss Eugenia helped and double checked to make sure she gave Addy their phone numbers in case they needed their parents. "And remember you can call me if you need any help." She yelled out to the kids, "Everybody, gonna behave? Yes?"

The handful of children in the back of the truck screamed out they would. CC felt a slight tug on her shorts and looked down to see Star gazing up at her. Her sweet expression reminded CC of Uncle Bud and her heart melted. She couldn't help reaching down and giving the small child a hug. When she stood up, Addy and Miss Eugenia were both giving her nods of approval.

CC held the door open and Star jumped in the cab between the two teenagers. Addy drove away from the church after opening the sliding window above the driver's seat. "Hey summer soldiers. Who wants to sing?"

A loud 'yay' rang out from the back and CC heard Star giggling. Addy started in with a chorus of "Row, row, row your boat," and the children picked up the tune and started singing. When they stumbled on the refrain, the laughter grew louder.

The truck rumbled along on the country road. CC noticed Addy glancing in the rearview mirror and she looked worried.

CC looked back. "What's up, Addy?"

"I think we have company. I'm not sure, but they are right on our tail."

"Who's on our tail?" and she noticed the laughter died down and it was suddenly very quiet in the back of the truck. Then she heard it – the loud honking from behind them and yelling.

It didn't take long for CC to recognize those voices. The annoying voices were the very same ones she heard the first day she arrived on the farm. The same idiots who gave Uncle Bud such a hard time. The same day she had to drag Uncle Bud away from the fence and tell them to shut up.

"They are idiots, Addy. Just keep driving. They'll give up and go away."

Addy didn't look too reassured, but she kept her eyes on the road and sped up a little bit. "I don't want to drive too fast cause we have these kids in the back of the truck, CC."

"Yes, you're right, but I think they'll get tired of following us."

The honking got louder and CC wondered how they could get them to stop. She didn't get a chance to figure it out because they pulled up on the driver's side of Addy's truck and honked and yelled, "Pull over, we just wanna have a word with you! Come on, now. We gotta talk to you."

Addy yelled back. "Leave us alone. We're just going to my house for a picnic. Go away."

"Aww. Come on now. We wanna go to a picnic too. Take us instead of them colored kids. Come on. Pull over." When the hickey boy sitting by the passenger window yelled, the driver veered towards Addy's truck.

Star let out a little squeal and CC cursed under her breath. "Addy, pull over, I'll take care of these idiots."

"No, CC. I can't do that with these kids in here. We have to take care of them."

When CC looked down, Star blinked with her huge brown eyes and a tear formed in the corner. She whispered to her. "I'm taking care of you. Don't worry."

The truck veered toward them again and this time the same boy yelled, "Hey, what are you doing with those little coloreds anyway? Don't you wanna take us instead?" When he said that, the other boys snorted and yelled, "Yeah, take us. We wanna go to a picnic."

There was another bang and CC managed to look behind her to see an old beat up truck ramming into the attacking boys' vehicle. A metal thud sounded, and the boys were jolted forward in their seats. It only took a second for them to start yelling, "Shit! Who rammed us?"

CC strained to see who was in the other truck, but before she could make it out, Addy shouted, "I can't believe it. I'm looking in the rearview mirror, but I just can't believe my eyes."

"Believe what? Tell me."

Addy's mouth was wide open as she exclaimed, "It's that boy. That drop-out. The one you said you knew. He works over at Gibbs' place. What's his name?"

CC was as shocked as Addy. "You mean Eric? That's Eric in the other truck?"

There was another loud bang as the old pickup in the rear rammed into the boys' truck. Addy watched the event unfold in her rearview mirror while CC smiled at Star to reassure her. There was loud yelling from both trucks and she strained to hear what they were saying.

Addy spotted a turnaround ahead and pulled over. CC hollered, "Stay here. I'm gonna see what's going on." She jumped out and walked around to the back of Addy's truck. The other vehicles were in the middle of the road. The guys who had been harassing them jumped out and ran around to look at the damage to their truck.

"You don't care, do you, man, about your old truck. Look what you did to mine."

Eric sauntered over and CC could see the grin on his face. He didn't seem concerned at all. "You idiots. What do you think you're doing? Running down these gals? Are you nuts?"

The driver of the first truck took his hat off and slapped it against his leg. "Just having a little fun. What's it to you, Eric?" The passengers bobbed their heads up and down in agreement and she heard one of them say, "Just chasing a truck full of coloreds. What're they doing with them anyway?"

Eric's grin turned to an icy stare and CC could swear those boys cringed and one of them almost fell. She turned to check on the kids in the back of their truck and other than being totally wide eyed, they seemed fine. She smiled at them anyway and leaned against the fender.

Eric moved closer to the group and drew himself up to his full height. He seemed to tower over them. The look of contempt on his face melted any thoughts they had of trying to scare Addy and CC and the children. They backed away and she heard one of them mutter, "Come on. Let's get out of here."

CC realized her heart was beating faster and her breathing accelerated. She wasn't sure if it was from fear of those boys or the sight of Eric, but whichever it was, she was sure glad he came along. Who would have guessed Eric would save them?

CHAPTER 28

CC heard the hayseeds' truck peel off in a final act of defiance. Eric's menacing stare turned into his familiar grin as he took off his hat, and made a little bow and asked, "You all right, Ma'am?"

She couldn't help but smile at that gentlemanly gesture, but coming up the rear, Addy yelped. "All right! What's this about? They could have hurt these kids in the back of the truck and driven us off the road. Not to mention the damage to my truck if they had rammed us!"

CC and Eric continued to lock stares at each other. CC couldn't take her eyes off him. She muttered," I guess you saved us from disaster." Then turning to Addy, "He saved us. We could at least thank him."

Eric got half-hearted thanks from Addy before she turned to the children to make sure they were OK. CC was touched by her friend's leaning over the truck's guard and murmuring to the kids. She reached out and patted a smaller boy on the shoulder and CC could see he was on the verge of tears. Then she remembered Star.

She ran around the passenger side of the truck where she had left the door open. Star was just sitting where she left her, and her beautiful eyes were as wide as ever. "You all right, Star? I needed to talk to the boy who rescued us."

In return CC got a wide smile which only accentuated Star's almond skin and dark eyes. Once again, she had the strong impulse to lift her up and hug her, but she wanted to talk to Eric.

He was already in his truck. He leaned out the window and said, "I'm going to follow y'all to make sure you get there in one piece. Where are you going anyway?"

CC rested her arms on his hood and smiled at him. "Going to Addy's house. The pool. We're taking the kids there for a picnic."

She waited for him to comment. Instead, he shrugged and said, "Go on. I'll follow."

CC stood and watched him for a minute before saying, "Make sure you park by the pool. We'd like to thank you again. Give you some lunch."

Eric didn't return her look, just turned the ignition and seemed to be fiddling with the radio. It occurred to CC that he didn't answer her, but she walked back to Addy's truck and hopped in next to Star.

"Everything all right?" Addy asked as she started the motor. CC didn't answer. She looked down at Star sitting next to her and smiled at Addy.

The rest of the drive to Addy's house was smooth and no one chased them. CC was glad to see Eric pull up behind them in the large semicircular driveway. "Addy, I'm gonna talk to Eric. I'll meet up with you guys by the pool." She didn't wait for an answer and walked briskly over to Eric's truck.

It was already beat up, but now the front fenders looked even worse. He hopped out of the driver's side and CC noticed a loud creaking as he opened his door. She thought he slammed it hard and when she looked at him, she saw a mean scowl that wasn't there earlier. Before she could say anything, he charged towards her. "What do you think you're doing? Don't you know it's dangerous to be driving around these country roads with colored kids? It's a good thing I spotted you all at the crossing by the church."

CC was speechless. She didn't expect him to fuss at her for driving the kids. He protected them from those hoodlums. "What are you talking about? You saved us. Why shouldn't we drive them here? What's the matter with you?"

"Look, CC. It's common sense. We don't mix it up around here. Those kids need to stay at the church where they're safe. And you and Addy need to stay where you won't get in any trouble."

CC stepped back so she could fire back at him. "Every time you do something good, you mess it up with this kind of foolishness. I'll drive whoever I want to, wherever I want to. These kids didn't do anything."

"No, they didn't. They are innocent. But driving them in the back of Addy's truck is crazy."

CC stared at him. Why was he so upset with her? He started to turn, but she pulled his arm. "Eric, if you think it's so wrong for us to throw the kids in the back of the truck, why did you rescue us? Why did you help and chase those guys off?"

Eric took his dirty hat off and slammed it against his leg. Before she could ask anything else, he said through clenched teeth. "Listen, CC, when I saw y'all, I knew there would be trouble. I followed you, and there it was. Those guys are friends of mine, but I couldn't let them run you off the road or yell at those little kids. They didn't do nothing wrong."

"Eric, that's what I mean. How can you protect us, them, if you feel we shouldn't have them with us?"

She could tell he was getting frustrated. She didn't flinch when he grabbed her arm and pulled her closer. "CC, all my life people have been putting me down. Telling me I'm no good cause I don't have a father and my mom, well, my mom has problems. Then I quit school and you know, folks look down on me for that. They don't understand, I needed to take care of myself."

CC wanted to hold him and tell him he was somebody, but she needed to know more. "So, you chased those idiots off because you didn't want the kids to get hurt. Right? Cause they are underdogs too?"

Before he could answer, CC heard a familiar voice from around the side of the house. "CC, are you over here?"

Before she could answer, Gran turned the corner. "There you are. I wanted to check on you. Addy said there was trouble on the road. What happened?"

CC didn't take her eyes off Eric. She had trouble understanding him since she arrived this summer. When she first got to the farm, he acted like he just wanted to make out with her, and she thought he was angry with her for turning him down. Then that day at Gibbs, he had been concerned about her arm.

"Gran, it's all right. Some guys chased us and yelled at the kids from bible school, but Eric took care of them." She smiled at him. "He chased them off and no one was hurt. What are you doing here?" She watched Eric and he was shuffling his feet back and forth like he was uncomfortable.

"Like I told you yesterday, I brought cookies. But, CC, we need to tell your grandfather about this. We can't just let it go."

Eric started to say something but stopped. CC took his hand. "Gran uh, this is Eric."

"Of course, Eric." And Gran extended her hand. "Clay's son, right?"

"Yes ma'am. CC, I think I better go now."

CC pleaded with her eyes. "Oh stay. Just have some food before you go."

Eric put his hat back on and did a slight tip at Gran with it. "Nice meeting you again, but I need to get to work." CC watched him saunter off towards his truck.

She heard Gran exclaim surprise. "If that's the result of this afternoon, that must have been quite an altercation."

"What do you mean?"

"His truck, CC. Look at it. It took quite a bit of damage."

"Yes. I guess so although it already had some damage." She turned to Gran before asking, "Are you going to call Sheriff Jack?"

Gran looked at her with a shocked expression. "You bet I am. We can't be careful enough. Come on. I'll use the phone in the house."

When CC rounded the corner, she was glad to see Addy laughing with the kids by the pool. It looked like they were having a great time. CC walked over and Star ran to meet her. "Hey, little one. Are you having a good time?"

"Sure am, CC. Addy told us a story about when she was little and fell in the pool. Her dog jumped in to save her."

CC took Star's hand and they strolled to the picnic table and sat on one of the benches. CC looked closely at Star and couldn't help but wonder if her baby was as pretty as the little girl in front of her. Star had such deep-set eyes and they were piercing when she looked at CC. For a little kid, she could convey such meaning in her face, especially those dark eyes.

They were distracted by loud yelling where Addy instigated a game of dodgeball. After the events driving over, CC was glad to see the children having such a good time. "Leave it to Addy to make things fun. Come on, Star. Let's join them, okay?"

CC watched Star run to the group and chuckled. The little girl had long, slender legs and reminded her of Lady years ago as a colt. Even though she was younger than the other kids, she was able to escape the ball's hits.

CC felt Gran's arm around her waist and turned to ask her about Uncle Bud.

"Your gramps said he's doing all right and brought him some food from home." As she talked to CC, she brushed a wisp of hair from her forehead. "You doing all right yourself after the run-in today?"

All CC could do was nod. She didn't want to tell Gran about her confrontation with Eric. She didn't understand his attitude about driving the children in the truck and sure wasn't going to discuss it with her. "Did you call the Sheriff?"

The look of concern on Gran's face from earlier returned as CC watched her. "Yes, I did, CC. You have to understand. There's been so much going on with attacks against Negroes. Not so much here, but I'm afraid what happened today could be a warning shot."

"Do you think so? I mean those idiots are so ignorant. They're helpless. Ran off with a shout from Eric."

Gran crossed her hands over her hips and stood akimbo. CC could tell it was a warning stance. "My precious granddaughter, things like this escalate when no one is around to protect others, especially Negro children. Who would have thought a man like Medgar Evers could be shot in cold blood outside a church or that police would hose down hundreds of Negro children to silence them? We must keep our guard up and answering these threats with the sheriff is the best way to answer them. You must be strong in this, Cicely."

CC smiled when Gran returned to calling her by her full name. Gran always resorted to Cicely when she wanted to make a point. As they stood in the backyard, CC heard the sheriff's siren coming up the road. It didn't take long for him to reach the driveway and thankfully turned it off. CC saw the children gathering around Addy, and they looked apprehensive.

Gran touched her by the arm. "After I speak to the sheriff, I'll go over and stay with the children, so Addy can come over here and give a statement. "There's Addy's father walking from the house. I'm sure he wants to stay with both of you. Don't worry. I spoke to him when I went in the house."

CC looked at him and wondered if he was going to support them or take the same attitude as Eric. She saw him put his arm around Addy's shoulder as they walked together. CC thought that was a good sign. She didn't know her parents at all and hoped they didn't blame her.

Her concern disappeared as she heard the sheriff getting out of his car. Mr. Nelson approached CC and put his hand on her shoulder.

"I hear you had a rough morning. Glad you knew the young man who helped out."

CC was relieved. It also crossed her mind that it must be wonderful to have a father who takes up for you. Actually, any parent who does but she didn't have time to think about that as she heard Sheriff Jack calling out to them.

"Ted, glad you're here. You know what went on today?'

He walked to the sheriff and they shook hands. "Thanks for getting here so quick, Sheriff. Yep. I know all about it and sorry to hear we're having that kind of trouble around here. I thought we have been getting along."

The sheriff shifted a little and CC waited to hear what he was going to say.

"Yep. Guess it's been kind of quiet compared to everything you read in the paper or see on the television. Still, you can't be too careful."

Mr. Nelson straightened up and cleared his throat. "Sheriff, seems to me those hooligans need to be careful. My daughter and her friend were just driving kids to a picnic. They're volunteering at the church this summer. They're not the ones doing anything wrong."

The sheriff stared at CC as he spoke. "I'm glad to see you're doing something constructive with your time, young lady."

Mr. Nelson spoke up again. "Do I need to go get Mrs. Scott, her grandmother, to talk to you, Sheriff? I believe she's the one who called you."

CC noticed at the sound of her Gran's name, the sheriff flushed a little and was quick to brush the idea aside. "Nope. Nope. That's fine. Tell me, Addy or you, young lady, do you know these fellas' names? The ones who tried to stop your truck?"

Addy spoke up. "I don't. Do you, CC?"

CC glanced at Gran. "I think they work for Mr. Gibbs. Farmhands, maybe."

The two men talked some more and the sheriff promised he would find the boys. Nothing was said about arresting them, but CC hoped Eric wouldn't get into any trouble. She thought he might not want to give their names up. He said they were his friends.

What would he do? Would he want to stay out of it?

CHAPTER 29

When she got home from the picnic yesterday, she went up to her room after telling Gran she was going to read her book. She felt confused about Eric. He was so strong when he chased the hayseeds off and then he criticized her for hauling the colored kids in the truck. They were just taking them to a picnic. What could be wrong with that?

Eric. Just saying his name made her heart quiver a little. He looked so handsome yesterday standing next to Gran at the picnic and tipping his hat. He seemed like two different boys. One was the cruel person leaning over the fence making fun of her uncle. Then he was the concerned person telling her to treat her leg after she and Johnny went over to Mr. Gibb's shed. She gave up on reading, and tossed and turned trying to get some sleep.

"CC, can you come down, please?" Gran yelled from downstairs.

She plodded down the steps but livened up a little as she rounded the door and noticed Gran had on what she called her Sunday best dress. Her hair was done up and as CC approached her, she realized she had a touch of makeup on with a light lipstick. She wasn't aware of Gran's looks before, but she must have been pretty when she was younger.

Gran poured a mug of steaming coffee. Without asking, she added a large splash of milk. "I thought I could hear you tossing around during the night."

CC took the cup and sat in the nearest kitchen chair. Blowing at the steam, she avoided Gran's piercing stare. She knew she was waiting for a response to her comment and was grateful Champ trotted over to her, nudging for a pet on his head. "Hey, boy. How are you today? Huh?"

When she looked up, Gran grinned, "Trying to avoid my question? No need. I know you had a lot on your mind last night, but I need to talk to you."

"Sure, Gran." CC let her head drop back. Her neck was sore from sleeplessness and she unconsciously rubbed it. She dropped her hand without looking down and scratched Champ, who settled under the table near her feet.

"Want me to fix you something while we talk?"

CC shook her head and Gran sat across from her. "CC, I'm glad we reported the boys for trying to drive you off the road. And I'm also glad Eric was around to chase them off, but I need you to be aware of the danger here."

Looking at Gran's face, CC realized she was totally serious. They returned the kids to vacation bible school and the teacher thanked them. She was grateful to Mr. Nelson for the escort.

CC stopped when she saw Gran's frown as a stern look crossed her brow. She seemed lost in thought, but spoke up again. "CC, you don't seem aware of what's going on. An incident like yesterday with those boys, and they are boys, may be a forewarning of what may be coming."

CC decided to keep her mouth shut while Gran explained what she meant. "This was a major incident. I hate calling it an incident. They may be hooligans but they almost ran you off the road. That's dangerous. Those children could have been thrown out of the truck and seriously injured, or worse. You could have been hurt too."

"But, Gran, Eric came along..." She didn't get to finish and trailed off because she knew she sounded feeble.

"Yes, he did. But what if he had not. Could you and Addy have saved those children? You all would have been lying in the ditch away from the farm and the town. I'm talking about a disaster. Not an incident, not some prank. This is dangerous, and those boys need to get arrested and charged. We need to make an example here that this behavior will not be tolerated."

Gran stiffened. "I thought you were supposed to be listening or watching the news for Miss Jessica. Don't you have any idea what's happening in the South? Here, I saved these news clippings."

She passed a folder across the table. CC looked at it like it was a snake and might bite her. She didn't want to look at it. Since the incident at the

Gibbs farm, she hoped everything would calm down and she could enjoy time with Addy and Johnny, Eric too.

"Go ahead sweetheart, take a look."

The top article showed a June twenty-first picture of a car surrounded by policemen. The headline read "Three Civil Rights Activists Disappear." She read the first paragraph describing how the Freedom Riders had not been heard from in days.

After reading the first couple of paragraphs, she laid it aside and looked at the second clipping. Dr. Martin Luther King, Jr. and children were arrested in St. Augustine for demonstrating outside a motel last week.

CC read the articles and passed the folder back to Gran. "This is all terrible. But do you think this could happen here? I mean it seems so quiet here and Sheriff Jack doesn't seem anything like that sheriff in Florida."

Gran sighed and twirled her coffee mug around. CC was shocked to see her usual bright eyes were now droopy and sad-looking even with a little make-up.

"Of course those boys who hit us need to be arrested. They tried to run us off the road. I want to see them punished. I just wanted to warn Eric that I was turning them in."

Gran grunted and shifted in her chair. "What if he is upset? What if he wants you to let it go and not identify those boys? What will you do then?"

CC stared at her. She couldn't believe Eric could forget the whole thing. He saw it. He couldn't fight with her about this, too. "I'll talk to him if that's how he feels. I think he'll turn them in. Anyway, he works for Mr. Gibbs. The sheriff can talk to him over there."

Gran stood and picked up the mugs. "Just be careful. Get Johnny to follow you and Addy to the bible school. Don't take any chances going out there alone."

CC thought to herself about Gran's comment. They weren't alone, but that didn't stop those guys from trying to run them off the road. "Okay, Gran, you're right. We'll get Johnny to take us or follow Addy's truck. She ought to like that anyway."

Gran grinned. "Does Addy favor Johnny?"

CC popped out laughing. "Sorry. Not laughing at you. Just don't know what favor somebody means. That's a new one."

"Just means kind of like him. But that's all right. You don't have to answer. By the way, what are you going to do the rest of the day?"

CC got up and walked to the window. "Before it gets too horrible hot out there, I thought I'd take the wagon out and pick some of those peaches. Help Uncle Bud 'til he gets back."

She heard Gran walking towards her and figured she was in for a hug, which is exactly what she did, wrapping her arms around CC. "Thanks for thinking of that. Clay has the starter rod for the tractor."

Without saying anything else, Gran picked up her purse and dug around for her keys. Walking out the door, she tossed a comment, "I'm going into town to meet with a couple of school board members. Meeting next week."

CC stayed at the window watching Gran drive the old Ford away. It was so quiet in the kitchen except for the whirring of the fan. She put her chin on her hands and found herself wondering what Marcus was doing back in New Orleans. He was kind of a loner, but he loved to read and he took music classes in the summer. She never thought about him getting hurt like those kids in Birmingham. Sometimes she didn't even remember he was colored until someone else brought it up. She buried her forehead for a minute and then said out loud, "Better get to those peaches."

The chickens scattered as CC strode out the back door. The tractor and trailer were already near Uncle Bud's garden. She looked for the starter rod, hoping she could go off by herself. Her plan was altered by the fact that the rod was not on the dash where Clay kept it.

Crunching on the gravel alerted CC to footsteps behind her.

"Morning. You lookin' for this?" Eric twirled the tractor rod and stood near her with that same mocking grin. "Did I scare you? You jumped just now."

CC shifted her weight and stood up straight. "Oh, Did I? You need to call out before sneaking up on a person."

"I didn't sneak up. I was standing right there by the barn. You didn't look around." There was that mocking grin again. "You want me to help you start the tractor? Drive you somewhere?"

"I can drive it. Give me that rod."

He hesitated a minute and CC thought he wanted her to walk to him to get it, but he took a couple of steps and held out the rod. "There you go, Miss New Orleens."

"Oh, for God's sake it is not..." Before she could chide him about his pronunciation, he broke into a big smile and she realized he was teasing her.

She took the rod and climbed into the seat. Sitting there, she tried to remember exactly how Clay started the tractor and where the rod went. Knowing Eric was watching her, she pretended to look like she knew what she was doing by fumbling with the controls. She sat back. "I don't remember how to start this."

"And? You would like me to?"

She turned to face the boy who rescued her on the road and was now looking at helping her in this situation. It was just too much. "How do you always manage to show up when I'm in... I mean when I need a little help?"

Eric didn't answer her, but strode around to the driver's side where CC sat. He leaned in and she moved over. "That's what I do. Look for ways to help you. It's my life's work now." She couldn't hold back. CC broke into the first real laugh she shared with him. "That's what I've been waiting for. You are pretty when you smile."

CC tried to stop the redness that she knew was spreading over her face. Since she couldn't, she slid over some more. "I'm going out to the orchard to help pick peaches. Someone needs to keep it up until Uncle Bud gets home."

"So, do you want me to drive you out there?"

CC nodded and she felt Eric sliding in the driver's seat. Her heart was fluttering again but not from fear this time. They were side by side, the closest they had been since the party. There was that same fresh hay smell again and it was all CC could think about until she realized he was asking her a question.

"You want to just put those peaches in the back of the trailer or you have baskets?"

She heard herself mumble to just use the trailer and when she turned and looked at him, he was smiling at her. It was not that mocking look and his eyes didn't look steely. They were dark, but had a softness she didn't see often.

The tractor rattled and creaked, so they didn't talk on the way to the orchard, but it wasn't uncomfortable. CC leaned back and looked around enjoying the slight breeze on her face and a quick glance at Eric's handsome profile.

When he pulled up at the first line of trees, CC jumped down and walked to the first tree covered in hanging fruit. She was always intoxicated by the sweet smell of the peaches, but also loved the sweet smell of hay behind her. Uncle Bud had left the ladder so she picked it up. She wanted to tell Eric she would get started but when she turned, she bumped into him. He grabbed her shoulders to keep her from falling and held her within inches of his face.

"You see, I'm rescuing you again. How many times is that?" His breath was on her face as he spoke in a husky kind of tone.

Pulling away gently, all she could think to say was, "I guess I'll get the ladder and start picking."

As though he didn't hear her, Eric sauntered over and picked up the ladder and braced it against the nearest tree. "Here, you climb up and throw the peaches to the ground and we'll pick 'em up after."

CC didn't like anyone telling her what to do, but Eric was different. She liked him taking control and found herself scurrying up the ladder. She picked peaches on the farm before, but this was different. It didn't take long to pick the fruit from the tops and they moved along until they finished the front tree line. CC threw the ground fruit in the trailer and scampered down the ladder.

Eric pulled out a knife from his front pocket. "Some of these are ripe. You want to snack?" Without waiting for an answer, he picked up a couple and plopped down by the fence. CC ambled over and sat near him. He concentrated on peeling slowly and then handed her a big slice.

She took a bite of the peach before asking, "You ever get tired of farm work?"

Looking at her sideways, he grinned and said, "What else could I do? I'm a dropout, remember?"

She grimaced at his remark knowing it hurt him to say it and hurt her to hear it. "Ever think about going back? To school, I mean."

"That's not going to happen. I support my mom. I send half the money I make here to her. Clay helps, but he don't make much either." He kicked at the grass. "Anyway, going back after all I been through, they'd give me a hard time."

CC saw the leer again before he added, "I'm learning a lot from the school of hard knocks. Think I'll stick with that."

CC finished her slice and Eric leaned over and got right in her face. "Don't move," and he pulled his bandana from his pocket and wiped her chin. "That juice is all down your face."

She could feel his warm breath as his lips brushed her cheek. She didn't have time to think as he cupped her face in both his hands and kissed her lips ever so lightly. If she were standing, she knew she might faint. Her heart raced and a tingly feeling washed over her body.

Eric pulled back a little and CC stared into his eyes. There was no mistaking the look of desire she saw, and she wondered if her eyes told the same story. Eric stood and held out his hand. When she took it, she felt her heart flutter some more and wondered if she could stand.

She didn't have to worry about that as he gently lifted her. They stood face to face and he kissed her again. The kiss lingered, but he didn't press into her like he did at the barn. Putting his arm around her shoulders, he led her back to the tractor.

CHAPTER 30

CC leaned into Eric as he kept his arm around her shoulder, and whenever she turned to go, he held her tighter. She felt the same way and didn't want to let him go either. He confided that he wished he hadn't quit school, but he didn't have any choice. He came to Ruston to work with Clay and make money to send home. He especially didn't like working for Mr. Gibbs.

"Why not?"

Eric brooded for a while before confessing, "Don't trust him."

He got quiet after that, so CC didn't prod him about Mr. Gibbs, and she didn't want to betray his confidence by telling Johnny about what he said. By the time they finished talking, it was late afternoon and dark clouds were gathering. CC didn't want to go inside, but knew Gran would be wondering where she was, so they loaded the fruit into a couple of bushel baskets to leave on the porch.

When she turned to go, Eric leaned towards her and whispered in her ear. "I'm sure glad you needed my help with starting the tractor."

CC turned her face towards him and whispered, "Me too." He brushed a quick kiss against her cheek, and CC's heart pumped so loud she wondered if he heard it. "I better get inside. See you later."

CC rushed through supper and as soon as the dishes were done, scurried up to her room. She collapsed on the bed and rolled around on the covers. Covering her eyes, she let out a wicked giggle. She wanted to scream but hugged her pillow and squealed into the feathery rectangle. "What a day! What a stupendous, fascinating, absolutely incredible day!"

CC had never felt like this before. Feelings bubbled inside her and made her feel like she could hold on to Eric and kiss him forever. It had been so different with Marcus. Not mechanical exactly, but more like good friends.

Marcus. She wondered if he thought about the baby. CC had never learned to pray like normal church-going people, but whenever she thought about her baby, she thought *Please let her be all right. Let her be safe.* Sometimes it felt like years ago since she gave her up instead of a few months. Like it was a dream and when she woke up, she wasn't pregnant anymore.

Could Eric ever understand about the baby? Having a baby and giving it up for adoption was hard to understand. Would he ever be capable of accepting that? He hadn't wanted her to drive the colored kids in the truck. How would he ever understand her being a birthmother to a half Negro baby.? That's what they called her at the home. A birthmother.

Her thoughts were interrupted by a knock on her door and Johnny called out, "CC, you up? I need to talk to you."

She sat up and threw her hair back before telling him to come on in. He came straight to the point. "Was that Eric Ralston I saw you with today? He got the rod for the tractor from the peg and took off with you. What were y'all up to?"

"He just helped me pick peaches. That's all. Why do you want to know?"

Johnny folded his arms across his chest "You know, he works for Gibbs. I was thinking he could tell us about when they spray and where. The sheriff is coming here tomorrow to look that area over. I wanted to be able to give him more information about the pesticide spraying."

CC stared at her cousin and then asked, "Is the sheriff coming for any other reason. You know there is the business of being run off the road by the boys in the truck."

"Yep. I heard about how Ralston chased those boys off. I know Sheriff Jack picked them up. He called Gran and told her. But Ralston works for Gibbs and I don't trust him. He's been in a lot of trouble. Did Ralston say anything at all about working for the old man?"

"He just said he had to work. He's sending money to his mother. And Johnny, his name is Eric." Frustrated with her cousin, she changed the subject again. "Johnny, what about Uncle Bud? Have you heard anything about his coming home?"

"That's another reason the sheriff is coming. He's going to tell us when we can pick him up." Johnny turned to leave.

CC yelled after him, "It'll be good to get Uncle Bud home." CC fell back into her pillow again. Her head swirled around with the thoughts of Eric, and she didn't want to have to talk about pesticides.

She walked over to the dresser. Looking in the mirror, she wondered if she looked any different because she felt like it. It seemed like a long time since the day she arrived at the farm, but she could tell the sun made her face glow and she was filling out her jeans. They weren't hanging on her in two big bags like they did when she saw herself that first day she arrived on the farm.

Feeling restless, she jumped back in bed and picked up her book. She didn't know when she fell asleep but it wasn't from reading her book. The last thing she remembered was throwing the book to the side, stretching out, and whispering Eric's name a couple of times.

CC opened her eyes to sunlight streaming through her window and the sound of Gramps and Gran in the kitchen. She padded to the door and opened it a crack. "I'm worried more about Bud. We need to get him home later today."

CC walked in the kitchen as Gramps hurried out to the porch. He met Sheriff Jack who lumbered in with Champ at his heels. The sheriff got right to the point after removing his hat. "Morning, Bess. Wanted to let you know we have those boys in custody and the judge will be deciding what to do with them."

"Don't you think they should get some jail time? How old are they?"

"They're different ages. One of them is seventeen and he'll be treated like an adult."

Gramps interrupted, asking her to wait and see what the judge decides. "And what about Bud, Sheriff?"

"He can come home this afternoon. I thought Bess might want to go pick him up while we go out to the field."

Gran didn't waste any time. She untied her apron hurriedly and picked up her pocketbook. Without looking back, she rushed out the screen door and CC knew she wouldn't come home without Uncle Bud.

Johnny almost collided with her. "Where's Gran going?" But when he saw the sheriff, he answered his own question. "Will she bring Dad home today?" Both men nodded and CC saw a look of relief break out on her cousin's face.

Sheriff Jack put his hat back on. "I need you to be aware, Johnny and Ethan, you will have to keep a close eye on Bud. He can come home, but you know he's been in a couple of fights before."

"But some of that happened because he's been teased and ridiculed so much," interrupted Johnny.

"Yes, true, but he still can't be running around handling things with his fists. You agree, Ethan."

Gramps answered before Johnny could defend his dad again, "Son, he's a big man. He's grown, and now that you're here I think you can spend time with him and help him out."

"Let's head on out for the front field. That's where you say you saw some damaged trees, young man?" the sheriff asked. CC thought he was changing the subject.

"Yes, Sir. Sure did."

While the group made their way out to the orchard, CC held back in case Eric showed up. Lady neighed as usual as CC approached, "I'll take you, gal." She looked around but there was no sign of Eric or Clay so she threw the saddle on and adjusted her bridle.

She started off in a trot this time. As she approached the tree line, she could hear voices in the distance. CC assumed the group was already by the state fences, so she dismounted and laid the bridle straps over a low branch. She remembered Eric's kiss on the ladder. The peach nectar smelled even more romantic after yesterday.

As she recalled the moment, she could feel her face flushing. She had never been kissed that soft and sweet. His lips pressed over hers made her want to stay with him all evening.

"Damn!! I better get a grip before I join this group by the fence," she said to herself so she moved closer so she could hear them.

She heard the sheriff say, "Go ahead, Johnny, tell us what's going on out here."

"I want you all to look at these trees in the back of the orchard, "Johnny said. "The leaves are all dying and we've found a few dead birds on either side of the fence."

"Listen," the sheriff said. "You're not supposed to go over his fence now. That would be trespassing."

"Sheriff, after we saw the tree damage, we spotted a couple of dead birds lying around. Dad spotted one by this tree and then I saw two of them by the fence." CC noticed Johnny didn't respond to the sheriff's comment about trespassing. "We started looking around and we saw an opening over by the fence between us and Gibbs' property."

The sheriff took his hat off and mopped his brow with his red bandanna. As he put the cloth back in his hip pocket, he asked, "Son, what are you basing this tree damage on? Have you ever seen DDT sprayed around? What does it look like?"

Johnny didn't hesitate. "It looks like the pictures we saw in this Rachel Carson's book we studied in science class last spring." Before either the sheriff or Gramps could gawk at Johnny's answer, Johnny blurted, "I know. It's a book. But we saw a lot of pictures of damage done to farms and what it does to chicken eggs. The egg thinning and all. If that stuff can do that to eggs, I bet it can do the same to trees and birds, too."

The sheriff didn't say anything for a few minutes but started walking around and looking up in the trees and on the ground. When he got to the fence, he twirled his hat around.

CC looked at Lady who was gently gazing and decided to leave her to follow the group to the fence. She heard Gramps confide, "Sheriff, I had a run in with Gibbs the other day at this same spot. He was carrying on with the kids about crossing over and I reminded him of his farmhands used to come over and take peaches from me. I let 'em until it got out of hand."

"Well, let's handle one thing at a time, and you're right, Ethan, this hole has been cut a while back. See it's a little rusty on the edges. Shows me someone sheared it away a while ago to slip through. Now enough room for spraying equipment. Right, Johnny?"

Johnny kicked his foot against some loose dirt before answering, "Guess so, Sheriff. But how did this stuff happen? I mean the things we say had to be caused by some kind of pesticide. The dead birds and the farm just feel different up here, don't you think? Gramps, what do you think?"

Instead of answering, Gramps looked at Sheriff Jack who stood up straight and scratched his head before answering. "You know, Ethan, I had to go to one of those Farm Bureau meetings about spraying pesticides, especially DDT. There haven't been too many cases around here, but in other parts of the state. farmers have been accused of accidentally spraying neighbor's land and of what they called drifting."

"What exactly does that mean, Sheriff?" CC perked up when Johnny asked that question.

"It means farmers can't be spraying on properties that don't belong to them. Even if it drifts over by mistake when a farmer is spraying his own land, it's still called drift. Whoever sprays is responsible and can be fined. They say at the bureau you have to be very careful with DDT and just spray on your own land if you're going to use it."

Johnny stepped in again. "What are they supposed to do? Damage done by DDT can't be wiped away. You cannot fix it."

The sheriff focused on Johnny and then on Gramps. "I have to look into this some more. But a farmer can't take it on himself to spray a neighbor's property even if it's by accident. I'm going to have to talk to the bureau some more about this, but Mr. Gibbs may have to answer for this. Could be fines involved."

CC heard the crackle of leaves and twigs and could tell immediately that someone was coming their way. Hearing the murmur of voices, she could hardly believe it. She saw Mama walking towards them in a pair of tight jeans and her long golden hair tied up in a ponytail.

Before she could say anything, Mama said, "Cicely, I knew I'd find you by the peach orchard."

CC stumbled towards her mother who held her arms out. She couldn't resist falling into them, but as she buried her face in Mama's neck, she narrowed her eyes at the lanky dark-haired man behind her. He spit at the ground never taking his eyes off CC.

She couldn't believe it. Randy. Mama brought that sleazy bastard Randy to the farm.

CHAPTER 31

"Randy," CC hissed. "You brought that good for nothing. How could you, Mama?" CC wanted to scream but the sheriff and Gramps were nearby, and she didn't want them to overhear.

"What are you doing, CC?" Mama yelled. "Let go of my arm."

CC didn't realize her grip was so tight. Releasing her hold, she implored "Mama, you know how I feel about him and how he treated me. How could you bring him with you?"

Rubbing her arm and shaking her head, her mother was clearly exasperated. She lifted her face and whispered through clenched teeth, "I will talk to you later about this."

"Well, I don't believe it. Johnny, look what the cat drug in. It's your Aunt Loreen. Lord daughter, when did you get here?" Gramps interrupted them.

Mama straightened up and smiled at Gramps. "Dad, I sure miss you. Had to come and see my favorite father."

"Only father you got, Loreen. And I'm glad you're here. Has your mother seen you yet?"

While Gramps and her mother bantered, CC never took her eyes off Randy. He stood with his hands in his hip pockets and still had that mean leer plastered on his face, the same look CC remembered back home. As she stared at him, thoughts flooded her memory and she was back in her mother's tiny living room forcing him off the couch and running to her room. Her heart started racing like it did that night but she took a deep breath to control her breathing.

"What's up, CC?" Johnny whispered over her shoulder.

CC continued to stare at Randy as she said to Johnny in a leveled tone, "I can't stand being around that creep, that's what."

"What creep? You mean that guy that came with your mother?"

Before CC could say anything else, Gramps hollered at the group, "Sheriff Jack wants to get back to town. Why don't we all walk back and have some coffee or sweet tea and some of Bess's peach pie. Know Bess would like to see everyone. She must be back with Bud by now."

CC noticed he didn't wait for anyone to answer but started walking towards the house with the sheriff alongside him. Mama and Randy followed. She stood there watching until Johnny prodded her. "Let's go, Cousin. Don't you want to talk about this in private later?"

Without answering, she took the bridle Johnny held and started a slow walk back. As she looked towards the house, she wondered how Gran would feel about Mama and her boyfriend just showing up out of thin air. She almost stopped in her tracks and thought about hearing Gran talking to Mama on the phone yesterday. Did she ask her to come? She would know soon enough, but hoped they weren't ganging up on her.

Gramps turned around and shouted to them, "Y'all coming? Thought the idea of Gran's pie would get you moving."

When CC didn't say anything, Johnny spoke up. "We're right behind you. Lady is a little slow. Been grazing." He added, "CC, I've got to get back to check on Dad."

As they approached the house, the unmistakable aroma of fresh coffee wafted towards them and a hint of something cooking. That meant Gran rushed back to the farm to bring Uncle Bud home and meet up with Mama and the idiot.

She turned to Johnny to let him know, "I wonder if Gran told Mama about what's been happening with me around here."

"You didn't do anything wrong, CC. It was my idea to investigate the DDT, and you were blindsided by those guys running you off the road. Anyway, you know Gramps and Gran'll back you up."

CC didn't say anything, but kept walking with her eyes glued to the house. As she got closer, she aimed for the barn. "You go on. I'll take care of Lady. I know you want to get inside and check on your dad."

Johnny raised his hand to motion he heard her and rushed for the back door. CC decided to tie Lady to the gate and head for the porch. She took a breath as she entered the kitchen. They were milling around the coffee pot so it gave CC a chance to stare hard at Gran who returned the look before jumping in, "Isn't it nice your mom is able to come today? I just talked to her yesterday."

"Yeah. Just fine, Gran, but you should have told me she was coming. This is not going to be easy." There was no mistaking CC's angry tone as she moved over to the hall door and leaned against the frame. She surveyed the room and saw Johnny in the corner whispering to Uncle Bud. She smiled and waved to them. It was nice to see Uncle Bud with that goofy grin bobbing his head up and down in response to Johnny.

She noticed Gran watched them too and smiled until she glanced Randy's way. Her face seemed to harden, but she poured a cup of coffee and took it to Johnny. CC heard her say, "Nice to have your dad home. Sure missed you, Bud."

Gramps spoke up first. "The sheriff wants to let us know Bud is home for good and he thinks Gibbs will drop the charges against him." Loreen started to speak up but before she could, Gramps added, "Sheriff Jack also wants us to know he is going to follow through on the charges against those hooligans who chased CC and Addy off the road."

Twirling his hat between his hands, the sheriff added, "Yep, Bess, I know you are concerned about that and I will do what I can about it." He looked at, CC. "We may need more witnesses, though. Talk to you about that later."

"We need to know they won't be harassing anyone, not just the girls, although that's bad enough." As she spoke, she looked straight at Mama, and CC hoped that meant Gran was standing up for her.

CC didn't miss the hard look on Mama's face, that unmistakable look she was used to, the one that said I know you did something wrong. Uncle Bud's mumbling was mixed in with the talk around the room and she also noticed Randy leering at him. Mama had wanted Gran and Gramps to put Uncle Bud in an institution and she had overheard her talking to Randy about it back home. Bud was her brother but she thought he should go away.

"Let's all sit and have some coffee or iced tea and pie." Gran said to the group. "CC, why don't you give me a hand?"

Before they all sat down, the sheriff motioned he was going and started for the door. Before Gramps could follow him, he said "Stay and eat, Ethan. I'll just hop in my truck and head back to town. Be in touch."

They all motioned to him. CC stayed near the door until Mama moved over to her. "Let's take a walk, Cicely."

"You're not gonna eat anything? That means you're not hungry or too sick to eat from drinking?"

As CC watched Mama throw back her shoulders and widen her eyes, she knew she was pushing her too far and there was going to be a blow up, so she started lumbering to the back porch. "All right, fine. I'll walk to the barn with you. Got to unsaddle Lady."

CC could feel the anger coming from Mama, but she was mad too. She was so mad she brought Randy with her, and to the farm of all places. And why just show up the way she did? Why was Mama here?

Lady neighed and waved her neck when she felt them approaching. CC started patting her and took the reins, walking her into the barn. Before she could take the saddle off, Mama geared up for action.

"Why do you think I'm here? What's the matter with you? You were supposed to use this time to cool down, but then I'm told you got into trouble on Gibbs' farm." She grabbed CC's arm which caused her to wince. "Look at this," as she raised her sleeve up. "You're all bruised up. What were you doing over there anyway? And how'd you get in a fight?"

"I didn't get in a fight, Mama. I was shoved by that man, and..."

Before she could finish, Mama started in again. "And what's this foolishness about driving around with colored kids? In this part of the country? Are you that stupid? Haven't you learned anything since you had your baby?"

CC's jaw dropped, and she drew in her breath over Mama's accusation. "People around here and in New Orleans don't like Negroes. Neither do you, Mama."

For a split-second CC thought for sure Mama would raise her hand and slap her, but fortunately, she heard Gran walking up behind them. "Wait. I thought I better check on you two. I heard a little of what you were saying. How about we listen to each other?"

Mama smirked when she heard that. "What are you saying? I shouldn't be worried about my daughter? Why would you even put yourself in that situation, CC?"

Gran and CC stared at each other. CC's teeth clenched as her anger started to take over. Once again Mama didn't understand her or even want to listen.

"Loreen, don't you remember when you were young? You played with the little girl on the edge of town. She was colored, and you used to love it when we picked her up and brought her to the farm to play."

Mama turned to the stall and put her forearms over the railing. She kicked at the dirt before turning back to Gran. "Yes, Mom, I remember. And it was wonderful. But it's different now. After everything that's happened, CC, I don't want you getting involved with Negro boys. I just don't."

"She has other friends now."

Mama grunted. "What friends? Are they all colored? Or white?"

Gran spoke up again, "Loreen, your daughter had been doing something wonderful. She is volunteering at the vacation bible school on the edge of town. The kids love her and she's made a couple of friends."

Mama sneered. "Good lord! You mean she's spending her days helping little colored kids and then driving them around? What about her schooling? Is she going to stay in the tenth grade?"

CC couldn't help it. "I'm working on my school stuff," she yelled. "I have a book up in my room. I read it every night."

She could feel Gran's soft touch on her shoulder. CC could hear Lady's whinny like she knew CC was in trouble and wanted to let her know she would protect her, but Gran was already closing ranks and stepped up between them.

"Your daughter has been through a lot in the last…"

Before Gran could continue, Mama started up again. "She has been through? What do you think I have been through? Finding out too late she was pregnant."

CC glared at Mama and looked at Gran.

When she did speak, her voice was very even and low. "I thought, Loreen, you came here to give Cicely some support and understanding. She has been hurt by a neighbor, albeit she shouldn't have been there, but he should not have grabbed her and twisted her arm. Look at it! She is black and blue. And then to be chased off the road for trying to help out some kids to have a good time. What is the matter with you? Are you going to keep punishing her for mistakes when she's trying to do the right thing?"

Mama glared at both of them, and then spoke in an even, fiery tone. "I'm going to continue to talk to my daughter as I see fit. CC, you can't be running around like this. It is plumb stupid to be riding around in this part of the country with a bunch of coloreds. You know that, Mom. And you should've stopped her from this foolishness."

With that final comment, Mama pushed past them and stomped out of the barn.

CC threw her head back and scoffed, "God, what does she know about me? Why did she even come here?"

Gran didn't waste any time after CC's tirade. "Wait a minute, CC. She is your mama and my daughter. Remember that. She's wrong, or at least I think she is in her attitude towards Negroes, but she hopes she is taking care of you. Coming here and checking on you, I mean, and worried about you."

"And coming sober? She stopped drinking to come here?" CC added. She couldn't avoid Gran's look of disapproval at that last comment. Her grandmother's eyes always went from soft to flaming in a nanosecond. She tightened her mouth into a downward frown that told CC she better lower her voice.

CC called a silent truce in the insult match and marched outside in search of a quiet moment. She knew Gran followed her and she was glad for her company now so she could stay in her good graces. She rested against the frame and took a deep breath. The horse sweat blended with the aroma of baled hay and fresh cut meadows. It wasn't exactly perfume, but it reminded her of Gran and Gramps and Johnny and Uncle Bud, and even Eric.

Eric. CC wished she could talk to him right now about Mama. She knew he would understand what she was feeling and she felt her heart actually skip a beat at the thought of him. Her mouth melted into a slight grin. But as Gran came up behind her and put her arms over CC's shoulders, she knew Gran loved her and was looking out for her. She also knew Mama would be on high alert if she found out CC had something going with Eric.

Gran pecked her on the cheek and started for the house, "I'll let you have some time. Come in when you're ready."

The argument with Mama left CC drained; it always did. She decided to walk out to the front field where she sat that first day here this summer.

Since the sun had gone down a little, it wasn't as hot. Late July on the farm was some of the hottest days of the year. It reminded her that August was around the corner and she needed to make some decisions and get on with the assignments from Miss Jessica.

As CC started towards the field, she heard Eric's unmistakable shrill whistle. As she turned, he stepped out of the shadows.

She heard him humming Elvis melodious "Love Me Tender" and rushed over to him. He motioned for her to follow him and when they reached the tree line, he turned to face her and put his arms around her waist. Pulling her closer to him, she marveled at how his touch could be gentle but firm at the same time.

The fluttering in her chest burned into an explosion as his lips brushed her cheek. She bowed her forehead into his face and his lips found their way to the top of her head and waited there until she was ready to lift her face and meet his dark eyes.

Her cheek felt the soft breeze of his words as he whispered, "God girl, I missed you today."

She fought the urge to ask him to take her away as fast as he could so she didn't have to face the intruders who arrived today. Instead she returned the kiss and whispered in his ear, "I was thinking about you all day."

He had such a tender expression on his face and she wondered what it would feel like to tell him everything – the baby, Marcus, Randy – but knew in her heart she wasn't ready. How could she tell him she had a half-colored baby? How could she tell him she had sex with a Negro boy even though he was the best friend she had in New Orleans? How could she tell him Randy had almost raped her and she ran away instead of forcing Mama to listen to her?

For now, it felt better to keep secrets. Dark secrets, until she was sure he could understand what happened. After all, if her own mother was ashamed of her, how could she expect anyone else to listen to her and understand?

These thoughts ran through her mind and she knew she would tell him someday, but not now. She knew she was reacting to what Mama said to her in the barn.

"What are you thinking about, CC? You've got the damnedest look on your pretty face."

She reared from his grasp and threw her long hair back and forth and exclaimed, "I am thinking about getting out of here with you and going for a long ride or drive, whichever. It's almost dark. Can we get away for a while tonight?"

Eric's arched brows registered surprised, but he recovered and beaming said, "Sure 'nough, Miss CC. We can and we will. Do you hafta sneak out or can I come knock at your door?"

At that she popped out laughing. "It wouldn't be any fun at all unless we sneaked out."

She thought about Mama's face if a new boy came to the door. CC wasn't ready for Mama's outburst about a boyfriend, and it didn't take too much thought to realize going out with Eric was a bad idea.

"I guess I better get back to the house. I didn't tell you this, but my Mama and her boyfriend showed up today, back at the field."

Eric's face mouth broke into a grin. He leaned over and picked up a grass straw and held it in his hands before putting it between his teeth. CC waited for him to say something but the goofy grin stayed in place.

"Say something. I told you Mama is here."

The grin stuck. "I'm waiting for you to tell me more about why she just popped in, darlin.'"

"Just checking up on me I reckon."

"Reckon. You are sounding more and more like a country girl. We may just keep you here."

CC saw the teasing look on his face turn to a slow smile as his dark eyes glossed over. He inched towards her and pulled her close again. A warning signal went off for CC. She understood what might happen if she let her guard down. At the same time, her whole body flooded with warmth and her face flushed.

But Mama's appearance at the farm today conjured images in CC's mind of that night with Marcus and everything that followed. She didn't want to make another mistake.

She glanced sideways and felt Eric take a sharp breath. CC knew the moment was broken. "I better get inside. Gran wants me to help her." As she turned to face him again, he leaned in as his lips brushed past her mouth and landed on her cheek. She sighed. "Oh hell, I have to go. See you tomorrow."

She marched to the house. As much as she wanted to stay, she knew she better get going.

CHAPTER 32

CC didn't have to worry about another run in with Mama after her meeting with Eric. Randy and Mama took off for Ruston. Actually, they drove off again the next morning and stayed gone all day. CC thought it was a good sign if they left early because her mother might not be drinking. It also meant she didn't have to see Randy.

She didn't see Eric either while Mama was gone, and she wondered if he was disappointed. She had heard about boys who dropped a girl if she didn't put out. She spent time helping Uncle Bud again and grooming Lady.

Later that afternoon, CC hurried to the house. She hopped over the back-porch steps and spotted Gran alone at the sink staring out the kitchen window. Even though she was still thinking about Eric, she was grateful for the familiar aroma of Gran's cooking and to have some alone time with her.

Gran spun around and flashed her familiar sweet smile "Glad you're back. I was watching you help Bud out there tending his garden. When he works that hoe back and forth, he looks himself don't you think?"

"Yeah. It's good to have him home. He's going to stay here, isn't he? I mean I heard Mama talking about you and Gramps sending him away, to live, I mean?"

"Cicely, let's not talk about that now. That's a decision your gramps and I will make down the road. We have enough to deal with now that your mother is here."

"What's she done now?"

Gran closed her eyes and rubbed the back of her neck before she let out a big sigh. "She hasn't done a thing. She hasn't had time to do anything yet. What made you ask that?"

CC paused before she answered. "I guess I'm just expecting the other shoe to drop like they say."

"I asked you earlier to give your mother a chance. You know she came here to check on you. I mean see you. She hasn't been drinking or at least she stopped to drive up here."

CC shifted her feet and looked at Gran a long time. "You're right about her trying to stay sober up here. I'll make an effort. OK? I'll sit next to her at supper and just talk about what I'm reading."

"You won't eat supper with her. She and Randy went back into town to look around some more and eat."

She thought she saw sadness in Gran's eyes. CC's mixed feelings towards Mama surfaced and she didn't know whether to be angry at her grandmother or hug her. Instead, she collapsed in the nearest kitchen chair and leaned over the table. The familiar whirring of the fan and the chicken clucking outside the window seemed far away.

Gran slid into the chair across from her. "Your mother still has friends in town. Girls she went to school with, and maybe she wants to see them and show Randy around."

CC looked up and said, "You don't sound very convincing, Gran"

"I have to convince myself. I can't go on thinking the worst about my daughter. She's not perfect, but, well, you know."

CC knew Gran needed to think the best of her daughter and decided not to argue or disagree with her. Even though she had been through so many of Mama's sudden disappearances, she decided to let Gran believe what she wanted. Maybe this time she would be right.

Pushing away from the table, CC started taking plates down from the cupboard. "How many places you want me to set?"

"Just us. Bud and Johnny will be eating with us, course."

Gran and CC worked putting the rest of supper together without saying much. CC thought about Eric's offer yesterday to meet her and wondered if she should try to find him, but decided it would be better if she stayed around the farm tonight.

Just as they were finishing up slicing the tomatoes and putting the other dishes on the table, Johnny and Uncle Bud came in, followed by Gramps. "The sheriff may stop by later. He's been over at Gibb's place looking into the spraying." He saw Gran arch her eyebrows so he added,

"Won't know any more about those boys about that until the judge hears the case."

After they finished eating, Johnny teased CC about being so quiet. "Man, you haven't said much. I know it's not a cat got your tongue. How 'bout a little birdie?"

CC didn't mind the teasing and announced she'd be in her room. She couldn't resist a counter over her shoulder as she left the kitchen, "Johnny, since you're so happy, you help with the dishes."

Gramps laughter over their banter and Uncle Bud's giggle eased some of her tension as she tripped up the stairs to her room. She opened the door and felt the slight breeze from the window near her bed. Her book was open on her night stand, and guessed Gran came up and straightened a little since her clothes were picked up too.

She stretched out on top of the cover and hugged the nearest pillow. As she looked around, she wondered if Mama ever just laid here and thought about things, like a boyfriend or a teacher she hated. It was hard to think of Mama giving too much thought to anything except drinking or riding her ass.

She felt her eyes droop and remembered thinking she couldn't possibly be sleepy. It just turned dark. But she was drowsy.

CC's eyes opened to total darkness in her room later except for the night sky from the window. As her eyes started adjusting, she turned to look out at the stars that cast a small amount of light. She listened for any sound from downstairs.

Her bedside clock stopped but she guessed it couldn't be too late. She heard a slight tinkle and guessed her Gran was in the kitchen making her nighttime tea.

She made her way to the door and saw the light on the stairs. Gramps always went to bed early so she creeped down the steps. When she reached the bottom, she saw Gran by the stove picking up the kettle. She held it with the red pot holder CC remembered from years before.

The gurgle of the hot water pouring into the china cup was a familiar sound from her childhood. When Gran put the pot down and turned to her, CC walked over to welcome the embrace and softness of her aging body.

"Want some chamomile tea with me? Just pouring."

"Yep, I heard you. I must have drifted off. What time is it?"

"Oh, 'bout nine. Want some?"

"No, not now. Did Mama get back from town?"

CC noticed Gran's smile fade slightly and waited for an answer.

"I think I heard a car a little while ago. Went straight to the bunkhouse."

"Should I have given them my room?" CC asked. "I mean her room I guess."

"No. I think she said Randy wanted a taste of farm life so they're still sleeping out there."

CC turned around so Gran couldn't see the smirk on her face. The idea of Randy wanting a taste of farm life was crazy. He just wanted to get away from everyone staring at him, giving him the evil eye.

"I'm going out to the barn to check on Lady. She can get a little nervous with strangers nearby. I see a light on out there. I'm wide awake now anyway"

"Okay, By the way, while you were upstairs, the sheriff stopped by to ask Johnny to take a ride with him. He needed a little more information on the statement about DDT before his meeting with Gibbs in the morning. I'm going up to bed in a little bit. Turn the lights out when you come back, please."

"Sure will." CC gave Gran a peck on the cheek. "Night."

She strolled past the light pole next to Uncle Bud's garden. The night air felt cool even though it was warm and sticky all day. She heard voices coming from somewhere but couldn't make out whether it was from the barn or the pasture.

There was no answer so she walked toward the voices. As she neared the barn, they became louder. The bunkhouse was attached on the far side of the barn, and she thought Mama and Randy were talking. As she got closer, she made out their voices and she heard Mama laughing. She knew that laugh. That was how Mama sounded when she was drunk. CC knew it well.

CHAPTER 33

She hoped for all it was worth that she was wrong. CC remembered there was a small window on the side of the bunkhouse. It was risky to spy on her own mother in case they were up to something. But if she walked in on them, it might be more awkward.

She edged along the side of the barn and saw a light shining through the panes. There were a couple of boxes Clay stored nearby where he put farm tools he kept outside. She pushed the nearer box over to the window. She could tell no one was standing near it, so she put both hands on either side of the frame and crouched until she could see what was going on inside.

She wished she hadn't. She saw Mama sprawled out on a chair with her legs propped on Randy's thighs. Her arms dangled on the sides of an unbuttoned blouse. Her skirt was hiked up to show off red panties.

Randy propped his chair back and a cigarette dangled from his thin lips. Mama stood up and swayed to nonexistent music. Then she heard her yell, "Where's the real music? I need some music, Hon. Turn the radio on."

"There ain't no radio out here, Loreen. There ain't nothing fun out here. 'Cept 'nother drink. Have 'nother drink"

CC could feel her cheeks burning from the sight of her mother so much like all the nights in New Orleans. She looked just like she did right before she passed out. Her hands hurt from squeezing the sill so tight. She thought she might throw up and she fought hot tears threatening to form. She wanted to scream but the choking she felt in her throat kept the sounds from coming out. And she knew screaming wouldn't make any difference. It never had.

She cringed at the sight. Just when CC thought she couldn't look at them anymore, she fell off the box and her leg scraped the splintered wood. She yelped at the pain.

"What? What's that sound? Who's there?" When CC heard Randy calling out, she felt a fierce throbbing in her forehead.

CC ducked on the ground and listened. She wanted to shriek at Randy and curse him. Her leg was burning from the scrape but she lifted herself up and took off running.

As she sprinted from the barn, her vision was blurry now from the hot tears she fought to hold back. She didn't know where she was headed and the voice in her head pulsed with blazing accusations at her mother. How could she? Coming to Gran's farm and getting stinking drunk? How could she be so disgusting?

She tripped and fell on soft grass. It was too dark to look at her leg so she rubbed her hands across her face. She heard someone moving through the grass in her direction and knew her mother was too drunk to make it in the dark. It could only be one person.

CC's heart pounded as she heard his voice laced with booze and lust.

"I know it's you out here gal. C'mon, Cicely, let me know where you are now. I just wanna make sure you're all right. I heard you let out a yell back there. C'mon now."

She didn't move but she knew she was trapped. *Oh no! This can't be happening again. I have to get away from him.*

She debated crouching where she was or darting for the house. She could see where she was now that her eyes had adjusted in the moonlight, and it was a pretty good distance to the back porch.

But Randy's eyes adjusted, too. "Gotcha, Gal. You won't get away from me this time."

He grabbed her bruised arm and she yelped again. He pulled her around and lifted her up to his face. She could feel the liquor spray from his lips and smelled his nasty breath. "Oh God. Don't let this happen again. Get away from me! I hate you!"

"I gotcha now. You can't get away this time. C'mon, I just wanna little kiss."

She twisted and fought to get free of his grasp. CC was surprised at how strong he was in spite of his drunkenness. She could feel his determination to trap her. Her instinct told her to shriek and fight. "Lemme go! Help! Somebody, help! Gramps! Johnny! Somebody! Help!" She tried kicking him and hit a spot because he leaned back and let go of her arm.

"You got me in the balls, you little bitch."

He backhanded her across the face. She swerved backwards and fell to the ground, gulping for air and trying to catch her breath. He pulled her bruised arm again and pulled her up. His heavy body landed on top of her and pinned her arms so she couldn't move her body. His breath nauseated her as he tried to kiss her.

CC shook her head back and forth but he still managed to press his slips over hers. Even though she had trouble breathing, she tried to bite him. He lifted his head slightly, snickering. "Hee hee. Nope you can't do that. I got'cha now." His laugh caused him to cough right in her face and she knew she would throw up.

Just as she was losing strength CC saw a huge figure over both of them. She recognized Bud as he pulled Randy back. CC rolled over relieved he was off of her and heard him howl, "Oomph! Git off of me you big animal!".

Randy was on his back in the grass and Bud was on top of him pummeling his chest and face with his huge fists. "Don't hurt Sissy. Don't hurt her. You can't hurt her! Won't let you!" With every word he punched Randy in the face. CC thought Bud was going to kill him. His face burned with fury.

CC pushed away from the two men to try and run for help when she realized there was a brighter light coming towards them. Someone was hurrying towards the three of them with a lantern.

"Dad. Dad. Stop. You have to stop," Johnny called out as he hurried to them and started pulling Bud off of Randy.

As hard as he pulled, Bud kept thrashing away at Randy. Johnny yelled, "Sheriff! Sheriff Jack over here. Help us!"

She could hear someone else running through the field. The sheriff's enormous figure carrying a flashlight appeared and he immediately began pulling at Bud, too. "Get off of him, Mr. Scott. Come on now."

Bud reacted to the sheriff's voice and stood up clenching and unclenching his fists, babbling about Randy trying to hurt CC. "Trying to hurt Sissy. Trying to hurt her. Had to stop him."

"Okay, Bud. I'll get to the bottom of this. Stand back."

Johnny was over CC pushing her hair back. When he did, he saw the welt on her face and her torn blouse. "CC, did Randy do this to you? Sheriff, look at her face."

"All right, I can see it, Son." CC squinted from the flashlight in her face and could feel the assaults on her face and arm already starting to throb. She lifted her knees to her head. She couldn't stop the sobs that wracked her body, but she managed to implore Johnny to get Gran. "Please go, go get her, Johnny. I, I need to tell her."

She heard the sheriff say, "Go ahead, get her. I see the lights on in the house," and saw Johnny running for the house.

He didn't have to go far. She heard Gran and Gramps voices as they hurried towards them.

Gramps rushed over to Bud who stood with his head and shoulders down. Johnny held his light on CC and Gran walked over to her. CC's sobs by this time could be heard over the others and when Gran knelt, she lifted CC's face to her. "Oh, good Lord, what on earth? What happened? Cicely, are you alright? Don't say anything. Oh child. I can tell you're not all right. That's a stupid question. Here, put my apron around you."

She wrapped the large garment over her shoulders and took CC in her arms and rocked her. CC continued to cry and thought she might throw up, but the more Gran held her, her tears fell softly and the nausea passed. She looked into Gran's eyes and Gran whispered in her ear. "Did he hurt you besides beating you?"

CC could barely speak. "No. He chased me and hit me and twisted my arm. He tried to kiss me and then pinned me down. He was gonna..." Her sobs threatened again.

"That's enough child. Where is your mother?"

CC motioned towards the barn. "Still in the bunkhouse I guess." She stood up and took Gran's arm. "Come on. Let's go get her."

"Mrs. Scott, can I ask where y'all are headed? I'm gonna have questions for your granddaughter."

"And they will have to wait awhile, but I can tell you right now, Sheriff, you better put that man on the ground in handcuffs when he comes to." They walked towards the barn and Johnny kept the flashlight on them. Gran turned her head around to the sheriff. "And you better pin a medal on Bud because he probably saved this child from something pretty terrible."

CHAPTER 34

CC's stride quickened as they approached the bunkhouse. Her jaw hurt but she wasn't letting that stop her from confronting Mama. She needed to know how much CC was hurt because she brought Randy too the farm. Gran's arm pressed closer to her side. As reassuring as that felt, CC wanted to let her mother have it.

The light was still on in the bunkhouse and she threw the door open. "Get up! Mama, do you know what Randy just did to me? No, of course not. You're drunk and passed out!"

"Damn," Mama opened one eye. "What? Who is it? Wha's going on?" She propped up on her elbows and looked worse than CC imagined. Her blonde hair frizzed up in all directions and remnants of red lipstick were smeared all over her mouth. Coats of black mascara bled down her cheeks. Her eyes were half slits trying to adjust to the one light bulb hanging from the ceiling.

The picture was more grotesque because Mama's open blouse showed off her pink bra and the exposed red panties. CC sensed Gran take in a huge breath. She hadn't seen Mama's hangovers like CC did in New Orleans.

"Is that you, Cicely?" She swung her legs off the cot when she realized Gran was standing in front of her. "Mother, what are you doing here? What time is it? Damn, it's still dark. What're y'all doing out here?" She blinked trying to adjust to the light and rubbed the back of her hand over her mouth. CC thought that made her even more hideous.

"Loreen. Get up and wash your face and put some clothes on."

CC took charge. "Wait. Just wait a minute. Look at me, Mama. Look at me." CC could see her own face in the aluminum mirror. She looked terrible herself from the redness and swelling from her injuries, but she pulled Mama up and swung her around. "I said look at me, Mama."

It took a few seconds but something in Mama's face changed. Her eyes softened and she touched the side of CC's face, but stopped when her daughter winced. "What happened to you, Cicely? Your face. And your blouse is torn. What happened?"

"You wanna know what happened. Mama? What happened is you brought that son of a bitch boyfriend of yours here. That's what happened."

Mama's face hardened again. She stumbled to the sink using the nearby chair as a prop. She didn't turn on the water after her first look in the mirror. CC heard her moan and then lean on the bowl. She turned and glared at CC. "Don't start on him again, Cicely. You tried to break us up at home and told that story about him trying to hurt you. You blamed him for you running off that night."

"What is the matter with you?" CC shrieked. "What has to happen to make you understand about him? Everything I told you was true. Now he has come here and chased me, slapped me down, kept me pinned under him until Uncle Bud saved me"

Gran grabbed Mama by the shoulders and shook her. "Loreen, what has happened to you? Are you so drunk you can't see your own daughter standing here beaten and almost raped by the drunken man you call your boyfriend?"

Mama's mouth quivered as she stared back and forth at both her daughter and mother. She plopped down in the chair and buried her head in her hands. CC knew what was coming. All that self-pity and slobbering.

Instead Mama sat there quietly.

CC watched as Mama stood and crossed the tiny room and found her jeans and another shirt in the suitcase. She put them on and turned back to CC. "Did he do anything else to you that night? That night in New Orleans when you ran?"

That question startled Gran. "You wanna ask her about that now? She was very hurt tonight, Loreen."

Mama approached CC and tried to touch the side of her face again. "Stay out of it, Mother. Cicely. Let me talk to you. Where is Randy?"

CC pulled away and unleashed all the anger she had stored for the last several months. "He is laying on his face half beaten to death by Uncle Bud.

That's right, Uncle Bud, the brother you make fun of saved me from that awful creep. He beat him up and the only thing that stopped him was Johnny and the sheriff."

She got close to Mama's face to make her point. "But in New Orleans, I was alone that night so I ran to Marcus' house where I had sex for the first time in my life. And yes, I got pregnant. I made a mistake. I don't know why I did it. But I did." CC took a deep breath and the anger grew. "And, Mama, I wish I could have kept my baby. Kept her and cared for her so she would never end up with someone like you."

CC felt like she could barely stand. Gran took her by the hand and led her to a chair. Before she could sit, she saw Mama's eyes widen again, but this time she stared at the other side of the room.

CC turned around wincing from the pain in her back. What she saw caused another kind of pain.

Johnny, Gramps and Addy stood in the doorway. Gramps' normal kindly expression turned to flaming red as he glared at his daughter.

Mama spoke first. "Dad, please I can explain."

No one said anything. Addy's face filled with sorrow and CC could tell her friend would start crying any second. Johnny stood in place, but motioned with his arm to ask her to come with him.

CC saw her family and friend staring at the scene. She groaned, "Oh no! You heard all of that!"

It was too much after everything that happened with Randy. She bolted for the door with her head down and pushed herself between Johnny and Addy. The last thing CC heard was Gran telling Gramps to make sure the sheriff arrested Randy and take him away.

CHAPTER 35

CC ran to the house and raced up the stairs ignoring her body's pain. Flinging the door open, she turned the light switch off and crumpled on her bed. It was hard to believe everything that happened. All in a couple of days.

She heard footsteps on the stairs and knew it would be Gran. "Can I turn the light on please?"

CC mumbled an okay, and the overhead light flooded the room. "Wait, CC, I'll put the lamp on." Gran quietly crossed the bedroom and turned the lamp on. "Let me look at you for a minute with all this light first."

CC didn't move, so Gran gently lifted her by the side. She had brought warm dish towels from the kitchen and started gently wiping CC's face. The movements felt good to her and CC suddenly felt tremendous love for her. Gran believed her. About everything. She reached up to hug her.

The embrace lasted a long time, and when she lay down again, Gran asked, "Where else is the pain?"

"My back is sore but not bad. It's my face. My head. But I don't need a doctor. Not now."

Gran pulled the stool from the dresser and sat close to the bed. "We'll have to get you to the doctor tomorrow to check that. Can you see all right? "I can see fine, Gran."

"Good. CC, the sheriff wants to talk to you."

CC winced. "Not now. I can't talk to him now," and turned her head to the wall. "God. This never ends. Randy tried to hurt me in New Orleans and now on the farm. How much will I have to tell them? Can't they just see what happened to me?"

"I know. It's hard to talk about it, but you have to give some kind of statement. It's what they call preliminary. He needs something to arrest that man. Bud is too confused, and well, you know. We have to make sure he doesn't get arrested again for fighting like he did at Gibbs' place."

CC turned back to Gran. "For fighting? He saved me! All right, I understand. Will you stay with me?"

Gran leaned into CC's pillow. "Oh, child, I'll stay with you all night if you want. She squeezed CC's hand. Can I go get the sheriff now? Wouldn't you like to get this over with?"

CC looked down at her shirt. "Why don't I cover with the sheet? Will he have to look at this?" as she pointed to the torn shirt.

"Don't know. We can ask." Gran didn't leave. She walked to the doorway and hollered, "Johnny, bring Sheriff Jack up."

It didn't take long. The sheriff lumbered up the stairs and stood in CC's doorway twirling his hat in his hands. "Sorry, Miss Cicely. Hate to go over this now, but that Mr. Benson is howling about you spying on him in the bunkhouse. Says he thought you were a burglar or something."

She looked at Gran who shifted in her chair and narrowed her eyes. CC could tell she was fuming over that comment. She pointed to the stool for the sheriff to sit. "Just tell me what you wanna know, Sheriff Jack."

She went over the chase and attack in the field without crying again. She felt numb. Gran said, "You've been through a lot, dear. Natural to feel shut down."

When the sheriff left, she got up and started taking off her clothes. Her knees felt like they might buckle so she asked Gran to bring her pajamas while she sat on the bed.

Gran was right. She felt so tired, but knew if she closed her eyes, she would see Randy looming over her again. She thought she could still smell that awful breath of his- alcohol mixed with cigarettes. Bile formed in her throat. She pushed it down determined not to throw up.

Gran brought a pair over and CC took off the torn blouse. She didn't want to look at it. "Here, Gran. Can you get rid of this?" and handed it over between two fingers.

"I'll put it in a bag for you."

"Why do you have to keep it, Gran?"

Gran sat down again and stroked CC's arm "We have to keep it as part of the evidence. I think. We'll have to talk to the authorities again tomorrow about his attack on you."

CC gazed at her and then sat up on her propped pillows. "Yes, I'll talk to them. Everyone needs to know about him. And I guess with everyone in the family being here, they'll believe me. It won't be like the time with Mama." CC brushed her cheek. "Gran, how did Uncle Bud know about the attack? And Johnny? It seems like they came so fast."

"I'm not sure of all the details yet, but pretty sure Bud heard you yelling and knew something was wrong. Johnny went looking for him when he got home. Just come back to the farm. Remember, I told you earlier the sheriff picked him up when you were upstairs."

Gran bent over and wiped CC's face again. "Why'd he have to go with the sheriff earlier?"

Gran straightened her back. "He went with him after supper to give a statement about Mr. Gibbs. You know that was settled, but the sheriff needs more information for the file."

CC sat up higher and started to protest, but Gran stopped her. "It's all right. Gibbs is not gonna file any kind of charges. Your Gramps seems to think he may be worried about the spraying on our field, so he's not making any noise about you and Johnny."

There was a soft knock on the door. CC heard Johnny ask if it was all right to come in.

CC nodded to Gran and she called out, "Come on in, Son."

Johnny opened the door and stood in the doorway. Gran stood up and told them she was going downstairs for a few minutes and patted Johnny on the shoulder as she left. "Don't keep her up too long. She's exhausted. CC, I'll be back in a while with some of my sleepy time tea."

Johnny watched Gran leave and turned to CC. "You Okay, cousin?"

She managed a slow smile. "I will be. Do you know what happened? I mean do you know more about Mama's boyfriend and before I came here." She bowed her head and mumbled, "I guess you heard an ear full tonight at the bunkhouse."

He stayed at the foot of her bed. "I heard some, but I know from Dad you were hurt by that man. You don't look as bad as that guy does, though. Dad put a hurting on him."

CC snickered. "Ouch, that hurts."

Johnny was thoughtful then said, "You know CC, you are something. The way you stood up to your mother tonight after fighting Randy off as best you could."

CC winced again when she tried to sit up more. "You want some ice for your back? That's what you need. Your face, too. It's swelling."

"You know that from all the fights you're been in?" She let out a little shaky laugh. "Yeah, some ice. And aspirin for my back."

Before she could say anything else, there was another knock and Addy stood in the open door holding a glass of water. "I have the aspirin. Gran gave me two on my way up." She squealed, "Oh my god! CC! Your face! On damn! I'm sorry." Addy regrouped. "It doesn't look that bad. Really."

CC managed another half laugh. "Like a horse didn't gallop over me. Just a little wagon." She covered her eyes to hide the tears she knew were forming and felt Addy moving to the side of the bed.

"I'm sorry, CC, that I bellowed like a cow just now. I didn't get a good look at you earlier, so, so... Oh God," and CC knew for sure her friend was going to cry now.

"You didn't bellow, Addy. That's not accurate. You screeched like a crow, actually, and don't do it again or Gran might run up here with a broom to chase you out."

Addy shoved the pills and water towards CC who took it gratefully. "Does it hurt a lot?"

"Only when you screech, Addy. Yes, it hurts some, but I'm okay." She glanced at Johnny leaning against the dresser with his arms crossed.

"You're gonna be all right, cousin. I'll get you tomorrow if your back can take it and we'll ride out to the orchard. Get some sun. You'll forget how you hurt. You'll be burning up again."

Addy chimed in, "That sounds positively awful, Johnny. She may not feel up to it." Before he could answer her, she turned to CC. "Gran said I could spend the night up here with you. Is that all right, CC? Already checked with my dad. He said it was fine."

CC frowned and gulped. "You didn't tell him what happened, did you? I'm not ready for everyone to know about the...you know. Addy, what were you doing here tonight? I mean, I'm glad, but..."

Addy slumped over and CC could barely hear her mumble, "No, of course not. Just wanted to tell him I'm staying over. Trying to spend time with you in case you go back to New Orleans. I called earlier and Gran said you were still up. I decided to bring my record player and records over. Then I drove up and saw those lights on by the barn, and, well…"

CC eyes softened as she patted the side of the bed. "Come sit down. We can talk about bible school and the children. But oh God, Addy, are you gonna play Elvis songs all night?" She fell back on her pillow in mock frustration and patted the top of her head pretending she hurt herself.

Addy started giggling. "Don't do that. If you fall back you may hurt something else."

Johnny shifted his head from side to side and laughed. "I'm getting out of here. You two are getting crazy." He turned to leave and over his shoulder told CC to use the ice. "I can hear Gran downstairs opening trays. Alert! She'll be here any minute!"

Both girls managed a laugh. After Johnny left, CC looked at Addy. "I can't believe I just laughed after everything that happened tonight. With Randy I mean."

Addy threw the comforter on the floor and sprawled on top of it. "I'm gonna stay here all night and read to you or something. instead of records"

CC grimaced at that last remark. "Are you serious? If you're going to read to me, I brought some very interesting and racy books from New Orleans."

"Oh God again three times. Just kidding." Her face crinkled the way CC remembered when Addy was thinking. "CC, you are something. I mean the way you fought that man off, and the way you stood up to your mother. And everything, I mean."

The room quieted and CC heard the clock ticking next to her bed. She thought Gran must have wound it when she was in the bedroom earlier. "I don't know how much you heard, Addy. I guess I kept everything a secret for so long. It's hard to talk about things, but it's nice to have you here tonight. We can talk about all that stuff some other time." She took a deep breath and closed her eyes. "I mean it. Glad you're here."

"Here I come. Emptied some trays for your face." The girls snickered as Gran turned the corner into the doorway. She stood in front of them with a big bowl and a towel draped over her arm. "Heard you laughing some. Good to see you girls in a better frame of mind."

She walked over to CC and wrapped some cubes in her dish towel. "Here. Keep this on your cheek as long as you can; it'll keep the swelling down. Does your neck hurt too? Saw you rubbing the back of it."

"Gran, where is Mama? And how is Uncle Bud?'

She put the towel on her cheek. Gran seemed to know CC wanted her to sit down so she took a spot on the bed and patted CC's arm. "Gramps made your Mama take a room at that little motel near the school. He told her to stay the night." She picked at some threads on the cover. "Your uncle Bud is good. He's downstairs in his chair. Course he has some hurt fists, but he's getting iced, too. Sheriff took Randy into town in the back of his police car in handcuffs. That's what Johnny said."

They looked at each other and Gran added, "Everyone's settled in where they're supposed to be." She looked at the floor. "Even Addy's falling asleep."

"That girl can sleep through anything. I think I'll keep this lamp on tonight though."

Gran smoothed CC's cover. "Be back in a minute. Gonna get a couple of pillows and a couple of blankets for you and me."

"Gran, I'm okay. Besides, Addy's here."

"I know it. And I told you I'd stay the night if you need me. I've decided you need me, so don't say different." She started out of the room, and turned back to look at CC. "Right?"

"Right, Gran. I need you tonight."

Within seconds she was back and settling into the chair in the corner. CC felt protected by her friend and her grandmother in the room tonight. She leaned her head back on the soft down pillow. Soon the purring of Addy's deep breathing and the ticking of the clock were enough to make CC believe she could close her eyes. Maybe she wouldn't hear Randy calling in her dreams.

CHAPTER 36

CC squinted at the sun beaming through her bedroom window and tried to stretch. "Ouch!"

As she felt the pain throughout her body, memories from last night flashed through her mind. Randy looming over her and spittle running down his chin. She felt like she couldn't breathe so CC made herself sit up.

She looked for Addy on the side of the bed. A note was propped on the dresser with large letters saying she had to get home and would call later. Just like Addy, CC thought, to write a note where she could see it from the bed.

She could hear Gran downstairs poking around in the kitchen and Gramps' early morning cough. "Guess I better get up."

She tried standing, but could see herself in the dresser mirror. "Damn. I can't believe it." Her eyes bulged back at her and she had to look away. "What will Eric think when he sees me? This is awful."

When she looked at herself, CC could still feel the sharp pain of Randy's slap last night. She could hear the sound of fist on face and her hand was drawn up to the spot where that explosion happened.

I wish Uncle Bud had killed him. Jail is too good for that...that... "God!" she screamed with disgust.

Uncle Bud. CC knew she needed to get downstairs and check on him. She held onto the side of the mattress and hobbled over to the chest. There were fresh clothes on top of the drawers and CC knew Gran left them. She reached for the shorts and blouse and threw them on the bed where she could sit down and dress.

"CC, do you want me to come up and help you?"

"No ma'am," She yelled. "I'm putting on my clothes now. Be down soon," as she struggled to lean over and get her feet in the pants legs.

With pure grit, she got her shirt and sneakers on. Taking one last look in the mirror, she hoped her face would look better once she was up for a while, but the redness and puffiness couldn't be disguised. Still here, she thought.

When she got to the kitchen door, she yelled, "Here I am, ready or not," hoping this would dampen shocked expressions when they saw her face. She turned the doorway corner, and surveyed the room, standing for a second to watch their reactions.

Johnny couldn't hide a quick glimmer of anger. His face got red and his jaw stiffened. Gramp's love and concern was written all-over his face. Gran, well Gran looked like herself, all poised to ask what she wanted for breakfast. She had gotten her fury out last night and was ready to get on with what had to be done today.

But it was Uncle Bud who softened CC's heart. When he saw CC, he lowered his head and started mumbling to himself. She couldn't make out what he was saying, but she knew he was upset by the way she looked. Champ lay at his feet, but when he saw CC, he ran over to her, and started whining and begging for her attention.

Johnny stood up. "It was Champ who started barking and running in circles to get me to chase after Dad. He sounded the alarm for the commotion in the field where... well, where the fight was going on. Might not have known if it hadn't been for Champ."

After patting the dog on the head and giving him a good boy, CC walked over to Bud and flinched when she saw his hands. One hand was wrapped and the other one was swollen and red like her face. She gulped and remembered Bud didn't like to be hugged or touched much, but CC gently stroked his shoulder.

"Sissy all right?" he asked.

"Sissy all right." When CC answered him, she fought back tears of love she felt for him.

She heard Gramps clearing his throat and knew he held back tears also.

"I mentioned something about a ride this morning," Johnny broke the awkwardness, "but we can bridle Lady and let her pull the small wagon. You don't feel like mounting the saddle, do you?"

CC held up her hand to Johnny to ask him to wait and moved over to Gran's side. "Do I have to go into town this morning to give another statement? "

"Sheriff Jack said to wait. He got enough from you last night for now. Plenty of witnesses, too." Gran wiped her hands on a kitchen towel. "But I do want you to eat something. You didn't even finish that tea last night. How 'bout coffee milk and toast."

CC smiled at her. "That enough to make you happy?"

"It is."

Before Gran could start on the coffee, CC asked, "Mama still at the hotel?"

Gramps spoke up, "I took her into town to give her a chance to sober up and get some sleep. Cleared out the bunkhouse this morning to get rid of that man's belongings. Gonna take her some clothes this morning on my way to the station. Going in late." He gave her a peck on the good side of her forehead.

Gran asked, "You sure you don't need to see the doc? Any dizziness or headaches this morning?"

CC shook her head. "No, but I would let you know."

Gramps kissed her again and Johnny followed him out the door. She looked over at Bud after the men left, and saw him sitting on his stool with Champ by his side. He was quiet and staring out the window. One of his birds on the sill started chirping like crazy and Bud giggled.

CC managed to eat buttered toast and sip on the coffee milk. When she was finished, she leaned over and kissed Gran. "By the way, if I didn't say it last night, thanks for everything. I love you, Gran," and headed for the porch. She didn't want to get all teary-eyed again so she started outside before she could.

The morning was bright and sunny. She took a minute to listen to the usual farm sounds, the chickens clucking, Lady neighing, a cow mooing. CC could hear Uncle Bud's favorite melodies in between those sounds: the bees buzzing in Gran's flower beds and his birds chirping away.

Her back throbbed and as the sun hit her face, it stung and she was glad she remembered to pick up her hat from the porch. CC closed her eyes and every time she did, she could still hear Randy goading her to kiss him.

"Hey, you coming with me? Got her hooked up. Old fashioned way."

She opened her eyes, and there was Johnny sitting on the wagon with Lady fastened up to pull them. She whinnied and shook her mane in recognition and CC smiled at them. "Looks like a good ride to me."

"Yep, but I'm gonna help you get up here 'til your back's better." Johnny hopped off the seat and took CC by the waist. "C'mon, let's do this together."

CC grimaced from the aches she felt even with his help. She settled on the cart's bunk.

"Thought we'd ride out to the pasture next to the front field. That OK?"

CC wanted to avoid the spot in the back field near the barn where Randy chased and attacked her. "Sounds good. Just feels nice being out in the sun."

They rode for a while stopping to look at the small herd of cows. Johnny asked about Addy's sleepover and what the sheriff had to say about jailing Randy. Just when CC settled in, they rounded a small clump of trees and there was Eric. He leaned against the fence in the same spot where they met when CC arrived at the farm.

Johnny clicked for Lady to stop and he turned to face CC. "I guess I better warn you. Eric must have heard all the commotion last night. I saw him at the bunkhouse." CC took a deep breath waiting for the rest of it. "I saw him running back to the field where the sheriff had Randy handcuffed."

She took another deep breath before asking, "You think he heard everything I yelled at Mama?"

Johnny didn't say anything so CC answered her own question. "How could he not hear me?" She slumped down and put her hands-on top of her head. "Damn! He heard enough. I wanted to tell him myself someday, but God, hasn't there been enough carrying on, Johnny?"

She dismounted from the wagon and held her side to hide the pain. She half turned so Eric couldn't see her wince. She didn't want him to feel sorry for her. Not now.

CC looked up at Johnny still sitting on the wagon. "Don't know what Eric's gonna say, but I'm going to stay strong. I am not gonna let Randy turn me into some little, little what?"

Johnny answered for her this time. "Like it's your fault. All this stuff. It's not, CC."

She pulled herself up to her full height and in spite of her sore back, she walked straight at Eric and kept her eyes on him. Even though her heart beat at full speed and she knew she looked like hell, she didn't look down. CC wanted to face him head on. She wasn't sure what he had heard but hoped she could make him understand.

When she got within a few feet, he straightened up and put his hands in his front pockets. "CC, I wanna ask if you're all right, but I can see you're not. How's your cheek? It looks bad."

He started to touch it, but pulled back when she drew away. "Sorry, it's sore. I can barely touch it myself. Gran's been giving me lots of ice to put on it."

Even though she didn't want him to feel sorry for her, she pleaded with her eyes for some kind of concern from him, for the same looks she had seen in the last few days. Like he still wanted to be with her. But he didn't look at her in the same way. He was looking at her like he was suspicious or something. She could swear she could hear her heart breaking.

She had to know. "What did you hear last night? Did you hear everything that was said in the bunkhouse?"

Eric shook his head slowly and CC could tell he didn't want to look at her. He swallowed hard and rubbed at the back of his neck. He muttered something CC couldn't make out and then, "Shit. I heard enough. You yelling at your mama about her boyfriend attacking you. I ran out to the field where the lights were. I was gonna beat the hell out of him. I mean beat the living shit out of him."

His voice got louder with each sentence. "Yeah, so I ran out there. And you know what that Randy," he spit out his name, "that Randy told me. You had a baby. I called him a liar. Yeah, I called him a liar. And you know what? He laughed at me. Called me a stupid kid trying to make out with you."

He kicked at the ground and bit at his lip. CC thought he might draw blood and reached out to touch him, to comfort him, but he drew away from her, yanked his arm up so she couldn't touch it. "So, me, stupid kid me," Eric went on, "I told him I was gonna beat him up. But the sheriff held me back, and then he yells at me even though his lip was mostly split from Bud's beating, he yells, 'you couldn't make it with her, but that colored did. He screwed her and she had a baby.' And he laughed with blood dripping down his ugly face and just 'bout coughed his head off. I wanted to kill him."

In spite of the back pain, CC leaned over and put her hands on her knees, anything to keep from listening to any more. She was tired of having to defend herself, but she knew she had to get up and face Eric. "Eric, you can think what you want about me, but one thing I've learned this summer is that I don't have to explain myself to anyone. I had a baby and I went to a home and signed her over for adoption. She was beautiful."

Eric stared at her. She broke the standoff. "I've been through a lot, but I'm not apologizing for having that baby."

Eric continued to stare at her and finally broke the silence. "I need to back off and talk to you another time. I don't know. I just don't know." He shuffled his boots some more and looked away. "I'm sorry he hurt you, but this is too much. I thought I knew you, but you never said anything about this. I never knew you had a baby. I gotta go." He jumped the fence and looked back at her. "How could you? How could you have that baby and just come here like nothing happened?" He turned towards Gibbs' place and sauntered off. He didn't look back again.

CC heard Johnny walking up behind her. Without turning around, she said, "I guess you heard that."

He put his arms over her shoulders. "Yep, I heard. C'mon. Let's get back in the wagon."

"What do you think is going to happen with him? Think he'll get over any of this?"

Johnny didn't answer but pulled her gently toward the wagon. "I'll help you up. Let's take that ride."

He let Lady meander along the line of juniper trees both keeping thoughts to themselves, until CC asked him again, "You think he could get over this?"

Johnny pulled the reins back, "Whoa, gal." He faced CC and brushed a fly away from her head. "It looks like he has some thinking to do. I would, too, if I was him. I'd let him be for a while, and when, and if, he comes around, treat him like you always have. Don't push. Just see what happens."

"If he comes around? You think he won't?"

Johnny didn't answer. He shook the reins and Lady took off again. CC was quiet, thinking about the baby. She remembered being ashamed about giving up her baby for adoption and wondering what people would think of her. A few folks back home knew she was pregnant, but she hadn't figured that anyone here would find out about her baby.

CC had seen her days after she was born at the home. It was almost magical that something so amazing could be born from her. The baby's skin was a pretty caramel color and she had these dainty little hands and feet. CC looked down at her own hands and the sun had turned her skin to almost the same shade.

They let CC see and touch her baby before she left the home. Last march. The baby had tufts of black curly hair on the top of her head that CC ran her fingers through. When CC first looked at her, she seemed so dainty. Then she opened her eyes and stared at CC like she had been waiting for her, waiting to see what she looked like, too. And the amazing thing was, her blue eyes matched CC's. She had CC's eyes.

Her little girl was beautiful. She was who she was supposed to be, just like God made her. CC could never feel bad about that. And she sure as hell wasn't going to apologize about it. Not to anyone. Including Eric Ralston.

CHAPTER 37

CC took a deep breath before entering the warm kitchen. She had started healing after a few days and began riding again. She wasn't in the mood to answer any questions about how she felt. She was tired of talking about it. Gran stirred a pot on the stove and Uncle Bud was in his usual spot by the window. She wanted to say hello and get upstairs so she wouldn't let anything slip about not seeing Eric again today. It had been three long days since the encounter when he told her how he felt about keeping her secret from him.

Gran stopped her. "Just been thinking about you. Let's sit and put more ice on your face. It's still bruised."

"Not now, and what good will ice do at this point. It's helped as much as it can." She immediately felt bad about snapping at Gran, but couldn't everyone leave her alone? Weren't things bad enough?

She thought quick and regrouped since Gran stood at the sink staring at her with those arched brows. "Have you heard anything about Randy? What they're going to do with him?"

"I just got off the phone before you came in." Gran looked at Bud. "The sheriff called the police in New Orleans. Seems that Randy is wanted there. The judge will decide what to do, but he's staying in jail. Not going anywhere."

"Wait." CC bolted up in her chair. "He's not going back right away to New Orleans, is he? I mean I want to have my say about what he did to me. He's not running out on these charges. He deserves to pay for what he did here. To me. I couldn't talk about it back in New Orleans, but I'm going to now." CC was adamant.

"I already told the sheriff to keep us posted and we want to make sure he answers for what he did to you. Your Gramps and I are not going to let him get away from this part of the state before he answers for his crimes here."

"Absolutely, Gran."

"Sheriff Jack is busy on our behalf. He talked to Gibbs again and he took Johnny's statement about what he saw in the shed. Apparently, the sheriff went to a county agents' meeting. There's more involved with this DDT spraying than your Gramps or I imagined, but we need to wait and get more information from him."

Gran continued. "Those boys are out on bail, but one of them, the youngest, said they didn't mean to run you and Addy off the road. He says it got out of hand. They didn't mean anything."

CC grunted. "They're making up some lies. They were yelling stuff at us when they forced us off the road. If Eric hadn't come along..." She stopped herself when she said his name and looked out the window.

"Anything wrong?" Gran twisted in her chair. "I know Gramps saw him running off from the bunkhouse the other night after your fight with your mother."

CC folded her hands together on the table. "I saw Eric when I went riding with Johnny, but too much is going on and I don't want to talk about it right now." She took a deep breath. "What about Mama?"

"Your Gramps is in town with her for a while. Do you want to talk to her?"

CC just shook her head. "No, not now. I was hoping she'd go back to New Orleans."

Gran patted her hands. "She's still at the hotel." Gran looked at Bud again and CC wondered if there was anything else on her mind.

"What? Is there something else, Gran?"

"Yes. There is. When you were yelling at your mother you said you wish you had kept the baby. Did you mean that? We can talk about it. We can talk about anything."

She thought about the awful things Randy said. What Mama said in the barn about Negroes. And the way Eric acted today. She straightened up in the chair. "No. I think I did the right thing. But I guess I would like to know that she's all right. And I don't know how to like, check on her. Do you, Gran?"

When she looked across the table, Gran had tears forming in her eyes. "Oh Gran. Don't cry."

Gran leaned back in her chair and took a big gulp of air. "Oh, my darlin'. Don't worry about me. I am just so proud of you. I'm not crying sad. And if it's possible on God's green earth, we will find a way to see about your baby. I will make some calls later today."

"OK, but let's talk about what you find out. I'm just not sure what I want to do."

CC lifted herself out of the chair. "Geez. I am still stiff. I'm going to call Addy and see if she wants to take a ride early tomorrow out to the bible school. I need to see Star and the other kids. Addy said they've been asking about me. And I need to think about something else." She stretched her back again.

"I'm going to my room. I'll get some more ice in a while." When she got to the landing, CC turned to see Uncle Bud waving at her. She wanted to let him know one more time she was okay. "Sissy all right."

When CC climbed the stairs to her bedroom, she was looking forward to time alone. She started looking through the records Addy brought over the other night. She didn't have a chance to bring any of hers from New Orleans because she didn't get much of a chance to pack when she left New Orleans. She smiled as she thumbed through them. Couple of Elvis, of course, and the Everly Brothers remembering how much Addy liked that country twang.

She wished she had her Supremes and Beatles records. She had that new forty-five of theirs. She remembered talking to Eric about the new hits. He was the only person at the party who knew much about them.

Eric. What will happen? Did he mean he would talk to her later? He was so different. Could he accept her the same way?

She rolled over in the bed. How could she expect him to understand? It was a lot. It just happened a few months ago but seemed longer.

I didn't lie to him, just didn't tell him everything. But why should I? It happened before I came here. And I'm tired of blaming myself for the baby. I made a mistake.

Everything CC felt for Eric caused a tightness in her chest and ached. She didn't know if it was the attack from Randy or the pain of what Eric said to her. Or both. He looked so different when he told her about knowing everything. Hell, he is different.

She thought about Gran's description of the boys who tried to run them off the road. She wanted to talk to Addy tomorrow and make sure they'd be going together to testify if need be.

CC put the radio on that local station that stayed on until midnight and turned the light out so Gran would know she was trying to go to sleep. She managed to sleep even with the bad dreams. Randy was chasing her across a field. She escaped from him even though he grabbed at her clothes and almost caught her. She woke a couple of times and was panting and sweating as though she had been running.

But when the first rooster crowed, her eyes opened. Addy told her to call if she couldn't sleep, but she didn't want to wake her early. She decided to slip her jeans and a shirt on and tiptoe downstairs to make coffee for everyone. On the porch she could watch the sun rising.

She tiptoed, but Gramps was already sitting on the porch drinking his first cup. She slipped up behind him and hugged his neck. "Thought I could beat you. Guess not. At least I can have a cup with you."

She brought her cup out and the two of them sat for a while. "Is Uncle Bud up yet?"

Gramps snorted. "Yep. He's back to his old self. Already getting them couple of cows out to pasture."

"I have to ask, Gramps. How is Mama?"

He cleared his throat and tossed the rest of his coffee off the porch. "She's messed up I guess is the best way to say it. She blames herself for everything – bringing Randy here, going out with him drinking after they got here."

"What about her own drinking?"

He ran his hand through his hair. "She didn't say anything, but CC, I think you need to talk to her. Understand you're mad, but you're gonna have to sit down with her yourself and explain how all this has hit you."

He turned back and smiled at her. "What're you up to today?"

"I'm taking a ride with Addy out to the bible school. There's this little kid I read to, and I want to check on her."

"Your face looks better. They'll be so glad to see you." He smiled again and picked up his mug. "I'm heading out. Going to work. Call Addy. Make her get an early start."

CC thought that was a good idea. The sun was up and she wanted to get a move on. In the kitchen she walked straight to the phone and dialed Addy's number. She picked up on the first ring. "Thought you'd never call, girlfriend."

That made CC laugh. "When can you pick me up, my number one and only girlfriend."

Addy laughed in turn. "I can be there in a few minutes. Already dressed."

CC called out to Gran she was leaving just as Addy pulled into the driveway. When she walked out to the truck, she heard "Walk on By" blaring on the radio and motioned to Addy to turn it down. Jumping in the truck, she asked, "You know who's singing that?"

"Dionne Warwick. Just heard the announcer intro it."

"Sounds good. Is it too early to go out to the bible school?"

Addy turned her way, "It'll soon be eight. Most of the kids are already there. They get breakfast there. Did you get any sleep?"

CC leaned her head against the seat. "Some. Had some bad dreams. Nightmares I suppose. He was chasing me and I barely got away."

"That would have kept me up. Your face is still a little black and blue, but it's not as swollen."

"Gran offered to put makeup on it, but she was still in bed. Gramps said to forget about it. You think it will scare the kids or something?"

"I hate to say this, but a lot of those kids are used to seeing people beat up. Let's just see how it goes."

The girls settled in to the early morning ride and Addy turned the music up again. CC had a little sad moment when "My Boyfriends Back" played, wondering if she'd see Eric at the farm again, but tried not to think about him. She wanted to see Star and Miss Eugenia, the teacher.

Addy pulled under the big oak in front of the white frame church. CC opened her door and sat for a minute. She remembered the first time she visited the Vacation Bible School with Addy and met Star. She felt the soft rustle of the branches and the birds' chirping. That hadn't changed. Uncle Bud would love it here, she thought.

Addy grinned a big one at her. "Come on girlfriend. Let's go visit the summer warriors inside."

CC grinned back. She loved Addy's nickname for the kids. They walked around to the side door that led to the school. The pretty cross still hung on the little stain glass window and a bell tinkled when they opened the door. She hoped Star was here.

She noticed the odor of paste as soon as they opened the door. Her eyes were drawn to the colorful mobiles hanging all over the room and someone was playing "Three Blind Mice" on the small phonograph in the corner. Miss Eugenia sat in the rocking chair in the front of the room. It's like walking into a fairy tale, CC thought, and Miss Eugenia is the queen.

She sure looked like a queen. Today her hair was up in some kind of twist on top of her head. As the girls walked closer to her, her face erupted into a wide smile, her full lips were colored with bright red lipstick. Her eyes grew larger as the smile expanded. CC knew now why she remembered her. She looked like royalty, just like in the stories CC read as a child.

"Why hello you two, glad you are back. The children are happy to see you."

CC turned hoping she didn't scare anybody. She thought about saying something to Miss Eugenia about her appearance, but before she could say anything, the lovely teacher asked, "CC, isn't it? So very glad you're with us. Star has been asking about you."

And with her soothing voice, CC knew she didn't have to worry. This was one place where she was accepted. "Where is she? Star, I mean."

"Right behind you. She was afraid you wouldn't be back after the incident on the road."

CC swung around and Star stood holding a copy of *Charlotte's Web*. "I remember that book. We read it last time I was here, didn't we?"

Star shook her head and whispered, "You want to read it again?"

CC didn't hesitate. "That's why I came. Let's sit in our spot. You remember the characters? Their names?"

CC had to lean in to her as she half whispered, "Wilbur. He was the pig. Fern, she was the girl on the farm who saved the pig. And Charlotte, the spider."

"That's right. You remember them." It was so easy to get comfortable with the little well-scrubbed pretty girl. CC loved looking at her as they read. Her beautiful mocha skin shone and her brown eyes sparkled as they moved through the pages. When Miss Eugenia announced snack time in the next room, Star whispered, "Can we stay here?" CC's heart melted as she thought about leaving her own baby but having a little friend here who needed her. She didn't have to abandon Star.

They read until Addy tapped her on the shoulder and said "Time to go," and made a sad face at Star. CC in turn made a sad face at both of them, but handed Star the book to put away. "But we'll finish it. I'll be back." It was hard to leave her.

On the way to the car, Addy asked, "You all right CC? I mean I noticed your face and you winced a little when you got down on the floor. I could tell Miss Eugenia was concerned."

CC looked up at the big oak tree. "Yep, I'm okay, I guess. It's two different worlds you know. A couple of nights ago getting assaulted by Randy. And then the farm and here."

They jumped in Addy's truck and she started to turn the radio knob. "Wait, let's talk first." CC swallowed hard. "I wanted to tell you about something. So, I saw Eric the day after the attack in the field. He heard everything about, you know, Randy, the baby."

Addy looked at her with raised brows. "You mean about the fact that you had a baby and she is part colored?" When CC nodded, she asked, "How'd that go?"

"He wasn't too understanding, to say the least," CC sighed. "But it got me thinking. Thinking about seeing the baby, my baby I mean" She turned to face Addy. "She was beautiful. Addy, she had blue eyes and this gorgeous skin, like Star's."

She heard Addy breathe, "Wow."

CC remembered how hard she tried to forget the baby when she left the nursery that last day. She walked down the steps when she left and looked straight ahead, willing herself to keep moving. She believed she could come to Ruston and keep acting like she was sixteen and go back to school and do what other kids do. But it wasn't the same. She felt different, like older. She wanted to crack jokes like she used to, but nothing was funny anymore.

"Addy, I think I'm going to try to see her. Seeing Star today made me want to, like check on her. I want to know she's living with someone nice and she'll be all right. I signed those papers with Mama, and I still know it was right, but Addy..." she stopped in mid-sentence. "I wish I had more time back then to see her."

She leaned back against the seat. "I'm asking Gran to help me see her. Don't know if we can, but I have to try."

CC was surprised when Addy pulled off the road and stopped the truck. After she put the gear in neutral, she turned to her with tears in her eyes. "CC, you are something. Whatever I can do I will. If you want me to go with you. I..." Addy couldn't finish her sentence. CC hugged her and both girls had a good girls' cry together without realizing it was almost exactly where they were driven off the road a couple of weeks before.

When they finished hugging, she tried to get CC to commit to living in Ruston and going to high school. "I'll be the class of sixty-five. We'll have a lot of fun. You can go to senior parties with me. I heard you tell Sar you'd be back. Think you'll stay? "

CC hadn't thought about it with everything going on. "We'll see. I guess it will take time to sort all this stuff out with the sheriff. There's a list." CC quipped.

By that time, they were on the farm driveway. CC jumped out of the truck and started for the back porch. She saw Uncle Bud leaning over in his vegetable bed and could hear him mumbling to himself, "Little bugs, stay away, come again another day," over and over again.

"Hey, Uncle. Weeding those critters out? Doesn't look like you have many weeds." When he looked up, he had a sweet smile she remembered from all her summers on the farm.

He dusted his hands on his pants' legs and called out to her. "Wanna help Sissy?"

"Hahaha." She chuckled. "It's sweltering out here. You don't get a burn?"

He giggled, "Nope. Always red. Look?" he held up both freckled arms and giggled again.

Watching him she thought about what Johnny said when he arrived at the farm this summer. He told her he wanted to help Gramps and take care of his dad so they could keep him here. "I know Gramps and Gran want to take care of my dad, but they are getting old. If I live here, they won't put him in one of those institutions."

CC thought about her talk just now with Addy. She believed if she stayed for a year or two, she could help, too. Wouldn't stay forever though. Couldn't live in the country the rest of my life, no way.

She waved her hand at her uncle and started for the porch. As soon as she hit the screen door, she could make out Gran in her house dress sitting in one chair and Mama perched across from her.

CC turned away and leaned against one of Gran's plant racks. Rubbing her forehead, she tried to take a breath before entering. How did Mama feel about her tirade the other night? Did she want to have it out again? Star made her feel calm and the ride with Addy helped. She didn't feel ready for another fight, but seeing her now, well, who knows what will happen.

CC took a deep breath and started for the kitchen door.

CHAPTER 38

CC exhaled as she pulled the handle on the creaky screen door. What would Mama's attitude be now? Would she want to continue with the accusations? She rolled her shoulders back, exhaled, and walked in the kitchen.

But CC's breath was taken away by the sight of Mama sitting at the table. She looked up at CC with what had to be the most sorrowful eyes ever. She had dark circles underneath her blue eyes and CC could tell she had been crying. Not drunk crying or beagle-drooping like she had seen so many times in New Orleans. This was red-eyed, honest drops of sorrow.

To make the sight complete, Mama's hands were shaking so bad they were a blur. More than the eyes, the sight of the shakes made CC want to run across the table and grab her and hug her just as she had held Addy minutes before. Before she could, Mama braced herself on the edge of the kitchen table and stood. "Cicely, CC, your face. It's still bruised. Are you all right? God, I'm sorry. I need to stop asking that question." She collapsed in her chair, mouth open, tears forming again, hands trembling.

CC stood still and felt Gran turning her chair around to face her. "Your mama asked Gramps if he would drive her out here to see you." With that Gran stood and walked over to the sink. With her back to both of them, she announced, "I baked the layers for that cake this morning for Bud. You know, before it got too hot."

"Would Mama would like to see Uncle Bud's swollen hands before we talk some more?"

When Mama's face dropped, CC was sorry she had gone for the kill. CC could hear the pain in Mama's voice as she murmured, "I did see him, CC. I feel terrible about all of it, and sorry you both were hurt."

CC walked back to the door and leaned against the musty screen. She could feel the pain from the last couple of days in her back when Randy shoved her to the ground. She hadn't noticed her head throbbing in the truck with Addy, but it ached now.

Resting her forehead on the screen she stared at the yard and barn. All the memories of Johnny walking across the yard the first time, of Eric finding her by the barn, of protecting Uncle Bud that first day were some of her best memories. They seemed to be overshadowed by Randy's attack and Eric's walking away from her.

She had forced herself to lock the image of the little one in a closet in her head. It was crazy, but the confrontation with Eric made her want to see her baby again. And spending time with Star and Addy made her want to see the baby even more. Was her baby safe? CC wanted to know.

She walked back to the table and drew up a chair. "Gran, did you tell her what I want to do? About the baby I mean."

Gran came back to the table and rested in her chair. "Thought you should tell her."

Not sure why, CC braced herself for an argument. "Look, Mama. I know you hated Marcus and the fact he got me pregnant." Mama started to speak, but CC continued before she could interrupt her. "No, I know he didn't get me pregnant. We both did it and had a baby. Mama, why didn't you want to see her? I have to ask. In Shreveport, before we left."

"Cicely, CC. That's not true, I told you before we left Shreveport, I didn't want to see her because I didn't know what to expect."

CC stared at her in disbelief. Mama hid her trembling hands below the table. CC wanted to ask her when she had her last drink, but decided to can that question 'til later. "What to expect? I didn't know what to expect. It was hard to see her alone, Mama. Without you. That's why I asked you to go to the cottage with me. Remember?"

For the first time, Gran spoke. "What's the cottage?"

"It was a little house, a nursery in the back of the home where they kept the newborns until the papers were signed." CC said in a faraway tone. "You could hear them crying at night waiting to get a bottle I guess."

Mama reached across the table to cover CC's hands but she drew them back on her lap when CC stiffened.

"Mama, that's not exactly what you said when I asked you to go with me to see her before we left. Remember? You told me you couldn't bear to see her because you didn't want to see your daughter have a half-colored child. You were ashamed of her, weren't you?"

Mama sat back in her chair. "Oh, CC. I guess you're right. I'm not proud of it, but it's how I felt. Wish I had gone with you. But, Cicely, I did my best. It was hard taking my sixteen-year-old daughter to a home for unwed mothers and leaving her with strangers. The whole thing was just, just..."

"Wait!" CC stood up. "You're not saying I embarrassed you?"

Gran interrupted. "Let's try to talk this out without yelling or accusing each other. Please."

"All right. One question. Mama, when did you have your last drink?"

"Is now the time to ask that, CC?" Gran looked exasperated.

"It's all right, Mother. CC wants to know how sober I am before we talk further. That right, Cicely?" She didn't wait for an answer. "Not for three nights ago after I left the bunkhouse."

She waited for Mama to say more, but she sat with eyes downcast so CC got up and walked over to the sink. She poured a glass of water and brought it back to the table and put it in front of her mother.

The three generations stared at their hands or at the faded walls. CC wanted to get up and go outside and saddle Lady. She was tired of this whole confrontation business with Mama, and she knew it bothered Gran. But she also knew she wasn't finished.

"Mama, it was hard for me because I didn't want to leave my baby. Not because I thought I could keep her. Because I wanted to make sure she would be with someone who could care for her and love her, no matter what. And I was afraid."

Both women stared at CC. It was Gran who asked first. "Scared of what, Sweetheart?"

CC started rocking in her chair. Her hands sat tightly in her lap and her eyes were downcast. "Scared that she'd think I abandoned her. Later, you know? Cause I didn't want her. That I just left her."

She rubbed the tears away with her fingers. Mama stood up quietly and walked around the table and pulled the extra chair by her side. She pushed CC's hair out of her eyes and stared gently into her moist eyes.

"Why didn't I even think about keeping her, Mama?"

The clock on the wall ticked and was the only sound, the three generations lost in their own thoughts. CC thought about her own question and tried to answer it herself. "Honestly, I didn't know if I was capable of taking her with me. Didn't know if I could care for her. I wanted to finish school and make a life. Is that terrible, Gran?"

She turned to the one person she knew would be honest with her and not just protect her feelings. Gran shifted in her chair and looked over at CC. "You did care for her in my book. You went to a proper home for unwed mothers, and she was placed legally with a family who will care for her, hopefully love her. You are so smart. You can go on and finish school, go to college, and be the big success in this family," as she raised her arms like scoring a touchdown.

"Along with Johnny, remember?" CC gave a little laugh at her own comment. CC noticed Mama's hands weren't trembling anymore.

"Gran, did you make that call we talked about?"

"I called our lawyer, Ted. You don't know him but that's okay. Your Gramps and I have known him for years. He said we just need a court order. Which sounds like a big deal, but he said he could get one in a couple of days around here. So, it's all up to you. Your Mama and I are gonna let you decide. Right, Loreen?"

Loreen settled back in her chair and nodded. "Yes, Mother. CC will decide."

CC looked back and forth at the two women and it occurred to her that Mama sounded better. She just hoped she would stay sober. "I just want to check on her. I don't even know yet if I want to go back to that place. To see Miss Dalton again. I just want to check on her."

CC looked up at the clock. "I'm going upstairs. I need to think about this some more."

She got up from her chair to leave the kitchen but turned back. She knew Mama needed a vote of confidence. "I'm glad we're talking about this together." Mama smiled in return.

Upstairs in her bedroom, CC noticed the slight breeze coming through her open window. She plopped down on the unmade bed and couldn't help thinking about Eric. It had been days since she saw him out in the field and she wondered if he felt any different about her. Probably not, because he could have found her again and talked to her.

Addy was right. If he still liked her, he would let her know. He's not going to change. He was brought up like the rest of the kids around here. She was tired of always having to be worried about what she said around these people.

She thought about the baby and wondered what she would be like. Will she be good at anything? Like Marcus? Or will CC ever know anything about her as she gets older?

CC sat up in bed and started thinking about her rights. Do I have a right to know anything about this little girl? What are my rights? Did I give them up when Mama signed the papers? What am I getting into by asking to see her? Do I even want to go back to that home and see Miss Dalton? She was okay, but do I want to return to that home?

CC remembered the trip to Shreveport from New Orleans and entering the home the first time.

It had been a long lonely drive to Shreveport from New Orleans when Mama took CC to the maternity home. She could tell Mama felt jittery at first like she did most mornings, but her hands stopped shaking as they got about halfway there. Mama tried to start a conversation, but the awkwardness hung between them.

"Let me know when you get hungry. We can stop."

Given the circumstances of the drive, CC thought eating was about the only common ground between them. "Not hungry, Mama. Haven't been lately."

"I guess you know you need to eat for the baby too." Then Mama sighed pretty loud like she was disgusted. "I can't believe this. I can't believe I'm driving you to a maternity home. You know, CC, you backed yourself into this. You waited too long to tell me. We had to do it this way. You should be in school instead of a home for unwed mothers. You're smart. I'll give you that."

"Not that smart, right, Mama? I wouldn't be sitting here pregnant if I was that smart." They glanced at each other and that shut down any further talk for a while. It took them eight hours to get to Shreveport and find the home. They had to stop a few times for CC to go to the bathroom and to grab a sandwich to eat in the car.

CC remembered standing on the sidewalk with Mama when they arrived. As lonely as the drive had been, it didn't compare to the awful feeling in the pit of her stomach as she approached the front door to that place. She thought she might throw up, and she knew it wasn't morning sickness. Something came from deep inside her and her arms felt like little needles were pricking her.

CC took a deep breath. It looked like a haunted house she and her friends found one Halloween. Large, dark shutters that needed painting framed the huge two-story monstrosity. The overgrown shrubs in the front yard almost hid the entrance, and CC stopped in her tracks when she saw the black door with green trim.

Mama grabbed CC's tattered grey suitcase and held her by the other arm. She gave her a slight push to get her moving toward the black door. CC fought the impulse to grab Mama and beg her to take her back home. To somehow make this all go away. But by the time Mama learned about the pregnancy, it was too late to turn back. CC decided to trust her mother when she realized her only choice was the home and adoption.

CC stood up and decided to go downstairs. Memories of the first day at the home made her realize she needed to talk to Gran and Mama some more.

On the way down, CC thought she heard Johnny in the kitchen but realized it was the radio. As she entered, Gran was back at the sink and Mama sat twirling an empty coffee mug at the table.

"I need to ask this, Mama. Do I have a right to do this? I mean we signed those papers. Do I have any rights?"

Gran came back to the table and patted a chair for CC. "Sit back down. I can understand what you're asking. Ted asked me a couple of things."

"Like what, Gran?"

"Loreen, did you have a lawyer present? I mean when you signed the documents?"

Mama and CC looked at each other, but it was Mama who spoke up. "I suppose we had made up our minds and didn't think about that. No, we didn't."

CC was also thinking about the adoptive parents. "Well, let's talk about the new parents, or the only parents she's known these last five months. Here we come, busting into those people's lives. I mean will they be mad or just scared that I want something?"

Gran spoke up again. "I think that's something you should think about. How much do you want to interfere and how much can you do legally? I think legally you can see them, but how will it feel?"

They sat looking at each other until CC finally spoke up. "I want to see her one more time. Like I told you before, Gran. I need to see that's she's all right and the family is happy with her. I need to know that I did the right thing."

Mama was still twirling the cup. "I would like that too, CC. If it's alright with you."

CC's voice broke. "She is your granddaughter, Mama."

CHAPTER 39

About ten days later they were in the car on the way to Shreveport. It happened faster than CC thought it could.

Gran talked to the lawyer and as she said, he obtained a court order in a few days. Since Mama knew Miss Dalton from the home, she called and made an appointment for a few days later.

"Did you explain what we wanted, Mama?" CC asked.

"I did. She didn't seem surprised. Like it happens every day."

They talked very little about going to the home once the plans were made. It had been a tough time for CC during the wait time for the court order and arranging an appointment. CC was accustomed to watching Mama when she wasn't drinking, but this was different. Instead of lying around all the time like she did in New Orleans, she took walks around the farm and chipped in with some chores. CC noticed her hands weren't trembling at supper and she ate a whole meal before picking up the dishes.

CC wondered if Mama was as nervous as she was. CC dreaded returning to the home, but dreaded even more facing Miss Dalton. It seemed so cut and dry the day of the signing, and she was still plagued by the feeling that she didn't have any rights at all.

She had signed the papers, hadn't she? So had Mama. Miss Dalton explained in the meeting that she was giving up parental rights. What parental rights CC wondered at the time? She never had any to begin with.

All these questions lingered in CC's mind, but she felt determined to go through with the appointment. Gran told her to take it one step at a time.

More than once, CC said, "Gran, the only reason I can do this is because you're helping me."

So far Mama stayed sober and seemed intent on going. After everything that happened in the last few days, CC knew that was a miracle. But she knew it was hard for Mama. She watched her so many times trying to stay away from drinking. CC just prayed she could make it this time, or at least long enough to see the baby. Deep down, she knew this was good for Mama as well as for her.

CC hadn't seen Eric in several days and wondered if he would ever come around again, but she was determined to hold her ground. No more apologies for mistakes that were made in the past.

She called Addy as soon as the plans were made. "Hey, girlfriend, just wanted you to know we're going to Shreveport tomorrow. Tell Star when you see her, I will be back soon."

"That's good, girlfriend. I think you're doing the right thing and I think you are so brave. Call me as soon as you get back. Okay?"

"Sure enough."

They took off and CC insisted on sitting on the back seat. She needed that time to herself without any kind of chatter between Gran and Mama.

They settled into a silence each guarding their thoughts. Mama never did answer CC's questions about how she felt about seeing the little girl. She had said to her, "She is your granddaughter. Are you curious after all?"

CC wanted her to say she wanted to see her. Instead Mama said, "You have to make the decision. I will go along with whatever you want to do."

They drove and CC heard the two women chatting in the front seat, but she didn't focus on them. Her thoughts were on the last days of her pregnancy before the papers were signed.

CC didn't remember her baby's birth in the hospital. Brief memories surfaced afterwards. In pre-delivery, she remembered being shaved in her pubic area. When she asked why, the nurse said, "so you'll be clean."

The nurse started to walk briskly out of the small room, turned and quipped, "It's all right young lady, you won't remember anything." She wanted to ask why but the woman in the white uniform left and never came back. Or at least CC didn't remember seeing her again. And she was right. She didn't remember anything after that.

The next thing she did remember was the obstetrician after the delivery. He was pulling her arms and shouting at her to calm down.

"Cicely, stop it! Calm down! You have to stop screaming and kicking! Stop it! You already had your baby. And you're going to be fine."

She wanted to ask whether it was a boy or a girl but she couldn't make her lips move. She stayed in the hospital for three days. One kind nurse told her she had a girl about seven pounds. When she asked another nurse if she could see her, she was told girls couldn't see their illegitimate babies until the agency approved it. CC rolled over and whimpered in her pillow.

The doctor told her later she panicked after the delivery and he had to give he a sedative to calm her down. When she told him she couldn't remember anything about the delivery, he told her she received a twilight sleep treatment. She had shots to keep her from remembering the pain and the ordeal of childbirth.

Living in the home was not easy. She had to get along with a group of pregnant women and girls of all ages. Fighting or at least arguments broke out, constantly, but laughter, too. She tried not to get close to anyone because she knew she would be leaving and would never see them again.

Lost in her thoughts as she watched the flat green fields roll by, she was surprised when Gran called out, "We're almost there. The city is up ahead. This is the outskirts of Shreveport."

CC's heart started thumping as she grew more nervous. She was going to upset lives, and for what? Just so she could see her five-month-old daughter. She asked herself again if she had any right to do this, but these plans had been made. She knew she had to do this. She would be going back to school soon after Labor Day. She couldn't wait until then. She might lose her nerve.

Gran explained to her that she and Loreen would try to handle the conversation with Miss Dalton. She might have to answer questions, but they were there for her.

Gran didn't have any trouble locating the home. CC wished it had taken longer. She needed more time to prepare. Prepare for what, she thought. To make it worse, Gran parked in front and the first thing CC saw was the black door. Mama turned around from the front seat and looked at her, and there was that soft smile. CC hadn't realized before that Mama smiled the same way as Uncle Bud.

Gran put the car in gear and they sat for a minute before she said, "I guess we're getting out, right?"

CC heard herself say, "Right," and surprised herself by immediately opening the rear door. It creaked so loud, she giggled.

"Giggling breaks the tension," Mama said. Then all three broke into the saddest giggle CC could imagine. Then out of the blue, Gran said, "I'm going to say a little prayer. Anyone want to join me?"

"Go ahead," CC said.

"Lord, open the way for us. This is hard for CC and Loreen and me. If this is the right path, lead us." They all said amen together and Gran said, "Let's go."

The three ladies started walking up the cracked sidewalk to the front of the house. CC gulped again as they approached the door. Mama stepped back so CC could walk in front of her and whispered, "Looks like I have your back."

CC nodded and kept walking. She knew she needed to keep moving. If she didn't, she might run back to the car, but there was no turning back now.

CC walked up to the front door and knocked. She remembered they were not allowed to open the door, so she wasn't surprised when Miss Dalton opened it. CC faced her but couldn't find the words to announce why they were here.

Mama took over and said, "Good afternoon. We're here for our appointment, The Scotts. Actually, all three of us. You remember Cicely and me. This is my mother, CC's, Cicely's, grandmother, Mrs. Bess Scott."

CC looked down at her hand and realized Miss Dalton waited for her to shake hands. CC began by feeling out of place, the same way she felt when she left the place.

Miss Dalton invited the three of them into her office. It was in the front of the huge house. CC didn't remember the room being so bright. Large windows flooded the room. She had only been in here a couple of times - when she arrived the beginning of January and when she left at the end of March - and it seemed gloomy then. Today, it was sunlit and airy.

Three chairs were already arranged in front of Miss Dalton's large desk. Gran and Mama took the end ones, leaving CC sitting in the middle in front of the woman.

Gran started. "You know why we're here, and Miss Dalton, we - I - want to be very clear. I know you followed all legal guidelines. You're a reputable agency both in caring for your residents and in adoption procedures. I, we're not here to question that." She looked at CC and Mama as she spoke. Mama nodded in agreement. CC remained silent.

"Then tell me why you're here, please."

Mama started. "As I said on the phone, we, actually, I mean Cicely..."

CC touched Mama's forearm to stop her in mid-sentence. "I would like to speak."

Everyone turned to face CC. "Before I start, may I ask you to pull the shade down in back of you. The glare is keeping me from seeing your face, and it's uncomfortable."

A slight smile crossed Miss Dalton's mouth as she swiveled in her desk chair and pulled the shade. "How's that? Any better?"

"I appreciate it." CC cleared her throat and folded her hands in her lap to hide any trembling. "I want to agree with my grandmother. You took good care of me when I was here. The housemother was very caring, and..." CC coughed again and tried to clear her throat.

Miss Dalton got up and poured a glass of water for her. Then asked, "How about you?" as she looked at Gran and Mama.

CC didn't notice what they said and continued. She knew she had to say what she came to say before she chickened out. "I'm speaking and requesting this because I'm the one who got pregnant and decided to come here and have the baby. Even though I am a minor and my mother had to sign the adoption papers, or release or whatever you call it, it was all up to me. And today is up to me. Gran and Mama told me I had to make my own decision."

"Do I want to see the baby? Yes."

"Cicely, you did see the baby. Every resident is allowed to see her baby before any signing takes place."

Gran broke in, "Yes, but that was a very emotional time, especially in a young girl's life."

"Excuse me, Gran." CC looked around the room again before she continued. "When I was here the last time, Miss Dalton, all I could think about was leaving. Getting back to New Orleans, to school. But now I've had time to think about it. To remember my child, the adoptive parents' child, in a little bed, so tiny, so healthy. All of that."

CC was determined not to cry because she needed to finish what she had to say. She pulled a tissue from the desk and wiped at her eyes before continuing.

"I remember she had curly dark hair, eyes like me, mocha like skin and she squirmed when I looked down, like she wanted me to pick her up. How old was she, do you remember, Miss Dalton?"

"I can look it up."

"I remember. She was seven days old. I saw her when she was seven days old. I was still recovering myself, but I remember."

The room fell silent.

"I remember what she looked like as a newborn. And all I'm asking now is to see her about five months later from a short distance, if that's what they prefer. To see what she looks like now. To see if she's still healthy and if the parents are happy."

CC wiped at her moist eyes again. "To be able to remember what she looks like and that she's okay. And that her parents love her. It will help me know I made the right decision to let her go, you know. That I didn't just abandon her."

"That's what I want, Miss Dalton."

CHAPTER 40

Questions lingered on the quiet drive home after meeting with Miss Dalton. CC wondered what Miss Dalton thought of her. And she still asked herself, *wouldn't it be better to leave them alone*?

Why couldn't she forget the whole business and go back to New Orleans? School starts right after Labor Day. She could go back in three weeks and act like nothing happened.

Oh God, she thought to herself. Would they make her stay in tenth grade? How could she live that down?

"Mama, if I go back home with you, what grade will I be in? Do I have to repeat tenth?"

Gran answered, "You can get those two credits from Miss Jessica if you finish the book and she said she could contact your previous counselor. You finished the first semester."

CC stopped her before she continued. "I guess those are crazy questions after just meeting with Miss Dalton. It popped into my head back here. What do y'all think about the meeting? She agreed to contact the parents. You have any idea how it will go?"

CC could see Mama nodding. "I guess we'll have to wait and see. But I got the impression that Miss Dalton is going to get on this as soon as she can. She said she would arrange a meeting."

CC knew Miss Dalton was satisfied with their answers and was glad Gran had the court order. She had said, "This way, we can move straight ahead if the parents agree. You have to understand. In most cases the adoption is sealed and there is little opportunity to contact them. I'm agreeing to speak with them. If they agree, I will let you know as soon as possible."

After going to all this trouble, CC hoped it would work out. It all hinged on the parents agreeing to meet.

When they returned to the farm, she called Addy to let her know it went okay. "You mean you'll get to see her?"

"It looks like the lady in charge will try to make it happen. We did everything we could. She's gonna talk to the adoptive parents."

"Wow! Did you talk? Did you say why you wanted to see her?"

"Yep. I tried and must have done all right. She smiled at me a little bit. She said I sounded mature."

"Ugh! Don't get too mature. Maybe you can start having some fun again soon. Let's spend time together riding or going to DQ while you're waiting. Take your mind off waiting to hear from them."

CC smiled. "Sounds good. Come over tomorrow. Johnny might be around, too."

"That sounds good. See you."

When she hung up, it was time for supper and she was exhausted. Gran had leftover chicken on the stove, so she nibbled at the food on her plate. Mama sat across from her. "CC, you did a great job today talking to Miss Dalton. You feel alright?"

"Yes. I'm glad you went with me. How about you? Are you staying here tonight?"

Mama grinned at her. "I'm fine and I'm gonna stay in that extra space down here."

CC hadn't thought about the bedroom upstairs in a while as Mama's room. "You know, Mama, that's still your bedroom. You want me to move down here?"

Mama put her cup down. "No, I'm good. You take that room and when you want to, we can fix it up to suit you."

CC looked over at Gran at the stove. "Why? Am I staying here?"

"Are you?" Mama asked in return.

They stared at each other, neither one not knowing what to say. Gran came over. "CC, you know you're welcome here. Do you know what you want to do?"

"I thought I should go back to New Orleans."

Mama reached across the table to cover CC's hands with her own. This time she didn't move away from Mama's touch. "CC, I'm going to be all right. Think about what you want to do. You're not supposed to take care of me. Not anymore. I'm all right. Really."

Their conversation was interrupted by Johnny and Gramps coming in from the porch. Uncle Bud trailed behind them.

Gramps chimed in when he walked through the door. "Yep, Johnny, you sure did a good job letting us know Gibbs was spraying around here. You know, Bess, it all worked out. I'm glad I never used that stuff."

"You mean the DDT?"

"Yep," as Gramps washed his hands at the sink. Johnny stood near him but looked at CC with a questioning stare. She mouthed 'okay' and gave him a thumbs up signal.

CC thought about the fight at the shed and wanted to know if that was settled. She didn't have to wait. Uncle Bud sat in his chair with Champ by his feet and Gramps settled in his chair at the table. "We told you about the spraying on a neighbors' property. The sheriff talked to the farmers' agency and learned that even if you spray another property accidentally, you're legally responsible for it. Gibbs has damaged our property and state land. He has to pay a penalty. Goes to us, Bess."

"Does Gibbs know that yet? Is he also going to be penalized some way for fighting with Johnny and hurting CC?"

CC noticed Gramps run his fingers through his wiry gray hair the way he did when he talked about something important to him. "Sheriff Jack thinks we all need to let that go. He'll pay the fine. After all, the kids broke into his shed. We're dropping it. So is Gibbs."

CC felt relieved hearing Gramps explain that part of it. Seeing Miss Dalton and trying to see her baby was enough for now. Not to mention taking legal action against those boys in the truck. She didn't want to get involved in any more legal stuff. She could tell by Gran's arched eyebrow that she waited for CC's reaction. CC mouthed to her also. "'Fine with me."

The table filled with everyone eating some of Gran's roast and potatoes. Uncle Bud sat quietly at his place and seemed content. CC waited for everyone to finish and watched Gramps walk out to the porch. Gran followed him but came back in the kitchen and motioned for CC to walk outside.

She stretched her back again and followed Gran out to the porch. Gramps sat in his rocker. The night air was cool for a change and CC noticed the sky was covered in stars. Champ trotted out expecting to go out for another walk but landed at CC's feet this time. She sat in the other rocker and scratched the top of the dog's head, and asked, "What's up?"

"Gramps wanted to tell you this out here himself."

He didn't hesitate. "Sheriff Jack needs you to come in tomorrow morning to file an official complaint and to identify Randy as the perpetrator. Since you're the only victim, he says this case rests on you. You can do it in writing and sign it, but you have to name him in person.

"He assaulted someone in a bar in New Orleans, too, and hurt him bad. May have to go back after he serves time here."

CC leaned back in the chair. Gran was standing near her and put her hand on CC's shoulder. She reached back and patted her hand before saying, "I will do it. I told Gran I wanted a voice in this. I want to make sure he pays for his crime here, too. Do you know what will happen to him?"

"At this point that's up to the judge. I don't think he is fighting this charge. Against you." Gramps twirled his hat in his hands while he talked. "You are the only victim, but we were all around you and him that night. We're witnesses. You and your grandmother can find out tomorrow."

CC realized again how tired she felt. Her eyes were red from lack of sleep and her back was beginning to hurt. She faced Gran to tell her she wanted to talk to Mama about going with her in the morning. "I'd like to have her with me to see how she faces Randy. See if it's finished. What do you think, Gran?"

"I think she'd want to see you through this just like she did today. You want me to talk to her? You can go upstairs and get some sleep. You look exhausted."

CC didn't need convincing. She trudged up the stairs reminding herself on the way up of the times she skipped up these steps, but not tonight.

Turning the light on, she was relieved she had this room to herself. She walked over to the window and breathed in some of the night air. It felt nice coming through her open window. She started looking for her t-shirt and bottoms and sat on the edge of the bed to take her sneakers off. Without looking over, she realized Mama entered the room.

"Good lord, the nights I laughed and cried in this room." She walked over to CC and brushed her hair away from her face. "How are you doing? I'm not staying. Wanted to tell you good night and tell you I want to go with you tomorrow." CC started to raise her arm to say something, but Mama stopped her. "I'm telling you again. I will be fine and CC, I need to do this with you. I am over him and want to protect you this time. Let me, please."

As tired as she was, CC stood up and gave her mother a hug. She finished changing and collapsed on the bed. Mama covered her and left the room softly.

CC slept through the night. Nobody chased her.

CHAPTER 41

Mama called CC from the back porch. "Time to leave for our appointment.'"

"Ugh. I wish I could forget that," she yelled at Mama. "Do we have to go right away?"

She could hear Mama's lilting laugh. "Let's go and get it over with. Have a nice lunch somewhere."

"All right, I need to go up and brush my hair." CC bounded up the stairs for another look at her outfit and hair. "May as well look my best for this."

She looked at her reflection in the dresser mirror and thought how different she looked since she got to the farm. She could see it now. She had a nice tan and her light brown hair was streaked blonde by the sun. Chestnut hair her mother always called it and she would always ask if she meant brown.

She bounced downstairs and received a big smile from Gran. "Glad to see you're in a good mood this morning. Should help you get through this appointment."

They walked out the kitchen with Mama jingling Gran's car keys. "Thanks, Mom. We'll be back after lunch."

CC avoided chatting on the way to town. Mama asked her if she was nervous about possibly facing Randy. "I wish I didn't have to face the DA and him, but I want to make sure he pays. How do you feel about it, Mama? Do you still have feelings for him?"

She noticed Mama tighten her grip on the steering wheel. She took a deep breath before saying, "I want to make sure he pays, too," as she pulled into a parking space in front of a brick one-story building. There were four long windows on either side of the large door, and CC could tell it was old.

Mama turned slightly after turning off the motor and said, "I'm sorry, Cicely. CC. I didn't listen to you and I will always regret it."

CC nodded and opened the car door. She wanted to face what she had to do.

They walked into the small building and Sheriff Jack came out of his office to greet them. "Want to introduce you to our assistant district attorney. She will take your statement, Cicely, with your mother's permission."

Mama spoke up. "CC will handle this. I'll sit next to her if that's all right."

The district attorney looked like she was still a college student with long, silky hair and little make up. Even though she was young, she got down to business. After shaking their hands, she led them down the shiny, clean tile hall. Her heels clicked on the smooth floor. She ushered them into a small office in the rear of the building. There was a polished empty desk with only four chairs in the room.

CC asked her, "Is the jailhouse here? Is he in this building?"

"No, the cells are in that brick complex next door, and he will be brought over when you're ready. You will see him behind one-way glass. Sound okay?"

CC nodded and sat up straight to signal she was ready.

It didn't take long. The young woman asked her to start at the beginning and tell what happened. CC gave her statement without any more tears. When she finished, the woman looked at her sympathetically and asked her to wait until it was typed up. When she returned to the room, they read the document. CC signed the last page and Mama signed the second line.

As the district attorney shuffled the papers, she said, "I don't know if anyone told you, but he pled guilty, no contest. You will identify him and the judge will sentence him later today."

Mama asked, "I'm surprised he didn't kick up more of a fuss. Has a temper."

"He has run out of options and wanted to get some kind of deal. Trying to stay out of a long-term sentence here and go back to New Orleans to face the lesser charge. But I think this judge will give him the maximum time."

CC turned to the district attorney. "May I identify him now? I'd like to get it over with as soon as possible."

They waited for a few minutes until they were led to another room and stood in front of a glass partition. It was stuffy and hot and CC could smell a disinfectant they used on the floors. The only sound was someone coughing in another room. CC stared at the streaked one-way glass. A door on the other side of the glass opened and a uniformed policeman brought a man into the room. She could hear him tell the prisoner to stand by a line marked on the floor.

CC gasped and felt her mother stiffen. She didn't recognize Randy at first. A different man stood in front of them. CC always thought of him as big, even tall, but he looked small. The man before them looked like he had shrunk to half of what she remembered.

It was over two weeks since she had seen him but his face changed. His eyes were bloodshot and sunken. His hair grew over his ears and his chin was hidden by stubble. The once cocky man had withered to this unkempt little man who looked like he needed help to stand.

CC heard someone ask "Is this the man who assaulted you, Cicely Scott?"

It took seconds for CC to realize the district attorney was asking her a question. She started to repeat it, but CC interrupted her the second time. "Yes, this is the man who assaulted me."

Mama put her arm though Cicely's and led her to the front door. When they stood next to their car, CC felt her legs buckle a little but she regained her strength and exhaled. She wondered if she actually breathed at all during the minutes looking at Randy.

Mama asked one question, "You okay?"

She nodded. "Are you?"

"I am. I decided to wait to tell you until this was over. Miss Dalton called first thing this morning. She talked to the parents and will arrange a meeting in a few days to see your baby and her parents. I thought you'd want this news as soon as possible."

CC looked into her mother's moist eyes. "Wow, Mama. I can't believe it. I'm going to see her!"

Mama remembered a little café in the middle of town but CC could barely eat after they left the police station.

"Why don't you at least nibble?"

CC chuckled. "Mama, all of a sudden, you're concerned about my eating habits? Sorry, I'm not laughing at you, but tell me everything. What did Miss Dalton say?"

"I told you everything already. She is going to call us with the arrangements. I just know we are going to meet her near this park where they take the baby all the time." She started fiddling with the fork and knife, rolling them over. She looked into CC's eyes. Do you want to know what they named her?"

CC thought for a minute. "I guess. It's kind of hard to know someone else named her." She curled a strand of hair around her finger. "Yes, tell me. "

Mama let out her breath, "Yes, this is hard. It is a beautiful name though. They called her Adriana."

"It is beautiful. Adriana." CC whispered the name three times.

Mama walked stood and walked around the table and CC stood to greet her. The hug between them in the middle of the café lasted a very long time.

CHAPTER 42

Mama opened her pocketbook and brought out a tissue pretending to blow her nose. She not too skillfully changed the subject.

"Would you like to buy a new outfit for the meeting? My treat. Here in town."

CC barely heard her. "No, I have a dress I never wore. There hasn't been any place to wear it since I've been on the farm."

After their late lunch, it was another quiet drive to the farm. CC was deep in thought. Everything seemed to be happening so fast. She was still plagued by the thought of whether she had any right to see her baby.

As they approached the farm, Mama asked. "I know you are going through a lot, but what are you going to do this fall? I mean stay here or go back to New Orleans?"

"I want to see the baby. That's all for now. I haven't thought about much else. Let's go to the farm. Please."

"All right, CC. I just want you to know I'm willing to make changes, work hard for us. I've already called ahead and told Jim I want my old job at the college. I'm not going back to the bar, and I'm going back to meetings."

"I know, Mom. I'm glad you have a plan. But I haven't made a decision."

CC barely slept that night. She kept waking up thinking about seeing her baby. She decided to spend the morning taking care of Lady, telling Gran as she left the kitchen, "I know Miss Dalton might call, but I haven't paid much mind to her lately. I'd like to brush her mane a little and let her now I haven't forgotten her."

"I understand. We don't know when she'll call."

She spent the couple of days with Addy. They went to DQ a couple of times and did some riding on Addy's land. She wanted CC to go swimming, but CC just couldn't stay away from home too long. "Take me back to the farm. It's hard to be away."

Addy said she understood and drove her back to the farm. She jumped out of Addy's truck as soon as they got back and could hear the phone ringing.

She dashed across the porch into the kitchen. Gran already held the receiver and shook her head to let CC know it was Miss Dalton. "That's all right, Miss Dalton. We're glad to hear from you. When do we meet you?"

Gran wrote something on a paper and CC heard Mama running across the living room. She looked at her with arched eyebrows and CC mouthed, 'Dalton.'

Mama went over to Gran and peeked over her shoulder so she could see what she was writing. Gran hung up and turned to them both. "I have the directions. We're going tomorrow. It won't be a long ride."

All three of them were up and dressed by daylight, sitting around drinking coffee. CC resorted to staring out the back door. Finally, Gran picked up her keys and they ran for the car.

With all the confusion they managed to get in the car and start down the driveway. Just as they drove by the massive oak tree where CC sat down her first day this summer, Johnny jumped the fence and hailed them down. CC leaned out the back window. "Hay cuz. I'll be back this afternoon."

He squinted at her even though he wasn't looking into the sunlight. "You take care and I hope it all works out for you."

"Yep. Me too. Say, make sure you let your dad know I'm coming back today. I think he was confused and thinks I'm leaving the farm."

"I will. Don't worry." He thumped the side of the car door and waved.

CC settled in before asking Gran about where they were going. "We're driving to a town called Natchitoches. I know, it's a funny name. It's an Indian name. Not too far - about two hours from here. Close, huh?" as she looked through the rear-view mirror at CC.

CC stared out the window but the view was the same. The hilly land was dotted with large old houses and fenced-in pasture. She noticed more cows than horses and occasionally a dog running along the fence line chasing their car

Mama didn't say anything, so CC asked. Do you know where we'll meet?"

Gran glanced at her again. "Miss Dalton wants us to meet her on the main street on the Cane River that runs through town. She said they want to meet us in a public place. Both parents will be there."

"Mom, do you know whereabouts on the street. I mean any address?"

Gran cleared her throat. "She said across from that fancy restaurant in the middle of town. The one they decorate for Christmas. It's famous."

CC didn't ask anything. She understood now what people meant when they said their heart might thump out of their chest. She could feel her heart beating away. But it was her throat. It was so dry she had trouble swallowing. She remembered she didn't run to the bathroom before she left. She hoped she could make it without having to stop.

CC needed time to think. What was she doing? What would she say? Did she look all right? What would they think of her?

There was no time to answer those questions because they were already in Natchitoches. CC saw the sign. To her left, were businesses and to her right she saw the river Gran mentioned.

"There's the restaurant. Are you going to park here?" Gran didn't bother answering. She pulled into a parking space on the side of the street and CC recognized Miss Dalton standing on the sidewalk waving to them.

CC murmured, "Oh God."

Mama turned around to her and said, "It's all right, Cicely. Your Gran and I are with you."

They opened the car doors and got out. Familiar smells from the restaurant wafted towards CC. Even though they were in a north Louisiana town, she recognized the strong odor of fried seafood.

CC tried to get out but she wasn't sure she could stand up. Her legs felt wobbly. Mama grabbed her hand and squeezed it. CC whispered to her, "Why didn't we discuss what we will say? What am I going to say to them? What if they're mad at me for doing this?"

Gran whispered in her ear. "Remember. You're here to see the baby. That's all that matters. "

Miss Dalton walked to them. "Good morning. This is the Cane River Park. It's actually a levee and the park is closer to the river. We can walk down these steps. The family wants to meet you here. They take the baby here sometime."

CC meekly asked, "Do they live here?"

"They live nearby. It's better if you don't know where exactly. "

Before they started down the steps, Miss Dalton added, "As I explained in the phone conversations, all the family allows is for you to meet them and see the baby. Adriana. Understood?" Gran and Mama nodded.

She turned to go and CC said, "Wait. Let me take a minute." The women looked at her. CC took a deep breath and exhaled. She straightened her skirt, and asked Gran, "Do I look all right?"

"You look lovely."

Even Miss Dalton said, "Yes, you look really nice."

CC took another deep breath before saying, "Let's go." She followed Miss Dalton down the steps to the Cane River Park below.

CHAPTER 43

Without looking back, Miss Dalton warned, "Careful. The steps are a little steep."

CC heard laughter in the distance and paused when she got to the last tread. Groups of children chased each other and a lemonade stand perched on the bank of the peacefully flowing Cane River. A vendor shouted "Hot dogs, twenty-five cents." The landscape before her reminded CC of the pictures in Gran's monthly magazines.

"There they are," Miss Dalton said.

CC didn't need directions. Her eyes settled on a woman sitting on a bench near a large oak tree. The dark-skinned lady's hands rested on a pink stroller's handlebar. Smaller hands reaching from inside the stroller grappled with a plastic toy on the tray. Overseeing the scene was an extremely tall Negro man holding what looked like a Polaroid camera. CC knew instantly who they were and walked slowly towards them.

She thought she heard Miss Dalton say, "Wait. I need to tell them you're here."

"They know I'm here, Miss Dalton. They're smiling at me. Is it alright if I go over? Have you asked them if it's okay?"

She felt Miss Dalton's hand on her shoulder as she leaned over and whispered. "Go slowly. They offered to meet you, but don't startle the baby. She's barely six months old and may be a little afraid when she sees strangers."

CC moved slowly. The lady continued smiling at her. She stood, and CC thought she looked like Miss Eugenia. Her lips were covered in bright red lipstick and when she smiled, her dark, soft eyes flashed in unison. A yellow and orange print dress hung from her tall frame and complemented her brown skin.

CC waited for the lady to motion to her and when she did, she opened her hands to CC. "You must be Cicely." Her outstretched arms beckoned as CC walked into them and sensed the woman's warmth. She let go and looked down at CC, still holding her. "Hello. I'm Bee, short for Beatrice."

An even taller man stood next to them. "I'm Roland. Bee's husband. And Adriana's father." A small mustache sat on his lip and his eyes shone out from underneath bushy eyebrows. He looked over CC's shoulder and peered questionably at his wife.

CC continued to stare back and forth between the couple until Mrs. Bee signaled for CC to face the stroller. Her breath caught in her throat as she stared at the beautiful little girl with almond skin sitting against a white lace blanket. Adriana held the plastic toy in her mouth and gurgled a sound CC could not understand. It didn't matter.

She marveled at the sight of the baby in front of her. She was no longer the newborn CC saw months ago in the cottage, but she still had the same black, curly hair which peeked from underneath a pink bonnet. CC searched her face and was astonished at the crystal blue eyes looking back at her.

Still staring at her, CC asked, "Her name is Adriana?"

Mrs. Bee answered quietly, "Yes, Cicely. Named after my grandmother."

CC said imply, "Yes."

"I have a blanket for the ground. Would you like to spread it? We can put Adriana down and you can visit with her. Would you like that?"

CC turned to face her. "May I?"

They spread the blanket and Mrs. Bee said, 'Would you like to pick her up and sit her over here?" She patted the blanket.

CC felt Gran and Mama behind her but neither said anything. She glanced at them and saw Mama searching for a tissue in her pocket while Gran put her arm around Loreen's waist.

"I think I need to sit down first." CC felt her legs shaking and wasn't sure she could hold the child. "Would you pick her up, Mrs. Bee?"

They sat and CC continued to stare at Adriana while Mrs. Bee fumbled with something in her bag. "Here's another toy, a plastic ball she loves," as she retrieved the one from the child's mouth. "Would you like to give it to her? Shake it and she can hear the little bells inside it."

There was a pause until Mrs. Bee spoke again. "She loves to come out here and watch the birds and listen to the children."

"I can tell she's happy here. I mean, well, you know..." CC remarked never taking her eyes off Adriana.

"Roland, why don't you take the ladies over and get us all lemonade at that stand. I bet CC would like some time with Adriana." When they were out of earshot, she turned to CC. "He's nervous and I guess that's why he's hovering. He means well."

CC spoke quietly. "How is she doing? I mean is she healthy?" Her questions were answered with a loud giggle and babble from Adriana as she held the ball and tried to bite it. CC laughed. "She's sitting up already, huh?"

"She's a good baby, sleeps a lot except the middle of the night. I am still giving her a bottle at night so she wakes up, but she goes back to sleep."

CC didn't respond. Mrs. Bee continued. "Her name, well, my grandmother's middle name was Adriana. Her first name was Pearl, but I think Adriana had more life to it. Do you like it?"

"Oh, I love it. It's a perfect name for her. Like she has exotic features. I think." CC blushed a little. "That's okay to say, isn't it?"

"It's a wonderful thing to say."

CC rubbed her hand along the blanket. "It's hard to say how beautiful she is, Mrs. Bee. She's the same as when I saw her in the cottage after she was born, but bigger. Her hands were so tiny then, but they've filled out I guess."

"Mrs. Bee, I just wanted to see her and make sure y'all are happy with her. You know. I guess I wonder if she will think I abandoned her." Her eyes pleaded with the lady. "Will you, I mean, if you tell her she's adopted, will you explain why I let her go?"

"Oh child. I will make sure she knows you went through a lot to bring her safely into this world and you loved her so much you gave her to us. Is that what you mean?"

"Yes. I guess that's exactly what I mean. But one thing. I guess I do want to hold her before I leave?"

Mrs. Bee reached over and held Adriana's hands. "If you help her, she will stand, but you have to hold onto her. Like this. Would you like to try?"

Adriana played with the ball so CC waited until she threw it down. She reached for her hands and lifted Adriana. Her chubby legs squirmed until she fell back down and sat on the blanket.

"Did she giggle just then, Mrs. Bee?"

"Sounds like it. She's very active and loves being outside. She looks happy with you. I'm going to give you some time. I'll walk over by the river with Roland."

CC just looked up at her and knew she looked panicky.

"It's all right. You can call me and I'll send your mama and grandmother back. Wouldn't you like a little time with her?"

CC nodded to her. "Does she prefer to sit up or lie down?"

Mrs. Bee chuckled. "Yes, prop her up with that half pillow and let her look around. She loves it."

CC couldn't believe she was by herself. "You smell so good. Like soap. I love your bonnet and your pink polka dot dress. Do you know your name yet, Adriana? Isn't that pretty? Just like you."

She enjoyed just looking at her on the blanket. "Adriana, someday your mom, Mrs. Bee, might explain to you about being adopted. I hope she tells you, or I might get the chance, that I had to go through living away from home and having you without anyone else around. But I need you to know, I'm glad I did, and I wouldn't change giving birth to you for anything at all. I love you in my own way, and I will always remember you."

CC kneeled on the blanket so she could reach Adriana's arms. "Okay. Here we go. Let me sit you up again. Don't squirm now. There we go." CC looked at Adriana and understood what people mean when they said their heart was full. Her heart was full looking at Adriana.

But there were other feelings too. She didn't feel like Adriana was her baby at all. She was so used to referring to her as her baby the last months. But now looking at Adriana, she was a stranger. She belonged to Mrs. Bee and Mr. Roland. CC realized that was all right. Like it was meant to be or something.

"She is so sweet." Gran and Mama stood near the blanket grinning at CC and the baby.

"She's a good baby." CC held her up again. Adriana giggled again.

Gran laughed. "She must love being outside. And she's comfy with you."

CC smiled in return and then a cloud crossed over her face. "Please call Mrs. Bee. I need to tell her something."

When Mrs. Bee came back, CC picked up Adriana and met her. "Can we go over by the tree?" CC spoke to her in a soft voice. "I want to tell you about her father. His name is Marcus and he's very smart and a good student. But he's talented also. Plays several instruments and his favorite music is jazz. I'm a good student and I write, but I'm not as talented." She looked up at Mrs. Bee. "He is a very nice boy. I want you to know that."

"I can tell you're a smart girl, CC. And I appreciate your telling me about Adriana's father." Mrs. Bee touched her shoulder.

"Hey, do you still want this lemonade?" Mr. Roland walked towards them with two cups in his hands.

"I'll pass, Mr. Roland. Thanks."

Mr. Roland looked back and forth to both CC and his wife, "Everything all right here?"

They nodded at him and then CC looked up at Mrs. Bee. "She's happy I can tell, and I know she'll have a good life with you. Let me give Adriana back to you. She's tired I think."

Mrs. Bee's eyes pierced hers. "You're sure? You're ready to give her to me?"

CC understood the question. "I'm very sure. She'll have a wonderful life. I know it."

Mama and Gran were already waiting at the steps. CC walked up to them and Mama put her arm around her waist. They waved at the group on the bench and the baby in the stroller.

Gran asked, "CC, you ready to go?"

"Yes ma'am. I'm ready. Let's go home."

CHAPTER 44

CC hopped in the back seat of Gran's old Ford and rolled her window halfway down. "Whew, still hot in here."

"It'll be better once we get going," Gran added.

They didn't talk for a while and CC was glad to have the time to think about the visit with Adriana and her parents. She was glad she went to the park even though she had been scared on the drive to Natchitoches and worried about what the adoptive parents might think of her. But seeing the baby was magical. The still, sleeping little baby she saw at a few days old was transformed into the beautiful bouncy Adriana. Instead of that nagging feeling she had felt of abandoning her, she now realized she did what was best for her. Giving Adriana up was a gift, a gift to two wonderful parents.

She saw Gran peering through the rearview mirror at her as Mama made a half turn to look at her. "You alright? Feel okay about the visit?"

CC sat up where she could lean over the front seat. Mama sat back and looked out her window. "I'm alright. Adriana looked so happy and healthy and I got to hold her. The parents are nice people. What do you think, Mama?"

She could see Mama smiling. "I hoped you would feel that way. I think it's best she's with Negro parents. How about you, Mother?"

Gran spoke up right away. "They are wonderful folks in my book. I know we just saw them for a short time, but you can tell they're very loving. Adriana's a lucky girl."

CC leaned back into her seat. "Miss Dalton did a good job finding them, right?"

Gran spoke up. "I understand some adoptive parents are on long waiting lists. It's hard for colored parents to adopt legally through an agency. I think they take over the care of children in their community. Adriana seems like the perfect child for them."

"I don't have to worry about her and I don't feel like I just left her behind. Right, Mama?"

"Right. It's the right decision for all of us."

CC smiled. "Right, Mama."

She looked at the hills going by and saw another farm with a couple of white mares in the green pasture. It made her think of Eric. It was hard to accept that he turned on her so fast. She knew he had feelings about Negroes like a lot of kids. And he was definitely shocked to learn she had a baby. But she knew he cared about her, the way he backed off from just wanting to make out. But then he left her standing in that field. It was hard to believe he was the same guy who stopped those boys from running them off the road.

CC leaned in again on the front seat. "Gran, I just thought of something. What about those boys who tried to run us off the road? Did the sheriff charge them with anything?"

Gran looked sideways at Mama before answering. "I'm glad you brought that up. The sheriff told me yesterday the boys think it was all a misunderstanding. They didn't mean to hurt anyone. They want to apologize for upsetting you and the children."

"Really? That's what they said? Wait until Addy hears about this."

"I know. It sounds suspicious, but I'd like to give you my thoughts. Sheriff Jack says there are three boys and you and Addy. Of course, the children. He's wondering if we can keep the incident tuned down. Not actually make this a criminal charge."

Before CC could interrupt, she continued, "You know, I'm on the school board and we are putting a new plan into motion this term. We're bussing those children from the bible school district into the brand-new elementary school, new books, good teachers like Miss Eugenia. She will transfer there too. We'll have a fully integrated school."

"What's that got to do with those boys apologizing? And if it's a misunderstanding, why apologize."

CC could see Gran taking a deep breath. "I think it's a good idea if the boys are taught a lesson, and at the same time we could start the school year without any big uproar. Criminal charges might make the paper, and there could be repercussions from the families, and on the children trying to start a new school year at a different school."

A dark car passed them and waved. Gran waved back so CC assumed she knew them.

CC started to speak up again, but Gran beat her to it. "Besides apologizing to you and Addy, they will serve some community service time. The sheriff wants to have them work the next three weeks before school starts cleaning up after the contractors and getting the school ready. They will be helping the children they hurt by their deeds and be punished at the same time."

CC fell back in her seat and mumbled, "Good Lord," under her breath. "Gran, what about the children? They heard what those boys said. They called them names."

"I'm going to their bible school to announce to the group that they are going to be punished for what they did. And tell them Miss Eugenia will be one of their new teachers at their new school. I think they'll be so excited; it'll be fine. "

She looked at CC again in the rearview mirror. "We'd just like to get these schools integrated as peacefully as possible to avoid any problems. I think we can do it. I've been hoping for this since the Supreme Court ruling."

CC stared at the back of the seat. "What court ruling? You mean that you can't keep Negroes and whites separate?"

"That's exactly what it means. And you remember what it was like in New Orleans a couple of years ago?" Gran added. "Those poor girls who tried to go to school were given such a hard time?"

"Mama, what do you think?"

"It's a small town, CC. This news will get out and when their friends hear what happened, they at least will see they had some consequences."

"I guess. I don't want them to apologize to me. I will stand with Addy if she wants to go along with this. It was her truck. Are you going to tell her father?"

"He already knows about it," Gran countered. "He's on the school board, also."

CC mumbled. "Of course, he is."

Gran sighed. "It's not the perfect solution and I wish it was different, but we're trying to move forward."

Mama spoke up. "CC, while we're talking about school, have you thought any more about whether you want to stay here, or go back to New Orleans?"

She pushed her head back against the seat. "What does that have to do with anything? No, I guess not. Still thinking about it."

She thought about Star at a new school with her friends. She stared out her window as she said, "I could help the children get used to going to a new school. I'm sure Addy would, too. But, Mama, what about you?"

"I have plans I told you about. Going back to my old job, away from the bar. I want you to do what you think you should."

CC wasn't sure. Spending the summer here had been fun at times. But living here all the time and going to school? How would that work? Then she thought about Uncle Bud. She could help out so Johnny would have some support for his dad.

"You know when I showed up here, I thought I didn't want any help and I didn't belong. I need to help out around here now. Help you with the new school and Johnny and Uncle Bud. And the farm."

Gran couldn't hide her enthusiasm. "Does that mean you're staying? Your Gramps and I would love it. But only if you want to."

"If Mama is okay with it? What about it, Mama?"

"I think it would be good for you." She snickered. "Not that you need it. I have a feeling you're going to be just fine no matter whether you stay or go. And of course, I will miss you, but I'll be fine. I don't want you to worry about me. That's my job."

Gran was barely audible. "I think so, too."

"Let me think about it a little more, okay?"

CC heard the familiar sound of the gravel highway. She hadn't noticed they were home. Home, she thought. When did I start calling it home?

She spotted Champ running down the road towards them. "Gran, can you stop here? I'd like to walk back with him." She hopped out of the car and he jumped up to greet her. "Hey, boy. How's it going?'

The car kicked up a little dust and when it cleared, a familiar shape appeared out of the white cloud. Eric stood on the side of the fence, hat in hand. He was still the tall, good looking guy she met when she arrived on the farm this summer, but the sneer and dark look were gone. CC wondered what he would say this time.

Her stomach was twisted in knots at seeing him. She wondered if she could handle seeing him after everything she had been through that day. But he was already walking towards her. CC took a deep breath.

CHAPTER 45

CC's heart still fluttered when she saw Eric. She wondered if that feeling would ever stop.

"Hi." He dusted the side of his jeans with his cowboy hat. He looked different, like he was tired. He had deep lines around his eyes. CC realized she hadn't seen him for over a week, and he wasn't the same cocky boy she met that first day on the farm.

What will he say to me now? Has he had time to think?

"I saw you drive off in your Gran's big ol' Ford Fairlane this morning. I waited a good while for you to come back. Hoped we could talk."

CC inhaled and let out a big breath. Her hands trembled and she wished she had her jeans on instead of this dress so she had pockets to hide them. But as nervous as she was, she knew she couldn't apologize for Adriana, not after seeing her today.

He twirled the hat and looked at the ground. *Does that mean he's sorry for what he said to me?*

"I know I hurt you the other day. You know coming on so strong, especially after that man hurt you. You looked so beat up. I wanted to protect you and I said I was gonna let him have it. But, well, you know."

CC's heart calmed. "No, I don't know Eric. Are you sorry for what you said to me? Are you taking it back?"

He leaned against the fence and bowed his head. CC could tell he avoided looking into her eyes.

She didn't want to make this easy for him, but she also didn't want to stand out here waiting for him to say whatever was on his mind.

He looked in her eyes. "I don't know how to handle it all now. I didn't know you had a baby. I began to have feelings for you, and I do. But I just don't understand it. You kept it a secret. I guess you had to. I don't know what you expect of me."

CC let out an exasperated sigh. "Expect of you? Nothing, I guess. Eric, I'm not apologizing for my little girl. Her name is Adriana by the way. And she is beautiful and I can understand how the secret I kept is shocking. I didn't do it because I wanted to hurt you or trick you. I did it because I was ashamed of all of it. But I'm learning to live with my past mistakes and accept them. I hope others will too."

CC looked down at Champ and patted his head before continuing. "I just spent this morning meeting with Adriana's parents and holding a beautiful little girl who is loved and cared for by someone else. And I'm happy for a change. Happy that she's loved and protected. I hope you can understand."

He kept staring at his hat. CC was impatient with the silent treatment. "Look, Eric. I don't know what you're saying to me."

He flipped his hat on and folded his arms over his chest. "I'm not saying good-bye. I just need to figure out what I can handle. I like you. Like you a lot. But I don't know if I'm ready for this. For you."

CC couldn't hide her frustration. She went through two major events in a matter of days by handling the complaint against Randy and seeing Adriana. Facing the parents. She didn't want to stand on a gravel driveway listening while he whined about his feelings.

"I know what I want and you know where to find me. Please, Eric, try to figure it out before we talk again. I'm going to go wait for Addy. Bye." The fluttering stopped.

She turned on her heel and called Champ. "Come on, boy. Let's take a little run through the field."

She skipped with Champ through the tall grass toward the barn. CC didn't look back.

CHAPTER 46

Johnny was on his way across the field with the three cows in tow and hollered at her, "Hi, CC. Y'all back? How'd it go?"

She caught up with him. "Went great, I think. Let's talk about that later."

"I saw you over there with Ralston. Don't let him get to you."

She snickered. "He's not. What're you doing?"

Johnny squinted through one eye. "I'm taking these cows in for the night. Say, I didn't get a chance to tell you, but with that fine Gibbs has to pay, Gramps and I are gonna get some more milk cows and I'll start a small dairy. There's not one close by. Gives us a chance to make a little money. Now that we took care of getting rid of the DDT spray, should be good."

CC smiled at him. "You're setting your sights on working this farm. Great plan. If you like cows." She couldn't help laughing, but it felt good to tease him.

"Yep. Why don't you stick around and help me?"

She leaned over and patted Champ on the head again. "I'm thinking about it. Wait and see, okay? By the way, Addy may come over later. You ever going to ask her out?"

He laughed and swatted at her with his hat. "That's a possibility. Been on my mind."

CC laughed again. "See you later. I'm going to wash up. Where's your dad?"

Johnny called after her. "You know he's in his garden this time of day."

The afternoon sun was settling and CC thought it cast a beautiful glow over the front of the house. It wasn't often she took a good look at Gran's flowers planted in a circular pattern in the middle of the yard. They were an assortment of colors, reds, yellows, and purples. She remembered sitting here with Gran last month trying to explain how she felt about the baby. Gran always listened to her. CC smiled when she remembered going with her to meet Miss Jessica at the high school and the driving lesson afterwards. No one else would have thought of doing that for her.

I'll have to ask Gran when I'll get to drive that big old Ford again. I may have to stay here to drive to school for the first day. Wow! That'd be something. And then drive out to the country to see Star. Addy could sit on her passenger seat for a change. This was sounding better and better. Did she want to stay?

When she turned around the corner of the house, she saw Uncle Bud tending his garden. He leaned over to pull weeds and get some more beans. She smiled remembering her first day when she had to pull him away from the boys and he brought the green beans to the kitchen. He was so proud.

Uncle Bud took care of her and she knew she could never forget how he saved her that night in the field. Randy hurt her and it could have been worse, but Uncle Bud stopped him. He saved her and he stopped Gibbs, too. He was so important to the family and they wanted him to stay on the farm. He could stay forever with Johnny while he took care of him. With her, too.

It wouldn't be so bad staying here. She could try it for eleventh grade. See how she liked it. Help Johnny and do stuff round here. It might be fun.

What was that smell coming from the kitchen? Gran was already cooking supper. Smells like chicken. And green beans. Wonder if she has any more peach cobbler. Yum! And that sweet tea.

Addy loved Gran's chicken. Maybe she'll stay and eat.

CC heard someone coming up the gravel driveway. She didn't have to wait long. That loud truck radio blared away with a different song than the ones the DJs played most of the time, but CC knew it well. There was a lot of yeah, yeah, yeah in the lyrics, but everyone knew the Beatles sound now. They had all the hits on the charts so far this year.

Johnny walked toward the house with Champ trotting by his side. CC could tell he recognized Addy's truck by his big grin as he looked towards the driveway. The hot "She Loves You" hit song blasted through the yard and even had Champ on alert. Addy started waving through her open window, her beaming smile matching her mood. Yep, CC knew they would all have a great time hanging out together.

CC couldn't wait to share her big news at supper and see how excited everyone would be that she was going to become a permanent country girl. Right here on the farm! Yeah, yeah, yeah!

THE END

ACKNOWLEDGEMENTS

I am grateful for two very special ladies I affectionately refer to as the Queens. First, Amanda Lee Thibodeaux, fellow dog lover and author, with whom I spent lovely afternoons soaking in love and inspiration. The second was Bunny (Bernadine) Thomas who did not live to see my novel published, but who always believed in me and in my character, Uncle Bud

I am fortunate to enjoy all the Mary's and Marylou's' in my life who offered guidance, great hair, coffee, lunch and laughter, not necessarily in that order. But it was thirty years of friendship with Mary D'Anna, who was a true believer in my work, and always, always in me.

In the earlier stages of my writing the East Jefferson Fiction Writer's group provided both praise and criticism for my short stories and initial chapters of this novel. My writing partners, Xavier DeSoto and Dee (Deidre) Boling each spent hours exchanging ideas, drinking coffee and pushing me to revise, revise, revise. Xavier DeSoto read my work with a critical eye and. Dee (Deidre) Boling's writing style and constructive suggestions sets the example, I believe, for fine writing.

D. Steven Russell, Doug, author and writing partner spent hours reading my third edited draft and helping me to trust in my process and to never give up on the heart of my novel. The emails from Doug helped to reinforce my belief in my story.

As a young adult author, I asked Ms. Jennifer Puccio's first period writing class to read my first chapters. They did a fine job encouraging my work, and I treasure the folder of critiques I received from them.

My daughter Stacey, a fine writer, read my short story, "*Red Shadow*," and commented, "It reads like the beginning of a novel." *CC's Road Home* was borne from her comment.

I have to thank my daughter in law, Elisa Huber, for all of her tireless work in helping me both in editing and formatting the novel. Her work was outstanding and matched only by her infinite patience with me.

Finally, thanks to Margo Dill, *WOW!*, for editing and reviewing my book, Charles Marshall for sharing his Louisiana photography and producing my cover photograph. A special thanks to the folks at Black Rose Writing, especially Reagan Rothe, publisher, thank you, thank you.

— LBE

NOTE FROM THE AUTHOR

Word-of-mouth is crucial for any author to succeed. If you enjoyed *CC's Road Home*, please leave a review online—anywhere you are able. Even if it's just a sentence or two. It would make all the difference and would be very much appreciated.

Thanks!
Leah

ABOUT THE AUTHOR

Leah B. Eskine grew up in small southern towns in Louisiana and Texas and moved to New Orleans in her twenties. Her first novel *CC'S Road Home* was inspired by the high school students she taught. She lives with her best friend and husband, Paul, and their two rescue poodles. When she's not writing, Leah enjoys country music and sixties rock, walking the dogs at dusk, lunch at neighborhood restaurants, and reading – a lot. Visit Leah at www.leaheskine.com.

Thank you so much for reading one of our **Coming of Age** novels. If you enjoyed the experience, please check out our recommended title for your next great read!

What the Valley Knows by Heather Christie

"A taut, compelling family tale."

–Kirkus Reviews

National Indie Excellence Awards- Young Adult Winner

Readers' Favorite Gold Medal Young Adult - Coming of Age

Maxy Awards Young Adult Winner

View other Black Rose Writing titles at
www.blackrosewriting.com/books and use promo code
PRINT to receive a **20% discount** when purchasing.

www.ingramcontent.com/pod-product-compliance
Lightning Source LLC
Chambersburg PA
CBHW011132100726
47898CB00009B/2943